D0949627

Read
and
Gone

Also available by Allison Brook

Death Overdue

Read
and
Gone

A HAUNTED LIBRARY MYSTERY

Allison Brook

CROOKED
LANE

NEW YORK

Copyright © 2018 by Marilyn Levinson.

Published in the United States by Crooked Lane Books, an imprint of The Quick Brown Fox & Company LLC.

Crooked Lane Books and its logo are trademarks of The Quick Brown Fox & Company LLC.

Library of Congress Catalog-in-Publication data available upon request.

ISBN (hardcover): 978-1-68331-734-0
ISBN (ePub): 978-1-68331-735-7
ISBN (ePDF): 978-1-68331-736-4

Cover illustration by Griesbach/Martucci.
Book design by Jennifer Canzone.

Printed in the United States.

www.crookedlanebooks.com

Crooked Lane Books
34 West 27th St., 10th Floor
New York, NY 10001

First Edition: September 2018

10 9 8 7 6 5 4 3 2 1

For my dear friends and fellow mystery writers, the Plothatchers: Krista Davis, Daryl Gerber, Peg Cochran, Kaye George, Ginger Bolton, and Laurie Cass. We've been together more than fifteen years, plotting books and sharing the good times and the bad. I love you all!

Chapter One

I glanced around my cottage at the thirty or so guests laughing and chatting, and grinned. *My party's a success! They're all having a great time!* Judging by the bulging plastic bag of discarded paper plates, it was time to serve dessert. I was on my way to the kitchen to instruct Mrs. C to put out coffee and tea, when I felt a tug on my pants leg.

"Cousin Carrie, this is the bestest party! I ate sushi and lasagna and lots of other things."

I smiled at my cousin's four-year-old daughter, with whom I shared a secret. "I hope you left room for dessert, Tacey."

"We're going to sing 'Happy Birthday.'" She shot me a piercing look. "Everyone will know how old you are."

I winced. "Pretty old, huh?"

"Uh-huh. You're thirty."

I found Mrs. C, efficient as ever, covering a platter of leftover deli meats with plastic wrap. Eager to help, I removed a chocolate cake from its box and placed it on a plate.

"I'll take care of that, Carrie. You return to your celebration," she instructed in her Scottish brogue.

Great-Aunt Harriet hurried into the kitchen, wearing an expression of dismay.

"Carrie, dear, I thought I'd packed everything so carefully, but I left the milk at home. Our car's blocked in, so Bosco can't get out to buy some for our coffee."

I'd consumed enough wine not to worry about such trivialities. "There's at least a cup of milk in the fridge."

"That won't be enough. What will we do?"

I felt an arm wrap around my shoulders and breathed in Dylan's cologne before I turned to see him standing at my side.

"I have a container of milk at the house. I'll run out and get it."

"Thank you," I said, kissing him quickly.

"I won't be long."

He wouldn't be. Dylan was my landlord. His mansion, as I thought of his large, elegant house, was only a quarter of a mile down the road.

When the kitchen door slammed behind him, Aunt Harriet grinned. "Dylan's such a nice boy. And I see that he makes you happy."

"Now, Aunt Harriet, don't rush things. We just started dating."

"Some things don't take long."

I left Aunt Harriet placing cookies on a tray and paused in the hall to gather my thoughts. I was happy—happier than I'd been for as long as I could remember. My cottage was filled with the people I cared most about in the world. All this was new to me. I'd had none of this before I'd come to stay with my great-aunt and -uncle last spring. Now I had a life filled with friends, family, and my job as head of Programs and Events at the Clover Ridge Public Library.

And I was dating Dylan Avery! Right now I was deliriously happy, but I didn't know how long it would last. Dylan's job took him away from home most of the time. And I knew from experience that something this wonderful usually had a limited shelf life.

My guests had broken into groups, the largest being that of my library colleagues: my best friend, Angela, and her boyfriend; my two assistants; my boss Sally and her husband; Marion Marshall, the children's librarian; and others. They sat around the living room, laughing and exchanging stories as Mrs. C cleared the tables of paper plates and plastic cups.

I could hear Uncle Bosco in the den, performing magic tricks for Tacey's brother, her parents, and a few other cousins I didn't know very well.

I walked over to the group gathered in the dining room. As soon as Jared Foster saw me approach, he put his arm around the girl he'd brought and seemed very interested in what she was saying. Jared and I had gotten pretty close when we were investigating the murders of his mother and Al Buckley. I wouldn't call the evenings we spent with his family and friends actual dates, but I had gotten the impression that he cared for me more than I did for him. After I told Jared I couldn't see him anymore and he realized I liked Dylan, I was sure he'd refuse to come to my birthday-housewarming party. But he must have decided to show me he could get someone else, and had brought her to the party. I was glad he'd decided to come and appreciated the many balloons and "Happy Birthday" and "Housewarming" signs adorning the cottage. Despite the change in our relationship, Jared had taken care of the decorations as promised.

"Coffee and dessert coming up soon," I said.

"Terrific party," Jared and Ryan's uncle George said.

"Yes, it is," George's girlfriend said. "Thank you for inviting us."

Gillian, Ryan's girlfriend, sent me one of her perky grins. "I hope you're planning to open your gifts soon."

I returned her grin. "I will. It seems no one paid attention to my 'No Gifts' instructions on the invitation."

"That's because you're an easy person to buy gifts for," she said.

Gillian was a sweetheart. I often wondered how she could be in a relationship with hotheaded Ryan, who took plenty of verbal potshots at his younger brother when they were together. Jared never responded in kind. Could be Jared knew that Ryan envied him because he was an accountant with a well-respected Clover Ridge firm, while Ryan went from one low-level job to another.

"Carrie, you should know that people never do the expected," Ken Talbot quipped.

"I should," I said, patting his shoulder. I'd grown fond of Ken, Uncle George's college roommate and the Foster family's lawyer. Ken's partner gazed at him with doting eyes. I was glad Ken had brought Adam, and I hoped to get to know him better.

"Carrie, come here! We've hardly seen you all afternoon."

I turned. Barbara Sills, my predecessor as head of P and E until she and her husband had moved to California, was beckoning me to the library group. Trish and Susan, my two assistants, made room for me on the sofa, so I plopped down between them.

"Sally was telling me you're doing a terrific job. I see I'm not missed at all."

"I wouldn't know how to run the department if it weren't for what you taught me," I said with heartfelt emotion.

"Carrie's still learning, but she's a terrific head of P and E. We're lucky to have her."

I blushed to hear such high praise from Sally, who hadn't wanted me for the position at first.

"Here! Here!" They chanted as Trish and Susan patted me on the back.

The lights in the cottage dimmed as Aunt Harriet carried a birthday cake with lit candles into the dining room. Everyone stood. Dylan appeared at my side as everyone began singing "Happy Birthday."

Too soon it was over. My guests enjoyed their cake, cookies, and ice cream as I opened my presents, mostly clothing and articles for the house. I doubted I'd ever use the waffle iron that Tacey and Mark's parents had bought me, but it was kind of them to get it. My cottage, which I rented from Dylan for a ridiculously low amount, had come equipped with every imaginable appliance.

By nine thirty, most of my guests had departed. Even Mrs. C, after reminding me to leave out whatever clothes I wanted her to launder when she cleaned the cottage on Tuesday, went on her way. Soon only Uncle Bosco, Aunt Harriet, and Dylan remained.

I hugged my aunt and uncle. "Thank you for my wonderful party and for my wonderful life here."

"I told you you belonged in Clover Ridge," Uncle Bosco said. "You have deep family roots here. I'm glad you invited some of your cousins today. There are plenty more. You'll meet them at the next Singleton family get-together. There's one coming up this summer."

Family was one of Uncle Bosco's favorite topics. I rolled my eyes. Aunt Harriet noticed and patted his arm. "Now Bosco, leave the girl be. Can't you see she has enough to take care of right now?"

"I asked Mrs. C to make up a package of leftovers for you to take home. You ordered enough for twice as many guests."

After some fussing, my aunt and uncle departed with several bags of food, and I had Dylan all to myself.

He drew me close for a deep kiss. Finally he pulled away. "I wish I could stay, but I have to get some shut-eye."

"I know. The limo's picking you up at four forty-five for your early morning flight."

"Clever girl." He stroked my cheek with his finger. "We'll make up for it when I'm home again."

"When will that be?"

"Christmas weekend definitely. Next weekend if we're lucky."

We. How I loved the sound of that small, two-letter word. "All right. I won't nag."

"I'm sure you have plenty of work to do, getting the library ready for the holiday programs."

"As if that makes up for it." I gave him a gentle push. "Go on before I pull you back. Then you won't get away till morning."

After Dylan left, I opened my bedroom door and turned on the light, waking Smoky Joe, who'd been fast asleep on my bed. He opened his green eyes and stretched his lithe, half-grown body, flicking his bushy tail in the air before jumping down to greet me.

I knelt down to scratch behind his ears. "You must be hungry since you finished all the treats I left you."

I carried his litter box back to the mudroom next to the

kitchen, then brought his dishes into the kitchen to refill them with food and water. I watched him devour his late meal, purring as he ate.

"Everyone asked for you," I said, "but the cottage was too crowded for you to run around as usual. And while you're generally well behaved, I was afraid that seeing all that food might tempt you to jump on tables."

He lifted his head to stare balefully at me, then returned to his meal.

"Anyway, you'll see most everyone who came to the party at the library tomorrow."

Though it was only a few weeks ago that Smoky Joe had turned up at the cottage, crying for food, it seemed he'd been a part of my life much longer. Through an odd sequence of events, I'd ended up bringing him to work with me that morning. The gray beauty proved to be the most sociable of felines. When Sally asked me what I thought he was doing in the library, I told her he was our new library cat. Thank goodness she liked the idea, and now I brought him to work with me every day. The patrons loved making a fuss over him, and Trish had written an article about him, which would appear in our next newsletter.

I was charged up with emotion and energy, too restless to settle down. I changed into my nightgown, then plopped down on the living room sofa and flicked through the TV channels. I paused briefly to watch the Sunday night news, but nothing caught my interest. I sat down at my computer in the spare bedroom, which I'd set up as my office, and read my latest emails. A few were from people I'd just seen, who had written to tell me how much they'd enjoyed my party.

I glanced down at the list of who had brought what that

Angela and Gillian had thoughtfully made as I'd opened my presents. I'd send out thank-you notes very soon, but not tonight.

Eventually the excitement of the day caught up with me, and I grew sleepy. I got into bed and slipped beneath the covers and switched off the nightstand lamp. I smiled as Smoky Joe nestled against me as he too settled in for the night.

A sound woke me. I jerked upright to a sitting position. Smoky Joe was gone. Someone was in the cottage!

"Who's there?"

Nothing.

For a moment I thought Dylan had decided to surprise me after all, but the illuminated numbers of my digital clock said three thirty, an hour and a quarter before his departure for the airport.

I turned on the lamp and surveyed the bedroom. Nothing seemed out of place. Why would a thief travel all the way to a cottage on a private road? I had nothing of value.

My heart began to pound. No one would hear me if I screamed. Dylan was in the Avery mansion a quarter of a mile away.

"Help!" I shrieked at the top of my lungs.

"Shh."

"Who are you? What are you doing here?" I screamed as a man appeared in the doorway.

"Caro, it's me."

Caro. The only person who called me that was my father. I stared at Jim Singleton, for that's how I thought of him these days. I remembered him as a handsome man—tall and slender with good, even features. Now he looked haggard and grubby, with a beard of several days' growth.

"Don't you know your own father?"

"Why would I recognize you?" I asked. "I haven't seen you in years."

"I'm sorry about that. I meant to contact you sooner, but things kept cropping up."

"Things," I spat. "Burglaries. Heists. Don't come any closer!" I shouted as he stepped toward me.

Smoky Joe chose that minute to amble into the room. He stopped to rub his face against my father's leg. Jim bent down to stroke his flank. "Good-looking cat. Come from around here? There was a farm nearby that had bushy-tailed cats."

Instead of answering, I slipped on my bathrobe and strode past him. He followed me into the living room, where I switched on a lamp and remained standing. My father surveyed the room with a practiced eye.

"Nice place. Does it still belong to the Averys?"

"Dylan lives in the mansion. His parents are dead."

My father sank down on the sofa and stifled a yawn. "And you're head of a department at the local library. I'm proud of you." His grin stopped my heart for a moment. As a kid, I would have done anything for one of his grins!

"Really? You have a funny way of showing it."

"No matter what you think of me, I keep track of your life."

"Sure you do," I jeered. "The library's newsletter is online for anyone to read. How did you find me?"

"I hung out behind Bosco's house. Heard him and Harriet talking about your party. Happy Birthday, by the way. Thought I'd wait an hour or two. Make sure everyone was gone."

I threw him a look of disgust. "You waited till three in the morning to wake me from a deep sleep? Why all the secrecy?"

"Well, darlin', some people are looking for me. I thought it best to wait until now to see you."

"How did you get in?"

"Your kitchen door lock isn't very secure. Do you have anything to eat, by the way? I haven't had dinner. Or lunch, for that matter."

Jim sat down at the kitchen table while I made up a plate with slices of turkey and ham. I also warmed up a huge piece of lasagna in the microwave. He ate quickly and neatly as usual. My father was a thief, but he believed in good clothes and good manners. When he asked me to serve him more, I knew he probably hadn't eaten since yesterday.

"Coffee?" I asked.

"Please. Black, two sugars."

"As always," I murmured before I could stop myself. I was annoyed that I'd kept his habits close to my heart.

He shot me a grin. "You remembered."

"Why are you here?" I asked as I slipped a French roast pod into the Keurig.

"I need your help, Caro."

I swallowed. Whatever he wanted meant trouble.

"Do you know Benton Parr, the jeweler?"

"I've met him since he's on the library board with Uncle Bosco. And I've spoken to him a few times on the phone. He's giving a talk Tuesday evening on 'Gems: How to Tell the Real from the Fake.'"

"I know he is." Jim suddenly sprang to his feet and paced the length of the kitchen. "What do you make of him?"

I shrugged. "He seems pleasant. Dresses well. He's strongly in favor of the new addition to the library."

"Benton Parr's a thief!"

I started to laugh but immediately froze when I caught his furious expression. "We nabbed seven million dollars worth of perfect loose stones. My retirement fund. Parr took the lot for safekeeping. I've tried contacting him several times this past month, but he refuses to answer my emails and calls." He patted my shoulder as he gave me a rueful smile. "Caro, I'm afraid I need to ask you to act as a go-between and retrieve my share of the stones."

Chapter Two

"You want to involve me in one of your crooked deals that could land me in prison?" My voice rose with every word. "How could you—your own daughter?"

"Caro, listen. All I'm asking is—"

"Why did you come here? I want you to leave." Tears sprang to my eyes. Angrily, I scrubbed them away.

Jim tried to touch my arm, but I moved out of his reach. "All I'm asking you to do is talk to Parr. Tell him I'm here to set up a meet and collect what's mine. Then let me know what he says."

"What's yours!" I said bitterly. "How did you get like this?"

His eyes filled with sadness. "It's a long story, Caro. I'll tell you someday."

"Don't tell me. I don't want to know. I wish you'd never come back into my life."

"I swear, if you help me with this one small thing, you'll never have to see me again. I'll have enough money to retire in South America."

"That sounds inviting," I said sarcastically.

"At least think about it, Caro. I'll contact you by the end of the week. That should give you enough time to talk to him—if you will."

He strode to the kitchen door.

"Where are you going?" I hadn't meant to ask, but the words had a will of their own.

"It's better that you don't know. I'll be in touch."

The door closed softly behind him. I peered out through the glass panel but saw no sign of him. I heard a car start up and drive off. It was as though he'd never been here.

Sleeping was out of the question. I gave up trying and went into the living room to watch TV. But I didn't watch, of course. Just sat there, thinking about Jim Singleton walking in and out of my life when I was young. At first, my mom would make up stories that he was away on business and would bring Jordan and me presents when he came home. He *did* come home with presents for us, but that only happened once. Later on, I found out from a classmate that my father was in prison. I went running to my mother, and she finally admitted it was true.

Of course, I had no intention of doing what he'd asked me to do. I was squeaky clean when it came to the law, probably a reaction to the shame of having a father who was a thief. In seventh grade, I never joined my two best friends the afternoon they went shoplifting candy bars. And I kept scrupulous records for my taxes. Still, as five o'clock approached, I was tempted to consider contacting Benton Parr if it meant I'd never have to see my father again.

Eventually, I went back to bed and fell asleep. I would have slept through my alarm, but Smoky Joe padded around my pillow, purring like a buzz saw until, feeling like a zombie, I got up to feed him. I showered and dressed, then downed a cup of coffee. He came dashing into the hall as I was putting on my parka. He loved being the Clover Ridge library cat and took his job seriously.

There wasn't much traffic, so my drive to work took just under ten minutes. I parked in the library's parking area behind the building. The library, like most of the shops, restaurants, and art galleries bordering three sides of the Green, was once a white, wooden-framed mansion. Aunt Harriet and Uncle Bosco's house, where I'd lived for several months, was one of the many private homes of similar architecture on the fourth side of the Green.

As soon as I set him down, Smoky Joe scampered off to the children's room, where I knew Marion and her assistant gave him treats despite my instructions that no one was to feed him but me. I tried to smile every time one of my friends stopped by my office to tell me what a wonderful time she'd had at my party. Only Angela, with whom I was closest, realized something was wrong.

"Spill it, Carrie. Did Lover Boy dump you last night after we all left?"

"Of course not! We're good."

"Then why the long face after that fab party? Even Steve had a great time, and he hates going to parties that don't include his noisy friends."

"It's nothing."

Angela's snort told me she didn't believe me for one minute.

"I'll tell you about it—soon." Though I wasn't up to discussing it now, I needed to run my father's visit by her and get a dose of her common sense.

"Lunch later at the Cozy Corner Café?"

"I've got too much to do today, finishing the holiday decorations. I brought in leftovers for lunch."

"Okay, girlfriend. I'm here when you feel like talking."

I went downstairs to the closet where the decorations were stored, and carried up an armload. I knew I didn't have to work on this right now. The Christmas tree, menorah, and Kwanzaa candelabra were already on display. Susan Roberts, my assistant, who was a whiz at decorating, would be in later that afternoon, but I needed to do something physical to keep me occupied.

Dorothy Hawkins stared at me as I passed the reference desk.

"Morning, Dorothy," I said, determined to maintain the fragile peace we'd established a few weeks earlier.

"Hello, Carrie. See my aunt lately?"

Evelyn Havers, a former library aide, had died six years ago. Dorothy discovered, to her dismay, that her aunt's ghost often visited me in the library.

"She stopped by a few days ago," I said. "I never know when she'll show up."

"When you see her next, tell her hi from me. And tell her she was right."

"Will do," I said, not even trying to fathom what she was talking about.

Smoky Joe was waiting outside my office, which meant he either wanted to use his litter box or eat. The litter box it was. I'd no sooner dropped the decorations on my desk than Evelyn Havers materialized not two feet from where I stood. Smoky Joe jumped into the air and hissed.

Evelyn laughed. "Calm down, kitty boy. It's only me."

I petted Smoky Joe to soothe him. "He can't see you, but he senses your presence."

"He'll get used to me," Evelyn said. Today she wore a white blouse and a violet cardigan over a black pencil skirt, looking very elegant for a sixty-something ghost.

"Your niece says hi and gave me a cryptic message to pass on to you: you were right."

"Hmmm, very cryptic. But I think I know what she's referring to, poor girl." She glanced at me sideways. "Is she behaving herself with you?"

"We're not BFFs, but she's civil these days."

"Good." I shivered as Evelyn walked past me to lean against the wall. "And how did your party go?"

"Wonderfully—well, until . . ."

I hesitated. I could trust Evelyn to keep my secret. Besides, the only other person in Clover Ridge that could see and hear her was little Tacey. "Until my father showed up."

"Jim Singleton," she mused. "I remember him and his brother when they lived at the old Singleton farm. His father wasn't much of a farmer; not like your uncle Bosco. Jim's father moved his family to Haddam, I believe, when the boys were in grade school."

"He's a thief, Evelyn. He's spent time in prison." It was the first time I'd said this to anyone.

"So I've heard." Evelyn glanced at me. "And you're ashamed of him."

"Most of my childhood, I hardly saw him. I missed him so much. And now he's trying to involve me in his criminal activities."

I told her what my father wanted me to do. Evelyn gazed off reflectively as she listened.

"Benton Parr. I never trusted the man, not even to clean my

rings." She laughed. "My husband thought I was paranoid, but I didn't like the way he strutted around town wearing a Rolex watch and a pinky ring big as a weapon."

I giggled. "These days he's added a diamond stud earring."

"Rumor has it he took his mother-in-law's emerald and diamond necklace and bracelet set and fenced them in Manhattan. Somehow, his wife managed to hush that up and get back her mother's jewels. Sweet thing, Mariel. I'm sure Benton only married her for her money."

"He's a thief two times over," I said. "It gives me the shivers to think he's on the library board. And he'll be here tomorrow night, talking about gems." A wave of panic swept over me. "What should I do? What *can* I do?"

"My advice is to do nothing."

"Nothing?" I stared at her in astonishment.

Evelyn's half smile was full of compassion. "You can't save the world, Carrie. You were almost killed helping to solve two murders. Tell your father you can't help him, and be polite when you introduce Benton to his audience tomorrow night. Their association has nothing to do with you. I'm sure they'll resolve their differences, and your dad will leave town."

I watched her disappear, hoping she was right.

Chapter Three

Early Tuesday evening I brought Smoky Joe home and ate a quick dinner, then drove back to the library. I stood outside the downstairs meeting room and checked off names as the patrons who had signed up for Benton Parr's talk arrived. All sixty spots had been filled immediately at registration, but there were always a few no-shows, and a few on the waiting list were standing by, hoping to be let in. Though I dreaded the mess the construction of the new addition would cause, I looked forward to the new stadium-seating auditorium and second meeting room that would showcase the library's events and programs I'd be presenting.

Benton had arrived twenty minutes earlier, dressed in a dark gray suit, light gray shirt, and a purple tie sprinkled with golden crowns. In his right ear, he sported what looked to be a two-carat diamond—at least it was the same size as the stone in his chunky gold pinky ring. Slick, slick, slick. He carried an iPad. A man's leather bag hung from his shoulder.

"Good evening, Carrie. Thank you for setting up the screen and the tables exactly as I requested."

"Of course." I forced myself to sound pleasant. "It's my job to make sure our programs run as smoothly as possible."

Benton observed me with narrowed eyes. I wondered if my contempt had seeped through, despite my best efforts to act in a professional manner. *No need to worry,* I realized, watching him beam as the two young people accompanying him wheeled a jewelry tray carrying cases, to where we stood. The tall, slender girl placed an acrylic display case on the table.

"Carrie, this is my daughter Dina and my assistant, Chris Crowley." He winked. "They're here to keep an eye on the merchandise."

"Thanks for helping out with the program," I told them.

"Don't mind us," Dina said. "We're only here to fetch and carry."

She was a pretty young woman in her early twenties and would have been stunning if she'd attended to her long, stringy hair that hung halfway down her back.

"Hi." Chris raised a limp hand in greeting. He had a stocky build and stood half a head shorter than Dina. Both were dressed casually, wearing sweatshirts and jeans under their parkas.

"Nice to meet you," I said.

Dina and Chris opened the leather cases and began placing open boxes of jewelry in the acrylic showcase. They chatted as they set up for Benton's program, giving me the impression that they were used to working together.

"Do you help out your dad at the store?" I asked Dina.

"I've been working there part-time since I was seventeen. This year Dad needed someone full-time, just when my course load started taking up more of my time." She bumped Chris playfully. "That's why Dad hired Chris."

Do you know your father's a thief? I wondered.

"Be right back," I said, needing to get away. I retrieved three bottles of water from the fridge in the small adjoining room and left them on the table, then went to open the doors to the waiting audience.

At seven thirty I introduced Benton Parr to a full house.

"Most of you know Benton Parr, a member of our library board, and have visited Parr's Precious Pieces, his jewelry shop in town. He's here to talk about gems—the real and the fake—and how to tell the difference between the two."

Benton waited for the applause to die down and began his spiel. I leaned against the wall beside the first row, the library's camera in hand. I was about to snap my first photo, when Benton stopped midsentence to glare at me.

"Please don't take any photos during my program."

Startled, I said, "We like to have them for the newsletter and records, but if you'd rather—"

"Thank you." He waited until I slipped the camera into my cardigan pocket and continued.

What was that all about? Had Benton brought the stolen gems as part of his program and was afraid to have them photographed? It didn't make sense, since whatever he'd brought would be exposed for everyone in the room to see. I took my seat in the first row, curious to learn how this was going to play out.

I had to admit that his subject was fascinating and his approach engaging. Benton certainly knew how to draw in his audience and keep their attention. He stood behind the table that now held his computer and began by talking about the appeal that gems have for humans.

A man called out to say he wore no jewelry and had a

twenty-dollar watch. When the laughter died down, Benton asked if he'd ever bought the woman in his life any jewelry.

"Well, sure," the heckler said. "I got the wife a watch last Christmas and a string of pearls the year before. Set me back a good amount, let me tell you."

"And I bet you're proud as punch when someone compliments her watch and pearls."

"Maybe. So?"

"So men might not wear as much jewelry in the twenty-first century as they did, let's say, during the time of the Tudors, when upper-class gentlemen wore heavy chains of gold to show off their position and wealth. These days they show off—if you'll excuse the expression—by buying baubles for their womenfolk. Such as an engagement ring with a stone weighing several karats." Benton glanced at me. "Lights, please."

I dimmed the lights and he began his slide show. The first slide was of two enlarged diamonds. "One is real; the other is a CZ, or lab-created cubic zirconium. In the next few shots, you'll see how each stone fares with the water test, the fog test, and the newspaper test."

The audience watched in absolute silence as the real diamond sank to the bottom of the glass of water, remained fogged for no more than one second, and they saw how the newspaper print was not visible when the diamond was placed over it, yet could be seen fairly clearly through the CZ.

"One failsafe way of making sure you're buying a real diamond is dealing with a reliable jeweler. Diamonds are rated according to the four C's: cut, carat size, clarity, and color. Carrie, lights, please."

I switched on the lights and Benton fielded questions: about synthetic high-pressure, high-temperature and chemical vapor deposition diamonds, the two common production methods; conflict-free diamonds not mined in war zones to raise money for rebel factions; and ethically free diamonds that were mined in mines safe for the men who worked there.

"I could talk to you about diamonds for a week straight without exhausting the subject. However, we only have an hour left, and I'd like to move on to rubies, sapphires, and emeralds as well as some of the more popular semiprecious gems like the amethyst." He paused for effect. "And of course, show you some wonderful examples of the various gems, all of which are available at Parr's Precious Pieces."

I tuned out much of what Benton had to say about the other gems, gathering that there were artificially created rubies, emeralds, and sapphires—many of which were held in high regard. Natural gems could be improved on in a variety of ways. Amethysts could be color enhanced. There was coating and fracture filling to fill inclusions or imperfections in diamonds. A diamond's color could be enhanced; laser drilling was often used to remove small, dark inclusions, where the inclusion is burned away and the space filled with a bleaching agent. "Feathers," or white fractures, are often injected with a glass-like substance.

My head was reeling. The subject of diamonds alone would be a wonderful subject for a program. I opened my mouth, about to make that suggestion, when I remembered that Benton was a thief. I wasn't about to encourage him to make any more presentations.

"Do jewelers tell potential buyers about these improvements?" someone asked.

Benton smiled. "They do if they're honest."

Do you *tell customers about corrected flaws in the pieces they're thinking of buying?* I wondered.

"And now for the part of the program you've all been waiting for," Benton was saying. "I've brought several genuine beautiful gems in lovely settings. They're all one of a kind, since I designed each piece myself." He winked. "They're all for sale at Parr's Precious Pieces."

Chris and Dina removed rings, bracelets, and earrings, still nestled in their boxes, from the acrylic case. They walked slowly up the aisle, showing the audience the pieces as Benton spoke about each one. They were gorgeous, I thought, especially a pair of gold drop earrings. But though I could now afford them, they cost more than I cared to spend.

Finally, Chris reached into the large bag he'd carried into the library and withdrew an elaborate gold, sapphire, and diamond necklace on a padded velvet bust display easel, with chandelier-length matching earrings. The audience oohed and aahed as Benton explained that the set had once belonged to a Russian noblewoman and was for sale for an undisclosed price.

I realized this was the grand finale and that none of the loose gems Benton and my father had stolen would be making an appearance. What was he planning to do with the gems? Or had he already sold them? No. Benton liked to make up his own designs, so I figured he hadn't touched them yet.

At nine fifteen, I thanked the audience for attending and mentioned the movie we'd be showing later that week. Several patrons rushed up to the table to get another look at the pieces as Chris and Dina were packing them away. A well-dressed gentleman asked to see one of the rings, and Chris handed it to him. The man examined it and said he'd be in the next day to buy it for his daughter.

Benton placed the sapphire and diamond set back in the bag. As I walked toward him to thank him officially for a successful presentation, a middle-aged woman beat me to it. I waited while they chatted for a few minutes. I heard snippets of their conversation: "a ring" "reset in yellow gold" then saw her smile as he spoke into his smartphone, noting the time and day when she'd be coming in for an appointment.

"Thank you for a wonderful program," I said.

Benton smiled. "It was quite a hit, wasn't it? And I've managed to snag a few sales. Always a pleasure."

Dina and Chris chatted in low tones as they packed up the articles of jewelry and stacked them in the leather carriers.

"Everything's accounted for," Chris told Benton.

He laughed. "I would hope so. I wouldn't expect anyone to walk off with any of our pieces here in the library. Right, Carrie?"

"Of course. Our library patrons are law-abiding."

"We're off, Dad," Dina said. "See you tomorrow."

"Bring everything to the house, Dina, and leave it in the hall." He lowered his voice. "But lock the sapphire and diamond set in my office safe. That goes back to Sheffield Jewelers tomorrow morning."

So that expensive necklace and matching earrings didn't even belong to him. He'd borrowed them for show! I couldn't bear to spend another minute with this man. Patrons stopped me to say how much they'd enjoyed the program as I headed toward the exit, where Max, our burly head custodian, was standing, broom in tow, ready to put the room in order once everyone had gone.

"Big crowd," he commented as patrons walked past us. "I suppose people want to know how not to get taken when they buy a piece of jewelry."

"The audience enjoyed it."

Max gestured with his chin. "Benton never misses a chance to do a bit of business."

I turned in time to see him pocketing what looked like a check, then handing a small box to a blonde woman. I felt a stab of anger at the idea of his making money here in the library. And yet our guest chefs were allowed to sell their books at their presentations, as were visiting authors. Still, the idea of someone selling expensive jewelry here rankled.

Especially someone who was a thief twice over.

"Go on home, Carrie. I'm flicking the lights," Max said.

I waited in the hall until the last stragglers had headed upstairs, Dina Parr and her father's assistant among them. The blonde woman hurried after them, leaving Barton to check his cell phone before gathering up his computer and leather bag.

I climbed the stairs to the main level, which was dimly lit and unoccupied as far as I could see. It irked me that Benton had managed to present himself as a solid member of the community when in reality he was a thief no better than my father. Did his wife know? Did Dina? I felt a stab of envy. They seemed to go about their daily lives in blissful ignorance, not suffering the shame that never left me because everyone in Clover Ridge knew that Jim Singleton was a thief who'd done time in prison.

I used the ladies' room, then walked to my office to collect my jacket and pocketbook. I was unlocking the door when I heard male voices. I peered around the corner. Two men faced each other in the main room. It was too dark for me to make out more than their silhouettes.

"You keep away from her, you hear, if you know what's good for you." The angry words were spoken by a large man with broad shoulders.

The other man let loose a laugh with fake bravado. "You're crazy. I've no idea what you're talking about." It was Benton Parr!

I covered my mouth as the larger man drew back his arm and punched Benton in the face.

"Ow! What did you do that for?"

"You'll get worse if you so much as call her!"

Benton raced past me. He yanked open the back door to the parking lot and fled outside. The large broad-shouldered man followed at a slower pace, his chest heaving as he inhaled gulps of air. But he wasn't gulping in air. He was sobbing.

Chapter Four

Who was he? Driving home, I marveled at Benton Parr's colorful life. Clearly, he was having an affair with the man's wife. The fifty-something jeweler was not only a thief, he was also an adulterer. I shook my head in amazement. *Benton Parr, you're some of piece of work!*

I considered calling Lieutenant John Mathers to tell him what I'd seen. The man had assaulted Benton in the library, my workplace. Surely this was a matter for the police. But knowing my father's connection to Benton kept me from making the call.

Smoky Joe was waiting for me at home. He meowed noisily as he wove between my legs until I set down a dish with a few late-night treats.

"Here you go, Smoky Boy. Eat up."

I undressed and got ready for bed, musing that despite my personal reasons to dislike Benton Parr, tonight's program had been a huge success with the patrons. As I brushed my teeth, I reveled in the fact that I didn't have to go to work until one the following day. Which meant I could watch TV till the wee hours of the morning.

* * *

Wednesday morning I was enjoying my second cup of coffee when the landline phone rang. Did Sally need me to come in early for some reason? My pulse quickened. Or had Dylan found a free moment in his busy schedule to call me?

"Carrie, you have to come and get me out of here!"

"Jim? Where are you?"

"In jail, dammit. They think I killed Parr, but I swear I didn't."

"Benton's dead? I just saw him last night. Why do they think you killed him? How did they find you?"

"Caro, slow down. I went to his store before opening time. The lights were on, so I went inside, figuring he was in the back room. Only he was lying on the floor. There was all this blood coming from his abdomen. The kid who works for him came in and called the cops. I took off, but they nabbed me a few blocks away. Knocked me down. I'm bruised and all scratched up."

"You need a lawyer."

"I don't have money for a lawyer."

"I'm calling Uncle Bosco."

He let out a long exhalation. "I don't know, Caro. I haven't spoken to the man in twenty years."

"I know a lawyer. He doesn't handle criminal cases, but he'll know who to call."

"All right, honey, call who you want. But please get down here as soon as you can."

Uncle Bosco was not happy to hear my father was back in town. "When did he get here, Carrie? Why did he come?"

"He arrived a few days ago. I think he wanted to see me." Both accurate statements, but far from the whole picture. "There's

28

more, Uncle Bosco. Benton Parr is dead. Murdered. And the police arrested Jim. He insists he didn't do it."

My uncle let out a long sigh that sounded very much like the one my father had exhaled only minutes earlier. "My poor brother. He'd turn over in his grave if he knew what his son has become."

I cleared my throat. "Would you be willing to put up bail? I don't have much savings, but I'll take out a loan if I need to."

"Of course I'll put up bail. Your father's a Singleton, whether I like it or not. I can't let him rot in jail until his trial. Meanwhile, I'll speak to John. Find out exactly what they have on him."

"Thank you, Uncle Bosco. I'm going to call Ken Talbot. Have him recommend a good criminal lawyer for Jim."

"The man doesn't deserve to have you as his daughter."

I called Ken's office and was almost surprised when his secretary told me he was free to talk to me.

"Great party, Carrie. I'm glad you got to meet Adam."

"Me too. He seems like a really nice guy. And he's clearly crazy about you."

"Well, the feeling's mutual. Now, what can I do for you?"

I told Ken that my father had been arrested and was being held at the jail in town. "Uncle Bosco will be bailing him out."

"If they're holding him as a suspect, I'm afraid that might not happen until he's arraigned."

"I need the name of a criminal lawyer."

"Phil Demuth. His office is right down the hall. We often work together. I'll stop by the jail after my next appointment."

"Thanks, Ken. I appreciate this."

"I know what an ordeal this must be for you, Carrie."

"He says he didn't kill Benton."

"They all say that, Carrie."

Is my father a murderer? I pondered that question as I dressed quickly and put out food for Smoky Joe. I called Sally to tell her I'd be late. "My father's been arrested for Benton Parr's murder. I need to see Lieutenant Mathers. I don't know how long it will take."

"You poor kid," she said. "Don't worry. Trish will be in soon. She can hold the fort till you get here."

Smoky Joe followed me to the door, expecting to be picked up and carried to the car.

"Sorry, Boy. No library for you today. I don't know when I'm going to get there."

I resisted the urge to speed, because the last thing I needed was a speeding ticket or to get into an accident. Traffic was light, and I arrived at the police station ten minutes later. I parked behind the small brick building and went inside.

Officer Gracie Venditto, who I'd met the last time I'd come to the station, was at the desk.

"Hi, Carrie. Your uncle and Mr. Talbot are inside talking to Lieutenant Mathers."

"I'd like to join them."

"Be right back." Gracie stood. "Meanwhile, you can go straight down that corridor and knock on the door. An officer will escort you to your father's cell. You can speak to him from outside."

I did as she said. Jim was stretched out on a metal slab covered by the thinnest of mattresses. He was snoring.

I stifled a giggle. Here I was worried about my father, and he was fast asleep.

"Jim, wake up! We need to talk."

Tremors ran the length of his body as he awakened. He

threw off the woolen blanket and sat up, rubbing his eyes. "Caro! Thank God you've come. I didn't kill Parr. I swear I didn't. He was dead when I got to his store. I shouldn't have . . ."

"Shouldn't have what?"

When he didn't answer, I got angry. "Shouldn't have gone there? Shouldn't have touched him? Shouldn't have hit him?"

Jim rubbed his eyes. "He wasn't hit that I could see. He was lying on his side with blood seeping from his abdomen. He must have been stabbed, but I didn't see a knife anywhere. Not that I looked very hard."

"Did you touch him?"

"Only to check his pulse. I could tell he was dead."

"Then Chris came in and found you beside the body?"

Jim shifted his shoulders the way he did when he was guilty of something. And wasn't he always guilty of something?

"Not exactly. I'd been checking things out."

"I can't believe it! A man was lying dead—murdered—and you stayed to look for those gems?"

"Benton told me he'd put them in a place where no one would find them. He swore I'd get my share, but he didn't say when."

"You spoke to Benton?"

"Uh-huh. Last night. I decided it wasn't fair to get you involved so I called him. Told him I'd stop by his house, but he insisted I meet him at the store this morning."

Gracie walked over to me. "Carrie, you can join your uncle and Mr. Talbot in the loo's office now."

My father's face lit up. "You got me a lawyer?"

"I said I would. And Uncle Bosco will put up your bond if needed."

"Great. Just get me out of here." He beamed his special smile at Gracie. "Good lady, do you think you could work your magic and conjure up a real cup of coffee for me from outside? Not the kind of dishwater they served me at breakfast."

The smile Gracie returned was radiant. "I'll see what I can do, Jim."

Had she known him from before, or was my father really that charming?

The three men were talking quietly when I entered John Mathers's office. They stopped to greet me as I slipped into the empty metal chair facing John's desk and chair.

"I was telling your uncle and Mr. Talbot the circumstances under which my men caught your father running from the scene of the crime."

I nodded. "Yes, he told me. He also swears that he didn't kill Benton Parr."

John pursed his lips. "We're not saying that he did either, but he's a person of interest. We're going to want to question him again."

"Can he leave?"

"Perhaps later today, as I was explaining to your uncle and Mr. Talbot. Your father's a suspect in a jewel heist that took place last year. We notified an agency that has been investigating the theft. One of their investigators wants to talk to him before he's released."

"John says there's no need for bail," Uncle Bosco said, "but Jim has to remain in Clover Ridge at present. Preferably with a reliable adult." He sighed. "I suppose we can put him up, if it's only for a short while, though your Aunt Harriet won't be happy about it."

"He can stay with me." *Did I actually utter those words?* I covered my mouth, but it was too late.

"Are you sure, Carrie?" Uncle Bosco asked. "You haven't seen your father in years. Having him underfoot might be emotionally draining."

"Given my work schedule, we won't have much together time. Which reminds me, I'll be at the library till nine tonight."

"Jim can visit with Harriet and me till then."

"Thanks, Uncle Bosco." I turned to John, "How was Benton murdered?"

"He was stabbed in the abdomen with a knife."

I thought for a minute. "My father's been sent to prison for burglary and theft, but he's never committed an act of violence. Do you really think he killed Benton Parr?"

"Chris Crowley, Benton's assistant, found him at the scene."

"Was he covered in blood?"

"I'm not at liberty to discuss it."

"I need to tell you something," I said. "Last night as I was leaving the library, I overheard a man threatening Benton. In fact, he punched him in the face."

John Mathers's face took on an expression of sympathy. "Carrie, I realize you're upset about your father, but making up a story about a man hitting Benton doesn't help the situation one bit."

"I'm not making it up! I saw it with my own eyes."

"Nobody else reported this confrontation."

"No one else witnessed it. All the patrons had gone home."

Suddenly John was all business. "Can you describe this person?"

"I didn't see him clearly, except he was over six feet and had broad shoulders. He was warning Benton to keep away from his wife."

"We'll look into it. Meanwhile, there's no point in any of you staying here at the station. Bosco, I'll call when we're ready to release Jim."

Outside John's office, I thanked Ken and my uncle for showing up.

"I'll notify Phil about the case," Ken said and took off.

Uncle Bosco and I walked more slowly to the rear door that led to the parking lot. He shook his head. "Your father brings nothing but trouble and dishonor to our family. I hate that he's put you in the position of having to look after him."

"I'll be fine," I said, sounding more confident than I felt. I'd seen little of my father these past ten years. Did I know the man at all? I wanted to believe that he hadn't murdered Benton Parr, but how could I know for sure?

Outside, I hugged Uncle Bosco. "Give my love to Aunt Harriet. I'll see you both soon."

I watched him head to his car, knowing how difficult this situation was for him. And suddenly Dylan was exiting his car and walking toward me.

"What are you doing here? I didn't expect to see you till the weekend."

Instead of the look of happiness I expected, his face wore a guilty expression. "Carrie, hi! I've come to interview someone. About a case."

A case? Dylan worked as an investigative investigator for an insurance company that recovered stolen art and jewelry. Of course! He'd been looking for Jim all this time!

My body stiffened with shock and betrayal. "You're here to question my father about a heist he was supposedly involved in."

I ran to my car, scrubbing away the tears that streamed from my eyes. Jim was a thief. He'd been an absentee father. But he was *my* father, and no one had the right to use me to get to him.

Chapter Five

Dylan chased after me. "Carrie, we need to talk."

I shrugged away his arm and spun around to face him.

"So that's why you let me have the cottage at such a low rent, why you pretended to like me! I was the perfect link to my father!"

"Carrie, listen to me. The case had just about come to a dead end. All leads to your father had dried up. I swear I wasn't thinking about him when you answered the ad."

"Sure you weren't!" I glared at him. "And you never asked me if I kept in touch with my father or asked where he was living."

"Well, yes. I admit I did. But I rented the cottage to you because you were someone I trusted, someone I knew when we were kids—"

"Someone you hoped would help you solve a case. Help you find some missing gems."

"Aha! So you knew it was gems that had been stolen."

I glared at him. "Gems, watches, bonds. Whatever was taken has nothing to do with me or with my father." I climbed into my car and slammed the door.

"I'm here to interview him because it's my job."

I opened the window. "You know what you can do with your job! I have nothing more to say to you—ever!"

I started the car and backed up faster than I should have, missing a parked car by inches. I blinked back tears. What a jerk I'd been to think for even one minute that my life was perfect. It was a mess as always. My father showed up out of the blue and turned everything into hash. Jim Singleton was Suspect Number One in a homicide case *and* a gem heist. My supposed boyfriend didn't care about *me*. To him, I was just a link to my father. A link to solving one of his cases.

As I drove back to the cottage, I tried to remember how often Dylan had asked me about my father. Only once or twice, if I remembered correctly. About the same number of times he'd asked me about my mother and her new husband, who were living in Hollywood.

The cottage! I was going to have to move. I'd fallen in love with the cottage the moment I'd set eyes on it—the layout of the rooms, the furnishings, the views of the river. It was the nicest place I'd ever lived in, and I considered it my home. I grimaced as I realized why Dylan had rented it to me for such a ridiculously low price. Perhaps I could arrange to rent it at a normal cost. It would be expensive, but I could afford it. I was making a good salary.

No, it would be better if I lived somewhere else, somewhere far from Dylan Avery. Maybe it was time to move on and leave Clover Ridge. I'd given the well-balanced, ordinary life a try, and look where it had gotten me!

Angela was exiting the ladies' room when I stormed into the library with Smoky Joe in my arms.

"Carrie, what's wrong?" she demanded. "You look upset."

"I'm very upset." I set Smoky Joe on the floor. He yowled and ran off. "Even the poor cat's had enough of his mother today."

"Tell me what's bothering you."

Trish was working in my office. The coffee shop was open, but I didn't want anyone to hear our conversation. "Come upstairs and I'll tell you everything."

We trudged upstairs to the attic. It had once been used as a room where librarians and aides could take a break, but now it was a storehouse of old furniture. I perched on a desk and Angela perched on another. I told her how my father had suddenly appeared at the cottage hours after my party had ended, and wanted me to contact his partner in crime to retrieve his share of some stolen loot.

"The total scuzzball! Sorry, Carrie. I know he's your father, but what he asked you to do is not something any father should ask of his daughter. Especially after not seeing you for how many years?"

"Too many. But to be fair, he reconsidered two days later."

"Well, bully for him," she said, her voice dripping with sarcasm.

I let out a deep breath. "His partner in this deal was Benton Parr."

"The *dead* Benton Parr?" Angela whooped with delight. "I always suspected he was crooked through and through. I heard he tried to sell his mother-in-law's jewels. Mariel managed to get them back."

"I heard that too," I said.

"You did?" Angela eyed me suspiciously. "I thought that was kept under wraps. I only found out because my mother and

Mariel are both active in the garden club and have become good friends. Poor Mariel." Angela shook her head. "The man was a snake. He ran around."

"I know."

"How do you know *that*? I swear, Carrie, ever since you solved those murders, you're a walking database of Clover Ridge secrets."

I laughed. "Last night I overheard a big, burly guy give Benton a punch in the face and warn him to keep away from his wife."

"Did he have broad shoulders? A rough kind of voice?"

"Yes, why? Do you know him?"

"Not really, but I think I know who he is."

"Please tell me. Lieutenant Mathers questioned my father as a person of interest. Benton's assistant found him in the jewelry store this morning, along with Benton's corpse."

"Oh, no, Carrie!"

"He says he didn't kill Benton, and I believe him." I drew a deep breath. "Maybe this man is the murderer."

Angela had a pained expression on her face. "I hope he isn't. I mean," she quickly amended when she saw *my* look of shock, "of course I also hope your father's cleared—of murder anyway."

"Please tell me the man's name."

"From your description, it sounds like Paul Darby, Jennifer's husband."

I stared at her. "Jennifer Darby? The gal who works in the coffee shop? I hardly know her, but I'd say she's only in her mid-thirties."

"Benton was good at picking them young, sweet, and vulnerable. Paul's been out of work for some time, and their marriage is shaky."

"Oh" was all I could think to say.

"Benton wasn't well liked," Angela said. "I bet there are plenty of people in Clover Ridge who are happy he's dead.'

"And who might have killed him," I said.

*   *   *

I felt better after talking to Angela. Not that I wanted Jennifer's husband to be a murderer. But if Benton was half the sleazeball he was proving to be, John ought to know his history and look beyond my father as the only suspect. At any rate, I was able to enter my office and greet Trish like a halfway normal person before beginning my day's work.

I'd managed to wade through my emails and phone messages, even called back four of the seven people, when Sally stopped by.

"Everything resolved?" she asked.

"Not really, but Uncle Bosco's taking my father home with him, where he'll stay until I go home tonight."

Trish looked up and shot me an inquiring look.

"My father will be staying with me for a while," I said.

"Really? The man you haven't seen in years?"

I nodded.

"I hope you know what you're doing," Trish said.

"So do I," I admitted.

"Do you think he did it—killed Benton Farr?" Sally asked.

"No, I don't."

"What?" Trish exclaimed. "Benton Farr was murdered?"

There was nothing for me to do but to tell her. "Chris, Benton's assistant, found my father in the store this morning, along with Benton's body."

Trish's mouth fell open. "How did he die?"

"Stabbed," Sally and I said together.

Sally cleared her throat. "Actually, I've come here for a much more mundane reason. Christmas is only two weeks away, and we did say that this year we'd have a Secret Santa."

Trish and I groaned.

"It was a total failure three years ago," Trish said.

"Sorry," Sally said. "You voted on it, and the yea's had it. Not you, Carrie, since you weren't a permanent employee back in September when we agreed to do this."

She handed an envelope to Trish and two to me. "Please give Susan hers," she said. "You're not supposed to tell anyone who you're buying a gift for—at least until we exchange gifts at our holiday party next week. And don't spend more than ten dollars. Fifteen at the most."

I opened my envelope and glared at Sally. "You can't do this to me!"

She held up her hand. "Don't tell me! I have no idea who you got. Marion put each name in a blank envelope and asked me to address and deliver them."

"What's the problem?" Trish asked.

"Dorothy, that's the problem!"

"I thought the two of you were friends now," Sally said.

"We'll never be friends, but this is awful!"

"Why?" Trish asked. "What's the big deal?"

"What if I buy her something she hates? Or, even worse, she gets it in her head that I'm insulting her? Then we're back to where we were when I started here as head of P and E. I'll have to dodge her pranks and tricks."

Sally made a scoffing sound. "Don't carry on so, Carrie. It's not like you to be a drama queen over something this trivial."

I sniffed. "Believe me, it's not trivial. And I'm not a drama queen."

Trish laughed.

"Thank you for supporting me."

"I'm laughing because I agree with Sally. Being Dorothy's Secret Santa isn't the big deal you're making it out to be."

"Marion's in charge of Secret Santa, and she said there can't be any changes," Sally said as she left the room.

Chapter Six

The rest of the day passed quickly. I checked my cell phone every fifteen minutes, but there were no texts from Dylan. No emails, no phone calls. *Good,* I told myself. He took you at your word that you never wanted to speak to him again. There was no way I could have a relationship with someone who used me to get to my father so he could charge him with a crime and put him in prison.

Not that Jim didn't deserve it, another part of me retorted. A father was supposed to be moral and brave, supportive and loving. And, above all, present. A father was supposed to be present in his child's life, but Jim Singleton was none of the above!

I wondered how the "interview" had gone. My father was too shrewd to give the slightest hint that he'd taken part in the heist. And of course he had none of the gems or the slightest idea where Benton had hidden them.

Uncle Bosco called me midafternoon to tell me that Jim had been released from jail and was now home with him and Aunt Harriet.

"I hope he's behaving himself."

"He is," Uncle Bosco said, but he didn't sound happy. "He's regaling us with stories of his travels. I'm sorry to say, your aunt is enjoying them. She just asked him what he'd like for dinner."

"She's only being polite," I said.

"I don't know. I can't remember the last time she asked me what I'd like for dinner."

Trish went home, and a few hours later Susan bounded in, cheerful and eager to work. I asked her to sit at the hospitality desk, where we took turns signing up patrons for various programs and answering questions they might have about upcoming events. She was happy to comply. In the two months since I'd taken over as head of P and E, Susan had evolved from an insecure waif who needed instructions every twenty minutes to a competent assistant. She even looked better now that her long, stringy hair had been cut and shaped to suit her thin face, and she'd forsaken her sack-like dresses for tunics and leggings that flattered her slender figure. I chuckled to think that my own makeover had been just as dramatic, though occasionally I got the urge to color my hair purple and slip into a black Goth outfit.

Smoky Joe came into the office to use his litter box. I fed him and ate the roast beef sandwich and baby greens salad I'd had delivered from the Cozy Corner Café. And then it was time to present the afternoon's foreign film. I brought it downstairs to the meeting room. While Max set it up, I gave my little spiel to the thirty or so patrons about the director and the accolades the film had won. Then I returned to the paperwork my job always seemed to spawn, trying not to think of what awaited me when I arrived home that evening.

*   *   *

My father was stepping out of his car, an overnight bag in hand, as I pulled up in front of the cottage. This time I made it my business to give his car a careful once-over. It was a far-from-new dark green sedan badly in need of a wash.

"Hi there, Caro. Have a good day at the library?"

He tried to kiss my cheek as I passed him to unlock the door, but I brushed him aside. He left the overnight bag in the hall and followed me into the kitchen

"Thanks for putting me up. Bosco and Harriet are good people, but I couldn't last there more than one evening."

"Let's hope you won't have to stay here too long," I said.

"My sentiments exactly. I hope they find Benton's killer ASAP. I understand how difficult I'm making things for you."

"Like a cup of coffee?"

"That would be lovely." He sat down at the table and stretched out his legs while I started the coffee in the Keurig and then fed Smoky Joe.

"Care for any cookies or cake?"

"Just coffee, thanks."

While his mug was brewing, I nuked the last piece of lasagna left over from the party and spooned some potato salad and coleslaw onto a plate. Two minutes later, I brought over everything to the table and sat down. Jim sipped his coffee, and I started eating my dinner.

When I was halfway through, I asked, "How did you leave it with Lieutenant Mathers? Are you a suspect?"

"I'm not sure. I heard him talking about blood spatter and the fact that there was no blood on my clothing. I hope that counts for something."

"I still don't understand how you let Chris find you at the store. You're smarter than that."

"What do you mean?" my father asked. He sipped his coffee, but not before I detected an odd expression in his eyes.

"I mean, were you busy doing something?"

His laugh sounded false. "I told you, I was looking around."

I gaped at him. "I hope you didn't steal any jewelry?"

"Of course I didn't!" He sounded indignant. "I would have been in a hell of a lot of trouble if they'd found any pieces on me when they took me in."

"Then how did you let yourself get caught?" I asked, marveling at how I knew to ask the right questions. Was it remembering my mother's interrogating him when I was little? Her constant fear that he was about to be arrested and get us thrown out of whichever apartment we were renting at the time?

"I took a look inside the safe, okay?"

Okay? No, it wasn't okay. "I suppose they'll find your fingerprints on the lock."

He sent me a withering frown. "This isn't my first rodeo, Caro. I wiped it clean when I locked it again."

"Were you looking for the gems?"

"Of course I was looking for the gems! But they weren't in the safe. I wiped my prints clean and was about to leave when that kid unlocked the door and started screaming."

I thought over what he'd told me. "Can John hold you as a suspect based on what you've told me?"

"He can't. Which is why I'm here and no longer in one of his cells. I've answered his questions, nice and polite. No doubt I'll have to go down to the station to answer them all over again, and then I'll be on my way."

I took a deep breath. "And Dylan? What happened when he questioned you?"

"Geez, I hadn't seen Dylan Avery since he was a kid. He was Jordan's friend, remember? They used to play together when you kids spent the summer on the farm."

"I know."

My father leaned over to pat my shoulder. "I understand you two are dating."

"Who told you that?"

"John Mathers."

"He had no business saying that! Besides, we're no longer going out."

Jim studied my expression. When I looked away, he reached over and, with one finger, turned my face so he could see me. "Because of me?"

I nodded. "I hate what you do, but I can't bear to think that someone would pretend to like me because he wants to have at you."

Jim laughed. "He questioned me about the heist, all right, and I told him I didn't know what he was talking about. This went on for the better part of an hour. He finally said, casually as you like, that he had some emails on record between Benton and me. That was a stupid move on my part. Happened while we were planning our little business venture. Before I could think of a good response, Dylan took a new tack. Mentioned the reward the owners are offering. Half a million dollars to whoever finds the gems and hands them over, no questions asked."

"Which you can't do."

"No, I sure can't do that." He yawned and stretched his arms overhead.

"You're exhausted," I said. "Where have you been sleeping these last few nights?"

"In my car."

No wonder I'd found him fast asleep that morning in his cell. "The bed in the guest room is made up. There are towels in the guest bathroom cupboard." I stood. "I'll move my computer and let you get a good night's sleep."

"Please sit down and finish your dinner. I'll put your computer in your bedroom."

"All right. Good night then," I said.

"See you in the morning." He bent down. This time I let him kiss my cheek.

I finished my dinner, cleared the table, and put the dishes in the dishwasher, feeling strangely adrift. My father was fast asleep in the guest room, I'd broken up with Dylan, and I had no idea what was happening next.

I watched TV in the living room, keeping the sound low so it wouldn't disturb Jim. The phone never rang. No one called me. I called no one. I got ready for bed at nine thirty, which was early for me, and read. I drifted off to sleep with Smoky Joe beside me. When I awoke in the middle of the night, the cat was gone. I used the bathroom and tiptoed to the guest room. My disloyal kitten was fast asleep beside my father.

Chapter Seven

It was odd but utterly delightful, waking up to the aroma of coffee. I glanced at the clock and saw it wasn't yet seven.

"You're up already?" I called out.

"Been up for hours. I fed your kitty."

I turned off my alarm and went into my bathroom to shower and brush my teeth. Smoky Joe came into the bedroom and kept me company while I got dressed.

I heard my father whistling before I entered the kitchen. "What are you so happy about?" I asked as I opened the refrigerator.

"Sit," he said.

I sat.

"To answer your question, I'm glad to be spending time with my lovely daughter." He set a mug of coffee before me and dropped a kiss on my cheek. He was clean shaven and wearing a tweed jacket over a robin-blue shirt and dark gray trousers. "Toast? Bagel? I see you have both in the freezer."

Who is this man? He's never served me breakfast in his life. "I'll have a slice of whole wheat toast, thanks."

He dropped a slice of bread into the toaster. "Butter, jam, cream cheese?"

"Cream cheese would be nice."

"I see you're well stocked."

"A lot of it's leftover from my party."

I sipped my coffee. My toast popped up and Jim served it to me. As I was spreading on cream cheese, he asked, "What do you hear from your mother?"

I shrugged. My mother, who had never been very maternal, showed even less interest in me since her remarriage to a man twelve years younger than her.

"She seems happy living in Hollywood. The last time we spoke, she was excited because Tom had gotten a small part in a movie. I don't remember which one."

Jim laughed. "Hollywood—the land of make-believe and dreams. The perfect place for Brianna."

My irritation toward my self-absorbed mother shifted to Jim. "Maybe that's because you never made things easy for her."

"That's true. I never did," he said, sounding thoughtful. "I always hoped . . ."

"Hoped what?" I demanded.

"That she'd make up for my absence, but it didn't turn out that way."

"It certainly didn't!" *Time to change the subject.* "Why are you all dressed up?"

"I have a few things to take care of today."

Ah! Secretive. Vague. The father I knew is back!

"What are you up to, Jim?"

"Always suspicious of your old man, aren't you?"

"I can't have you staying here if you're planning to rob someone," I said.

"I'm not planning anything of the sort." He sat down and sipped his coffee. "John Mathers wants me to stop by around eleven for another little chat."

"He does?"

I must have looked frightened, because he placed his hand over mine. "Don't worry, Caro. There's no evidence that links me to Benton's demise. No blood spatter on my clothes. But Dylan put a bug in Mathers's ear, and now he's trying to link me to the gem heist, though it happened way out of his jurisdiction. Frankly, I think he's trying to put the thumbscrews to me to get me to tell him where the gems are so he can collect the reward."

"I don't believe that for a minute! John Mathers isn't that sort of man."

"Well, maybe I'm reading into things, but he called to tell me to stop by, and it wasn't a request."

"That can't be why you're dressed so nicely."

He coughed, a tell when he was feeling guilty. "They're holding the wake for Benton this afternoon."

I gaped at him. "You're not thinking of going, are you?"

"Why not? Benton was a friend of sorts, and poor Mariel deserves all the support she can get."

"You know Mariel, Benton's widow?"

"Knew her when we children. We were sweethearts, in fact. In fifth grade."

"I hope you won't do anything foolish. You'll be leaving Clover Ridge, but this is my home now."

"Don't worry, Caro. I don't plan to ask if she knows where her devious husband hid a bagful of stolen gems."

I sent him a fierce look. "Don't tell me you're still trying to get your hands on them."

At which point he stood and wiped his mouth with his napkin. "Gotta go."

"Where, at this hour? It's not even eight o'clock."

But he was slipping on his jacket and was halfway out the door.

*　*　*

Jim was up to something, I just knew it. I was in worry mode as I drove to work amid the morning rush-hour traffic, hoping he wasn't about to do something rash. He didn't have to spell it out for me that he was still determined to find those gems—probably more so now that he no longer had to split them. If he hadn't killed Benton, and I didn't think that he had, it was possible that someone else was after them too.

But maybe I was being paranoid. Maybe Paul Darby killed Benton, and Benton's murder had nothing to do with the gems at all. As far as I knew, my father and Benton were the only people involved in the theft. Benton had taken the stones and had no intention of splitting them with my father. Somehow my father knew that Benton hadn't tried to fence them. I snorted. Probably because he knew all the fences.

Why hadn't Jim and Benton divided up the gems immediately? Perhaps my father had been in one of his traveling phases and hadn't had a safe place to keep them. Benton had a safe, but the gems weren't in it.

Smoky Joe nestled against my hip. "Sorry I've been ignoring you," I told him as I stroked his back. "You're getting so big, and your tail's bushier than ever."

He snuggled closer and began to purr.

I arrived at work fifteen minutes early. I decided to call John Mathers at the station. As my father's daughter, it was only logical that I'd want to know if he was still considered a suspect. Gracie greeted me warmly and put me right through.

"Hi, John. It's Carrie Singleton."

"Hello, Carrie. What can I do for you?"

"My father told me you wanted to talk to him this morning. Do you still consider him a suspect in Benton's homicide?"

"He's still a person of interest since he ran from the murder scene."

"I suppose he was frightened you'd see him as a suspect, given that he was in the store and found the body."

"Then why didn't he call us? That's what an innocent person would do. And Carrie, we found his fingerprints outside the big safe where Benton kept his merchandise."

My heart was thudding when I asked, "Was anything taken?"

"Nothing's missing, according to Chris Crowley."

I hesitated a moment then plunged ahead. "And you didn't find any jewelry on my father when he was apprehended, right?"

"That's true."

"And there was no blood on his clothing. So why do you still want to question him?"

"Your father and Benton did some business together. We're inquiring into other avenues of their relationship."

The heist! "Did you follow up on that man I told you about? I think I now know who he is."

"Is that so?" John sounded annoyed. "Carrie, I hope you're not getting involved in another murder investigation. You almost got killed last time, remember?"

"I'm worried about my father," I said, surprised to hear my voice breaking.

"I hope neither of you does anything stupid. Leave the investigating to me and my men."

"The man's name is Paul Darby."

"Yes, we know. Jennifer Darby's husband."

"Oh. So you know about all that."

"We do, and I appreciate your telling me what you witnessed."

"You thought I was making it up. I'd never do something like that."

"I apologize." His voice softened. "Carrie, I'm sorry you have to deal with all of this. Your father's a career criminal. I'm sure you love him and want to keep him safe, but he's done some bad things. Don't get caught up in his shenanigans. Be well."

Tears welled up in my eyes as I disconnected. John Mathers felt sorry for me. Precisely what I'd been running from all these years. The phone rang.

"Hello!" I said more gruffly than I'd meant to.

"Carrie, it's me. Dylan."

I set down the receiver and covered my face with my hands, then snatched it up again. I had to get my emotions under control.

"Hello, Dylan," I said as calmly as I could manage. "I really can't talk right now."

"Carrie, please don't shut me out."

"How can it be any other way? You're determined to put my father back in prison."

"I'd like to talk about that. Can we at least meet and discuss it before I fly out?"

"What's there to say? We're on opposite sides."

"Your father—"

"My father's been a thief all his life, but he's my father." I drew a deep breath, hating to say the following words but knowing I had to. "Tell me if you want me to move out of the cottage. I'll understand."

"Of course I don't want you to move."

"I have to go, Dylan."

"We'll talk over the weekend when I'm home again."

"Yes. I'll see you then." I disconnected.

The moment I hung up, I longed to call Dylan back to tell him . . . *what*? That it was fine for him to question my father about gems he'd been paid to recover? A sense of despair came over me. I'd never be free of Jim Singleton's legacy. His absence during my growing-up years coupled with the shame of being a felon's daughter had taken a toll on my confidence and pride. And now he was back in my life, ruining my relationship with the only man I'd cared for in years.

I leaped from my chair in desperate need of a break. Maybe Angela could spare a few minutes to give me a pep talk. For some reason, I hadn't told her about Dylan's part in all of this.

Smoky Joe came bounding toward me as I crossed the reading room. I petted him absentmindedly and continued on my way to the circulation desk. A line of patrons was waiting to have their books and movies checked out. I waved to Angela, said I'd see her for lunch, and made a beeline for the coffee shop beyond the magazine area. I wanted to speak to Jennifer Darby. My father was a thief, but he wasn't a murderer. I needed to clear his name of this charge, and to do it, I had to talk to the people closest to Benton Parr.

The shop was located in an alcove off the reading room. I glanced around the small eating area and behind the counter. There was no sign of Jennifer. I heard the sound of running water and realized there was a tiny back room that might have been part of the kitchen when the library had been a private home. I eyed the brownies and chocolate chip cookies in the display cases on the counter and told myself that despite my miserable mood I would not buy either one. I sat at one of the small, round tables, glad that no one else was there.

A minute later, Jennifer appeared, a coffee carafe in hand. She had a girl-next-door vibe about her. A headband held her long brown hair off her face, making her look ten years younger than her actual age. She offered me a wan smile. "Be right with you. I'm making a fresh pot of coffee."

"Carrie!" she said, realizing who I was. Her hand trembled and water splashed as she slammed the carafe down on the counter.

"Hello, Jennifer. I'd like a cup of coffee, please."

"What are you doing here? You never come in here."

"I thought we might talk."

"About what? How you sent the police after my husband? Yesterday they questioned him for hours. And he had to go back to the station again today. I have to find him a good lawyer so he doesn't go to prison for something he didn't do!"

"I'm sorry, but I heard him threatening Benton. I had to

tell the police. At the time, I had no idea he was your husband. Turns out they already knew about the incident."

"You're just trying to divert their attention from your father. Chris found *him* with poor Benton lying dead on the floor. Why don't the police arrest *him*? We don't need any more aggravation in our lives."

Jennifer burst out crying, deep wrenching sobs. I wanted to comfort her but knew she didn't want solace from me. I left the shop and returned to my office. So far, the morning was a total failure.

Chapter Eight

I turned on my computer and began answering my email. Most of it required short, straightforward answers—a chef's question about his upcoming visit; a reminder from Sally about Friday morning's meeting. Just enough to keep my mind occupied and not dwell on my father or Dylan or how I'd just upset Jennifer Darby, who had enough troubles of her own.

"Why the glum expression?"

I glanced up to find Evelyn perched on my desk.

"So far, everything's gone wrong today." I ran down my list of woes. "I need to find out who killed Benton. I need to find those gems."

"You're worried about your father."

"Of course I'm worried about him. He could get himself killed, chasing after those gems."

Evelyn began pacing the width of my small office. Today she wore the same black pencil skirt, a gray print blouse, and low-heeled black pumps. "Do you think the person who killed Benton was after the stolen gems?"

"Could be. Or maybe Jennifer Darby's husband killed him because he was sleeping with his wife! How would I know?"

"Please calm down, Carrie. You're not helping matters by getting worked up."

I covered my face with my hands. "Jim Singleton's back in my life and making a mess of it."

"Don't let him."

"How can I stop him? This afternoon he's going to Benton's wake. I know he's going there to find out what he can."

"Like father, like daughter," Evelyn murmured.

"I'm *not* like him!"

"I only meant you both want to find the gems."

"I want to find them so he can't get at them. I'll hand them over, and there'll be nothing else for him to do but leave town."

"And you?"

"What about me?"

"You'll be left drained and exhausted and without the man you love."

I slumped into my chair. "I know. But I can't get past the fact that all this time Dylan was searching for my father. He knew he'd taken the gems."

"I wonder how he knew."

"Good question." A thought occurred to me. "What if there was a third partner involved in the heist? Not that Jim said. But what if there was a silent partner who provided information and never got his share? My father's so secretive, he might only have told me what he thinks I need to know."

"Interesting possibility," Evelyn said. "You're thinking this partner might have assumed both your father and Benton were double-dealing, so he ratted on them?"

I shrugged. "Maybe. Maybe not. The problem with that is neither the police nor Dylan seemed to suspect that Benton was involved."

"Are you sure of that?"

"Not exactly."

Evelyn grinned. "You could ask Dylan if he'd ever questioned Benton about the heist."

"I don't want to ask Dylan anything."

"He's been trying to explain matters, but you're refusing to listen." When I didn't answer, she said, "Don't make the mistake of backing the wrong horse."

I glared at her. "What's that supposed to mean? I shouldn't care about my father?"

"Of course, care about him, but Jim Singleton isn't part of your world. Once he finds what's he's after, he'll disappear from your life again. Don't lose Dylan in the process."

"I'll think about it," I said, none too graciously.

"Good." She faded and disappeared.

* * *

Trish arrived a few minutes later. We discussed the day's schedule. I asked her to visit all the programs in progress, to check if any of the instructors needed anything and to make sure all was running smoothly. At twelve thirty, Angela and I walked over to the Cozy Corner Café, where she bestowed on me a dose of cheerful common sense as we chowed down on sandwiches and coffee. I drove home, ruminating over her and Evelyn's advice, and promised myself I wouldn't do anything drastic, either about my father or for his sake. As for Dylan . . . I wasn't ready to tackle that problem yet.

Jim must have heard me drive up to the cottage, because the front door swung open as Smoky Joe and I exited the car.

"What's all this?" I asked, staring at the wreath on the door. Once inside, I breathed in the lovely aroma of pine even before I caught sight of the tree in the far corner of the living room. It stood at least seven feet tall.

"Christmas is practically at our doorstep, and here you are in your new home with none of the trimmings. I decided we needed to get in the holiday spirit."

Smoky Joe scampered over to sniff the lower branches. I opened my mouth to say I thought he had no money, then shut it. I didn't want to know anything about his financial state.

Jim pointed to the four boxes lying beside the tree. "I bought a few ornaments and tinsel. We can trim the tree tomorrow."

"All right, or we can start on it later tonight," I said.

Jim clapped his hands. "What are we doing about dinner? I see you still have plenty of cold cuts left over from your birthday party, but I was hoping for something a bit more along the lines of home cooking."

I laughed. "In that case, you've come to the wrong place. But I have some prepared Indian dinners in the freezer. They take minutes in the microwave. And I'll cut up a salad."

"Sounds perfect."

I fed Smoky Joe then chopped up lettuce, tomato, cucumber, and carrots for our salad. I prepped our Indian meals for the microwave and made up a salad dressing. Then I took an open bottle of Chardonnay from the refrigerator.

"Care for some wine?" I called to my father, who was watching the news on TV.

"Sure, honey."

I brought him a glass of wine and poured one for myself. "Dinner will be ready in five minutes."

I hummed as I nuked the two Indian dinners and set the table. A few minutes later, Jim joined me in the kitchen and poured himself another glass of wine. The microwave beeped. I spooned the heated food onto plates, and we sat down to our dinner.

My father took a bite of his chicken tikka masala and shot me a look of surprise. "This is great!"

"Glad you like it. I used to eat it a lot before I moved to Clover Ridge."

He scoffed down a few more forkfuls, then started in on his salad. "This is real nice, the two of us having dinner together."

"It is," I agreed. "Too bad we didn't do this when Jordan and I were growing up."

"Oh, honey, I'm truly sorry."

"Of course you are."

"It's the truth. I think about all the time I lost away from my family. It was stupid of me to get involved in things the way I did." He sighed. "But now my life is as it is, and there's not much I can do to change it."

And the less I know about that life, the better. "What happened at the wake?"

"The usual. I signed the book, offered my condolences to Mariel and her kids, hung around a bit, then left."

"See any people you know?"

"Of course. I lived here once upon a time, remember?"

"Were Uncle Bosco and Aunt Harriet there?"

"They were."

I grimaced. My father was acting cagey again—like a CIA agent refusing to discuss top secrets. "How did Mariel react when she saw you?"

A big smile wreathed his face. "She sure was happy I'd come. We talked a bit. She let on that things between her and Benton had been strained for some time."

I stared at him, wondering if he was pulling my leg. "Really? After not seeing you all these years, she suddenly opens up and tells you about her marital problems at her husband's wake?"

Jim shrugged. "What can I say? We go back a long time, and maybe there's no one else she can share this with. Anyway, we only had a few minutes to talk. A young woman showed up and went straight to the coffin. She stayed there, sobbing into the casket. People began to notice. Mariel's son went over to her and told her to leave. At first she resisted. Then someone from the funeral home came over and escorted her out. She left in tears."

"Oh, no! That must have been Jennifer Darby."

"The girlfriend?" Jim asked.

"She works in the library's coffee shop. I tried to talk to her this morning, but she was terribly upset, so I left. She was angry because I'd told the police about her husband's altercation with Benton the night before he was killed."

"You did the right thing, telling them what you heard. Otherwise, Mathers might still be liking me for Benton's murder."

I shook my head. "Come on. We don't know if Paul Darby killed Benton."

"You're right. I'm thinking anyone of several people at the wake might have killed Benton. He was a real snake in the grass."

Jim laughed suddenly. "Turns out I know one of them. I'm surprised he dared to show up today."

My pulse quickened. "Who was that?"

"Tom Quincy. Benton and I had some dealings with him in the past."

"Was he involved in your heist?"

"Are you kidding?! We learned real quick he wasn't reliable. NTBT."

"What does *that* mean?" I asked.

"Not to Be Trusted."

"So, it sounds like the wake was more interesting than you first let on."

"I suppose. But I didn't learn one damn thing about the gems or where they are."

I prepared coffee in the Keurig and served cookies and small pieces of cake leftover from the party. I made a mental note to freeze the rest of the desserts before I ate any more of them.

I cleared the table and began stacking dishes in the dishwasher. I was feeling content. It was nice having dinner at home with my father, chatting a bit about the days when I was small and the four of us had spent time together as a family.

"Want to get started on the Christmas tree?" I called out to Jim, who was drinking the last of his coffee in the living room.

He didn't answer. I was about to call out again, when I noticed he was speaking in low tones into his cell phone.

Finally he looked up and I repeated my question.

"Sorry, Caro, I have to go out tonight."

"Where?" I demanded.

"I'm meeting an old friend. It's important."

"Oh."

He came into the kitchen and put his arm around me. "Why don't you start decorating the Christmas tree? I promise I'll help you with it tomorrow night."

"You're leaving," I said bitterly. "Just like old times."

He held out his hands, palms up, as if he had no choice. "I'm doing the best I can," he said softly and went into his room. Fifteen minutes later he appeared. "Don't wait up for me," he said.

"Don't worry. I won't."

I turned on the dishwasher and then ran to open the four boxes of ornaments. I oohed and aahed like a little kid over colorful glass balls, icicles, snowflakes, and candles. Instead of an angel, Jim had bought a laughing Santa Claus to stand at the top of the tree. While Smoky Joe sniffed them, I carefully placed each ornament on the carpet. I longed to start hanging them, but even more, I wanted to share the trimming with my father.

We'll decorate tomorrow, I told myself. I'd spent so few Christmas holidays with him. *Maybe I'll make a real Christmas dinner. Invite Aunt Harriet and Uncle Bosco, Randy, Julia, and their kids. Shall I make turkey or ham?*

Who was I kidding? Jim would probably be long gone from Clover Ridge by the time December twenty-fifth rolled around.

I walked toward the sofa, ready to switch on the TV remote, when I heard a muffled sound. It came from the window facing the river. I hadn't bothered to close the blinds since there were no other houses around. I ran to the window and looked out in time to see a figure disappear from sight.

Someone had been watching me! I managed to unlock the front door just as a dark blue sedan turned onto the road and sped away.

I shivered with fear. Occasionally cars drove down the road

despite the "Private" sign. But no one ever left their vehicle to walk around the house and peer into a window. Whoever had been out there must have been looking for my father!

I called his cell phone and frowned when it went to voicemail. I left a message. "Someone came here and looked into the cottage through the living room window. Please be careful."

I called two more times. Still no answer. The land phone rang at ten forty-five.

"Jim?"

My heart leaped in my chest when a gruff voice said, "Is Jim there?"

"No, he isn't."

"When's he coming back?"

"I have no idea."

The caller disconnected. *Where are you, Jim Singleton?*

He still wasn't home by eleven thirty, when I drifted off to sleep. I woke up before my alarm went off and hurried into the guest room. I felt a sliver of dismay to see clothes strewn across the bed, a bed that hadn't been slept in.

Chapter Nine

"Hello, Carrie. This is John Mathers."

"John! What's wrong? Is my father . . . ?"

John let out a humorless chuckle. "He's got himself in a spot of trouble. But he'll be all right in a week or so."

I gulped down the panic rising to my throat. "You haven't put him back in jail, have you?"

"Nope. This time he's the guest of South Conn Hospital."

"The hospital." I collapsed onto my bedroom chair and closed my eyes. "What happened to him?"

"Danny Brower was out patrolling last night. He found Jim in Due Amici's parking lot out cold. He's concussed, and I'm afraid he has a ruptured spleen."

None of this made any sense. Questions swirled around in my head. "What was he doing at a restaurant? We had dinner before he went out. What time did Danny find him?"

John paused. "Just after two a.m."

I jumped to my feet. "And you're just calling me now? Why didn't you tell me as soon as Danny found him?"

"Easy there, Carrie. Your father made us swear up and down

that we wouldn't disturb your night's sleep. I spoke to his doctor. Jim will be fine."

"I sure hope so. Thanks for the call."

I was about to disconnect, when John asked, "What's he looking for, Carrie?"

Information about the gems. "I have no idea."

"Do you know who he was meeting?" John asked.

"I don't. He went out after dinner. Didn't tell me where."

"What time was that?"

"Seven thirty. Eight."

"Sounds like he was out and about for quite some time."

I hesitated, then plunged ahead with my question. "Did anyone at the restaurant see him?"

"Not in the restaurant, but the manager saw two men talking in the parking lot when he finally left at eleven. His description of one of the men sounds like your father."

"The other man?"

"Shorter, gray-haired, wearing a leather bomber jacket."

Could that be the man who was looking in the window last night?

"Do you think they had an argument and the man hit my father?"

"Sounds that way. Punched him in the area of the spleen. Jim fell and hit his head."

"And he was lying there for hours in the cold?"

"I'm afraid so. Danny called for an ambulance. As soon as the EMS brought him in, they gave him two CT scans to make sure he wasn't bleeding internally. He's in a great deal of pain, but he'll be okay."

"Oh, Jim, what are you up to now?" I covered my mouth when I realized I'd spoken out loud.

"When he gets home, do me a favor and tell him to stay out of trouble."

"I will, John, but will he listen to me?"

* * *

I called Sally to tell her I'd be late to work because my father was in the hospital with a concussion, then drove to South Conn Hospital. It was an old building with two additions that had obviously been added at different times. I parked in what turned out to be the wrong parking lot and had to walk through the emergency area. I finally found his room. My father was lying on his back in the bed near the windows. His eyes were closed. They fluttered open when I grasped his hand.

"Caro, thank God you came. You have to get me out of here."

Not again. "Sorry, Jim. You'll be here for a while. Who did this to you?"

He tried to smile, but it turned into a grimace. "Honey, what you don't know you can't tell John Mathers."

"What were you thinking? Who is the man you were talking to behind Due Amici?"

"It doesn't matter."

"Of course it matters! A man called the house looking for you. And someone peered into the living room window. Is that the same person who landed you here in the hospital?"

"Don't worry about him. He's gone, Caro. I told him nothing."

A chill snaked down my spine. "So he's after the gems too. Did he kill Benton?"

"Maybe. I don't know."

"We have to tell John!"

"No! Don't mention him to the police."

When I didn't answer, he tugged at my arm. "Please, honey. If Mathers tracks down Quincy, he'll spill the beans about the heist. I only managed to make him leave town by promising to send him a few grand."

"A few *thousand* dollars?"

"That's right." He scrunched up his face. "Could you please call my nurse? I need more pain medicine."

"Of course."

I pressed the call button just as a bald doctor wearing glasses pushed aside the privacy curtain and greeted us. "Hello, I'm Dr. Brodsky. I bet you're Jim's daughter."

"Right. Carrie Singleton." We shook hands.

Dr. Brodsky listened to my father's heart and lungs and asked him how he was feeling. "I've scheduled CT scans for you this afternoon."

"Again? I had CT scans when they brought me in."

"You have a tear on your spleen that needs monitoring. We're very concerned about internal bleeding caused by the injury to your spleen. Your hemoglobin count is low, which means you may need a blood transfusion. It's too soon to say. And you've suffered a concussion."

"When can I leave?"

Dr. Brodsky released an exasperated sigh. "Now Jim, we've been through this. Your blood pressure's dropped a bit and you're having blurred vision, all indications that we need to keep an eye on you. You have to stay here until your symptoms have cleared up and your CTs are okay. I'd say, figure on being our guest for at least a week."

My father tried to sit up but fell back. "A week! I can't stay here a week."

The doctor turned to me. "Carrie, I need your help here to make your father see reason."

"Don't argue with Dr. Brodsky, Jim," I said. "You have to stay in the hospital until he says it's okay for you to go home. I'll bring you whatever you need."

His answer was a frown. Doctor Brodsky beckoned me to follow him into the hall. "Your father has some serious injuries, but they'll heal as long as he calms down and stops fighting me."

"I'll do my best to see that he does," I said.

When I returned to Jim's bedside, he gripped my arm. I stooped down so he could whisper in my ear. "If I can't get out, you're going to have to find the gems."

I snorted. "I wouldn't know where to start."

"Of course you do. You've already solved two murders."

I stared at him open-mouthed. "Who told you that?"

"Harriet and Bosco. They told me how resourceful you are." His voice took on a wheedling tone. "You can start by attending Benton's funeral. It's tomorrow morning at ten o'clock."

Chapter Ten

Thoughts bounced around in my head like ping-pong balls as I headed for home. My father's assault had shaken me badly. Where was his outrage at the man who had attacked him? And why had he agreed to pay him off? Jim didn't want me to tell John the man's identity. What's more, he seemed to bear him no ill will and was very nonchalant about having nearly been killed. Maybe beatings and attacks were common occurrences in Jim's so-called line of work. If that were the case, I was glad he'd stayed away from us all these years. Glad too that the doctor wanted to keep him in the hospital for at least a week. It would keep Jim out of trouble while I did my darnedest to find the gems so I could hand them over to Dylan.

Smoky Joe was happy to see me when I walked through the front door. I fed him, and then we headed for work. Word that my father was laid up in the hospital with injuries had already spread to my colleagues. They assumed he'd been mugged, and I made no attempt to correct their erroneous assumption. I'd tell Angela the truth over lunch, where curious ears couldn't overhear us.

There were plenty of phone calls and emails to respond to, which kept me occupied until Trish showed up at eleven. I peeked in at the craft group making Christmas stockings and felt menorahs, then looked in on the current events group, which was already in the midst of a heated discussion about the president's latest unilateral decision.

Back at my desk, I read over the May–June newsletter to check for typos and to verify dates and course numbers, then brought it over to Harvey Kirk, the head of the computer department. Harvey was a slight elf of a man, in his early fifties, who used to work for one of the big computer companies. He knew everything there was to know about computers, tablets, and smartphones. I asked him what could be causing my computer at home to be slowing down, and he gave me a few suggestions to try out.

"If none of them work, bring it in and I'll look it over," he said as I was leaving.

"Thanks, Harv. I will."

Dorothy Hawkins called to me as I was passing the reference desk. She had been my nemesis since I had become head of P and E, believing she should have been given the position instead of me. She had tried to make me look incompetent in various ways. Once she had hidden a film we were about to show. Another time she had called a few presenters and told them their programs had been canceled. I'd managed to broker a truce between us, but the scowl on her face let me know that truce was about to be broken.

"Carrie, I wish you'd leave your cat at home like the rest of the world." She stood up, brushing the front of her skirt with both hands. "He's getting hair all over my clothes."

"Really? I'm sorry about that. I'll make sure to brush him more frequently."

Just then Smoky Joe came up to me and rubbed against my slacks. I bent down to pet him. When I stood up, I smiled at Dorothy. "No hairs on my pants, or on any of my clothing for that matter. I wonder if the hairs on your skirt came from Smoky Joe or from some other animal."

I felt the heat of her glare on my back as I walked away. *And I'm supposed to buy* her *a Secret Santa gift?*

"I see Dorothy's been acting up again."

I turned to Evelyn, who had suddenly manifested. She kept pace with me as I continued on to my office. "Your niece is a most unpleasant person." I spoke softly so no one would hear me and think I was going bonkers.

Evelyn sighed. "She's been that way since she left my sister's womb." As I was about to turn the doorknob, she said, "Carrie, I'm going to ask you to do me a favor."

"Certainly. As long as I don't have to invite Dorothy over for dinner."

She laughed. "Nothing like that."

I released the knob. I couldn't talk to Evelyn in my office with Trish there. "In that case, why don't you come downstairs with me and tell me what you have in mind?"

We took the staircase down to the supply closet, where I signed out a package of paper for my office printer. There was a folding chair against one of the walls. I sat down and looked up at Evelyn.

"What can I do for you? I know it must be important or you wouldn't ask."

Evelyn's face took on a faraway look. "It's something Robert and I used to do every Christmas for many, many years—until I left this plane."

"I'm listening."

"We had an elderly neighbor." She laughed. "That is, Morgan seemed elderly when we moved into our house thirty years ago. He must have been in his mid-sixties, the age I am now."

That is *old,* I thought.

Evelyn shot me a shrewd glance. "Age is relative, my dear. You'll learn that soon enough. Anyway Morgan Fuller was a retired widower, a carpenter who kept his house and lawn in tiptop condition. He was very welcoming to us when Robert and I moved into our home. If we had a plumbing problem or needed a new roof, wanted to wallpaper the kitchen and redo the bathrooms, he always offered sound advice. What he couldn't do himself, he recommended reliable workmen he could vouch for. He had no children and we didn't either, so we spent most holidays together."

"He must be in his mid-nineties now. Is he still living in his home?"

"No, he had a stroke ten years ago that left him partially paralyzed. Robert and I helped move him into a nursing home. Poor guy—we adopted Snuggles, the cat he was so fond of, because he couldn't keep a cat in the nursing home."

She looked down at the floor. "Robert died less than a year later. When I wasn't working at the library or visiting my sister, Dorothy's mother, I often stopped at the nursing home to visit Morgan. I always brought him a box of his favorite cookies around the holidays."

She reached out her hand. Though it remained inches away, an icy chill ran along my arm. I knew she wished she could touch me. I wished she could too.

"I'd like you to visit Morgan and bring him a box of linzer cookies." Evelyn giggled. "He's already seen a ghost or two in his lifetime and won't panic when you tell him I sent you, and give him my love."

"Of course. I'd be happy to. But are you sure he's still alive?"

"That I don't know."

"Where's the nursing home?"

"I'm afraid it's quite a distance from here. An hour's drive at least."

I gulped. With everything going on in my life and the holidays approaching, spending an afternoon away from Clover Ridge before Christmas was going to be difficult.

Evelyn's face took on an expression of chagrin. "Please forgive me for being so presumptuous. Silly me—I think of you as my niece and forget that you're not a relation."

"The thing is, my father's in the hospital with a concussion and a ruptured spleen. One of his cronies attacked him last night, and Jim refuses to tell John Mathers his name. I have to find those gems he's after so he'll stop looking for them himself."

She sighed. "You certainly have more than enough on your plate."

"At least I can find out if Morgan Fuller's still alive."

"The name of the nursing home is the Hopewell Home for Seniors. It's in Bantam."

"I'll find out if Morgan's still a resident there. If he is, I'll do my best to find the time to pay him a visit."

"You're an angel, Carrie," she said as she faded.

I laughed. "I'm far from that, but I'm glad you think so."

At lunchtime, I drove Angela to our favorite Indian

restaurant on Mercer Street, a few blocks north of the center of town. Though the only other diners were a party of four men who were laughing it up at a front table, I asked to be seated in the semicircular booth in the far corner. Here, no one but the four human-sized statues of Hindu gods and goddesses behind us could hear what I wanted to tell Angela.

We went up to the buffet and filled our plates with chicken tikka, rice, palak paneer, and other vegetables. As we ate, I explained why Jim would be spending at least a week in South Conn.

"Wow! The man's one tough dude! A guy clobbers him, demands to be paid off, and he stays mum."

"Angela, please! You're making him sound like the lead singer of a rock band when he's a thief after his loot. He's fifty-eight and acts like a kid who never grew up. He's so hot on finding those gems, he's blind to the danger he's in. Someone may have killed Benton for them."

"Who knew about the heist?"

"My father said he and Benton made a pact not to tell anyone, but somehow that Quincy guy found out." I frowned. "Maybe Benton told him. He cut my father out of his share, so we know he's not a man of his word."

Angela laughed. "They say there's no honor among thieves."

"Exactly. The other possibility is Benton contacted a fence to sell the gems, and the fence told Quincy."

"How do you know Benton hasn't already sold them?"

"My father spoke to him the night before he was murdered. He wanted to stop by Benton's house, but Benton convinced him to come to the store early the following morning. He told Jim he'd hidden the gems where no one would find them."

"Okay, so that's why he went to the store. But why did he stay when he saw Benton had been murdered?"

"The idiot started searching for the gems. He managed to open the safe before Chris arrived. No gems."

"So that's why the police arrested him! Even with a dead body on the floor, he kept on searching."

I frowned at Angela, not liking the admiration in her voice. "It was pretty stupid, if you ask me. John arrested him, and hours later Dylan was at the station questioning him."

"Dylan?" Angela's eyes widened. "Oh, no."

"He'd been working a case of stolen gems for months. My father was a suspect but was nowhere to be found. Dylan used me, Angela. That's why he rented me the cottage and started taking me out. To get to my father and solve his case."

To my shame and embarrassment, I burst into tears. Angela reached over to wrap her arms around me.

"Oh, Carrie, Dylan adores you. I've seen how he looks at you."

"Yeah. I'm the perfect stooge."

Angela handed me a napkin, and I blew my nose. The young Indian waiter came dashing over to us.

"Is everything all right?" he asked nervously.

"Of course," Angela said. "My friend just ate a very spicy piece of chicken."

Relieved, he left. Angela and I burst out laughing.

Angela slid back in her seat. "I'm glad to see you've regained your sense of humor. What do you plan to do about your father and those gems?"

"Find them as quickly as I can and hand them over to Dylan or the police to return to their owner. I don't want Jim to live on stolen goods, and I don't want to see him back in prison." I sighed. "When he realizes he can't get the gems any which way, he'll probably disappear again, and I won't see him for another few years."

"Won't you miss him?"

I shook my head vehemently. "Absolutely not! He's caused me nothing but grief since he arrived. I can well understand why my mother divorced him."

I drove back to the library in better spirits. I was lucky to have Angela as my best friend. She was resourceful and always upbeat, and I could count on her to be straight with me.

"I suppose you're going to try to find out who killed Benton," she said as I turned into the library's parking lot.

"Looks that way, since Benton and the missing gems are connected. Can I count on your help?"

She shot me a broad grin. "You sure can! What would you like me to do?"

"Find out all you can about Mariel and Dina Parr and Chris, Benton's assistant. Money issues, love affairs, scandals."

Angela giggled. "Will do."

"Are you at all friendly with Jennifer Darby?"

"Not really."

"I'm going to try talking to her again," I said. "She might know something about Benton's business—the legal and the illegal."

"I'll find out what I can about her husband, Paul," Angela said.

"Great. I'm planning to attend Benton's funeral tomorrow morning. Maybe I'll learn something useful."

Chapter Eleven

The rest of the workday went smoothly. After Trish went home, Sally stopped by with the month's expense sheets for me to fill out.

"I know you're swamped with holiday programs, so don't worry if you can't get these back to me till mid-January."

"Thanks, Sally."

We exchanged smiles, both remembering how two months earlier she'd given me the sheets to fill out within an unreasonably short period of time. To her surprise, I'd handed them back, properly filled out, before her deadline. She had no way of knowing, of course, that Evelyn had helped me. I thought part of Sally's hostility toward me when I'd first accepted the position as head of P and E was because her friend Dorothy had egged her on. Or perhaps Dorothy had been holding something over Sally. Whichever it was, Sally had changed her mind about me, and now we were good friends.

Which reminded me. "Dorothy complained that Smoky Joe got hairs all over her clothes. I don't believe it for a minute. I pick him up all the time and don't have any gray hairs on me."

Sally laughed. "She whined about it to me too. I told her to keep out of his way. Too many patrons are happy to have a library cat to pet and make a fuss over. He's a big hit with the little ones, of course, and with our retirees who spend hours reading newspapers and magazines in the reading room. Many of them love animals but are unable to keep them at home for various reasons."

"Yes, I've noticed."

"There's something else." Sally leaned closer to me, though no one could possibly hear her inside my office. "I've seen a mouse scampering across the floor near my office. Max is all for setting mousetraps, but I'm afraid the sight of them would put off our patrons."

I shuddered. "I agree."

"I'm hoping Smoky Joe catches the little varmint. See you later."

I thought about mice as I drove home that evening. The idea that we had a few in the library was repugnant, but the idea of my half-grown kitty murdering a little mouse didn't please me either. I tried to convince myself that catching mice was something cats did naturally, and only managed to stop dwelling on this fact of nature when I remembered something else Sally had said. Smoky Joe had a special affinity for our older patrons. It gave me an idea.

My evening was busy, almost too busy to think about Dylan. I missed him terribly, especially knowing the weekend was coming and I wouldn't be spending it with him.

It's your own fault! I thought, then remembered how he'd had plenty of time and opportunity to mention that he'd been working on a case that might involve my father and hadn't bothered to tell me.

I fed Smoky Joe his dinner and heated up leftovers for mine. Then I called Jim, who complained about the hospital food. I hung up, relieved that he hadn't complained about pain, which meant it was probably easing. And thank goodness he hadn't demanded that I bring him home immediately.

Time to decorate, I told myself, though the thought of adorning the tree by myself had me feeling lonely and bereft. My father had managed his disappearing act once again. And this time right around the holidays.

He planned to decorate the tree with you tonight, only he's in the hospital, you ninny!

I would *not* feel sorry for myself! I switched on the radio and found a station with upbeat holiday music and turned up the volume. I spent the next hour hanging every decoration on the tree and spreading the tinsel about the branches in what I liked to consider an artistic manner. I took occasional breaks and danced around the room to the beat of the lively songs.

Smoky Joe dashed from one decoration to another, sniffing each one and trying to make the balls roll. When that didn't work, he snagged a section of tinsel in his mouth and tugged until I lured him away with one of his toys. He finally wore himself out and curled up in a furry ball at the base of the tree.

On impulse I called Jim. As the phone rang, I glanced at the clock and saw it was past ten o'clock. I hadn't realized it was that late. I was about to disconnect, when he picked up, sounding groggy.

"Sorry I woke you up."

"Caro? Don't give it a thought. I can sleep anytime."

"I just wanted to tell you I finished decorating the tree."

"Good girl. I'll see it when they let me out of this place." I heard a female voice in the background. "Have to go now. My nurse wants to take my vitals."

"See you in the morning," I said.

"Sleep well, dream sweet dreams," he signed off, the way he used to when Jordan and I were little.

*   *   *

Thank goodness the following day was another late day for me at the library, and I didn't have to take time off from work to attend Benton's funeral. I woke up early and drove to South Conn, arriving as Dr. Brodsky was finishing his examination of my father. The two men were engaged in a friendly conversation. I gave my father a peck on his smooth cheek. A nurse must have shaved him. He looked rested.

"How's he doing?" I asked Dr. Brodsky.

"Coming along." He glanced at Jim. "His vitals are good. He's getting CTs this afternoon to check the internal bleeding and the skull hematoma."

When the doctor left, Jim asked, "Did you find out anything? Do you know who has the gems?"

I burst out laughing. "I was working all day yesterday, but I'm going to Benton's funeral this morning."

His expression turned grim. "Let me know if Quincy shows up there. He's short, has gray hair and the face of a boxer who's lost too many fights. I want to know if he's still hanging around Clover Ridge."

So he wasn't feeling that kindly, after all, toward the man who had sent him to the hospital. "I'll let you know," I said and changed the subject.

I left shortly after and drove to the large Congregational

Church. I remembered when the old church had been located on the Green, a few doors down from the library. The membership must have grown too large for the seventeenth-century building, and some time in the many years I hadn't been back to Clover Ridge, a new church had been erected on Elm Street, a few blocks north of the town center.

I arrived early and took a seat a few rows back from the front of the church, amid the fifteen or so mourners, and waited. The ceremony wouldn't begin for twenty minutes. Hopefully, I'd have the opportunity to talk to the few people who'd been closest to Benton.

But the opportunity didn't present itself. Ten minutes later I spotted Mariel in the hall, who had just arrived with her son, Richard, and his wife and Dina. They disappeared into the small adjoining room. The seats began to fill up. When Aunt Harriet and Uncle Bosco arrived, I called them over to sit beside me.

"How's your father?" Aunt Harriet asked.

"He has a ruptured spleen and a concussion, but he's improving."

Harriet tsk-tsked and Uncle Bosco frowned. "Your father—always finding himself in a mess of trouble. Will he ever grow up? I wonder."

I giggled. "My thoughts exactly."

Uncle Bosco reached over to pinch my cheek. "Thank God you turned out fine."

I tried to catch some of the comments being whispered around me, but all I could make out was "poor Mariel" and "not doing well." Were they speaking about the jewelry store or Benton's widow?

The organist began playing a doleful hymn. Like everyone

present, I turned to watch the procession walk down the center aisle—first the minister, then the pallbearers wheeling the coffin, then Mariel and her children bringing up the rear.

Knowing what I did about Benton Parr, I was surprised to see the rows behind me were filled with Clover Ridge residents wanting to show their respect. Or was it the titillating fact that Benton had been murdered? Sally was sitting across the aisle, here no doubt to represent the library. A few rows behind her, Chris Crowley whispered to an older woman—possibly his mother. I wondered if he and Dina were good friends, dating, or had been simply kidding around the night of Benton's library presentation because they were working together.

The minister gave his blessing and the page number of the first hymn the mourners would sing. As the organist struck a chord, I glanced back and noticed John Mathers standing in the rear. Was he hoping Benton's murderer would show up wearing a guilty expression on his or her face?

The minister began his elegy, praising Benton for having been a good citizen and member of the church, and expressing his fervent wish that his murderer would soon be apprehended. When he finished, he asked if anyone would like to speak.

Richard Parr, a slender, good-looking guy about my age, stood at the podium and talked about the wonderful father Benton had been when he was young—teaching him to pitch and catch a ball when he was seven, and how the two of them had gone fishing together when Richard was in junior high. Nothing about the present, I noticed. Had they been estranged? If so, for how long? And why?

I'd gotten so engrossed in my speculations, I'd missed Dina's opening comments and only caught her last words, stating she hoped the police caught her father's murderer very soon. She sat down, and for a minute or two no one stirred. Then Uncle Bosco went up to the podium to say Benton had been a valuable member of the library board and would be sadly missed.

Sally stood to say pretty much the same thing. A few friends and neighbors mentioned the times Benton had helped them out. I felt a twinge of sympathy for Jennifer Darby when I recalled what Jim had told me of her reception at the wake.

Then it was over. We rose to exit the church. Aunt Harriet kissed my cheek. "Don't be a stranger. Come for dinner soon. Any night that suits. We miss you."

I smiled, remembering the seven months I'd lived with her and Uncle Bosco after I'd arrived at Clover Ridge last May. "Will do," I promised as I hugged her.

It was slow moving up the center aisle, with people from both sides joining the exodus. I found myself walking beside Chris Crowley.

"Hi, Chris. How are you?"

"Still recovering from finding Benton lying dead on the floor. I'd never seen a dead person before."

"I can imagine," I said. "Will you still have a job at the jewelry store?"

"Are you kidding? Mariel can't wait to sell it to the first person that makes a decent offer."

"I imagine she doesn't know much about the jewelry business," I said, "since she didn't work there."

He snorted. "That's for sure. She only knows how to wear it."

"What about Dina?" I asked. "Is she interested in jewelry? I mean interested enough to run the store? She told me she'd been working at the store for years."

A speculative gleam came into his eyes. "She might be if her mother gave her half a chance. But money's tight and Mariel's out to get it ASAP any way she can."

So finances were tight in the Parr household, and neither Chris nor Dina's opinion of Mariel jived with the sweet, kindly facade she presented to her neighbors.

Chris stepped up his pace. Clearly he wanted to end the conversation, but as far as I was concerned, it was just getting interesting.

"Are you and Dina good friends?"

"Why do you ask?"

"When I saw you two together last week, you seemed to get along so well. I got the idea you were dating."

He hesitated, then said, "We were, but Mariel doesn't think I'm good enough for her daughter. Gotta go."

He scooted around a small group of people who had stopped to chat and were holding up traffic.

That was interesting, I thought, glancing at my watch. I had just enough time to stop in the supermarket and pet store and then drive back to the cottage for Smoky Joe before beginning our workday.

"Playing detective again, Carrie?"

Startled, I looked up into John Mathers's eyes. He neither looked nor sounded amused. "I most certainly am not. Benton had just presented a program at the library, so I thought I'd pay my respects."

"Sure you're not after something?"

"Of course not. I'm leaving the detecting to you."

I joined the line of people offering their condolences to Benton's family. "I'm so sorry," I said to Mariel, Dina, Richard, and his wife in turn and received their words of appreciation for having attended the service. Now was not the time to raise questions.

I headed for my car, which I'd left on the street, and stopped when I saw Jennifer Darby in a car parked two spaces in front of mine. She was sobbing. I knocked on the driver's window. At first she didn't hear me. When she looked up, I saw devastation in her face.

"Jennifer, I'm so sorry."

She rolled down the window. "I missed Benton's funeral. Mariel left instructions that I wasn't allowed to enter the church."

"My father told me what happened at the wake." I reached inside my pocketbook and handed her a tissue.

"Thanks." After she blew her nose, she said, "I knew better than to come here, but I couldn't stay away."

"You must have cared for him a lot."

She nodded.

I wanted to advise her not to waste her emotions on a man who had had many affairs and was a thief to boot, but I kept quiet.

"We were in love."

"Jennifer . . ."

She gave a little laugh. "I know. You probably think I'm a foolish innocent that got involved with a Lothario. But it wasn't like that between Benton and me."

I pointed to a small coffee shop across the street. "Would you like to have a cup of coffee?"

She sighed. "I may as well. This has been building up for weeks. I need to talk to someone and get it off my chest."

Chapter Twelve

Angela's eyes popped wide open like a frog's. "You're telling me Benton was really in love with Jennifer and ready to leave Mariel?"

"That's what she said. More wine?" I asked, holding up the bottle. We were sitting in my living room the following evening.

"Of course. By the way, dinner was superb."

"Thank you." I refreshed both our glasses and sipped. "But anyone can make an omelet stuffed with mushrooms and cheese."

"Here's one gal who can't. Steve wishes I'd learn how to make some of my mom's recipes so we can have great dinners when we're married. I told him he could do the cooking."

"How did he take it?" I studied Angela. She and Steve were talking marriage?

"Not that well, but he's agreed to think about it since he's better in the kitchen than I am. But getting back to Jennifer, what else did she say?"

"Once we sat down and ordered muffins and coffee, she was like a faucet you couldn't shut off. She'd met Benton when she went into his store to buy her niece a pendant for her birthday almost four months ago. They found each other easy to talk to, and when he asked if she'd like to have coffee with him, she readily agreed. They met a few times just to talk. She cried on his shoulder about how unhappy she was with Paul. Being out of work had made him distant and grumpy. Even worse, after going on interviews where nothing panned out, he quit looking for another job. She resented having to sell their second car and doing without anything but the basics, including handing over their puppy to her mother. She'd had it when he told *her* to get a job that paid more money.

"Benton told Jennifer he'd had enough of Mariel's rules and regulations. She was ice cold as a person and only concerned with appearances." I looked at Angela. "What does your mother think of Mariel?"

"Mom thinks Mariel's a lovely person who married beneath her. She said Mariel comes across as formal and dogmatic until you get to know her, but she's warm and has a terrific sense of humor."

"Did Mariel ever complain about Benton?"

"Not in so many words, but Mom had the feeling Mariel was planning to sue for divorce."

"Oh! I wonder if that's because Benton told her about Jennifer. Or somehow Mariel found out that this affair was more serious than the others."

"No idea," Angela said. "Mariel didn't say."

"Jennifer said after a few meetings, things got hot and heavy. After they made love in a motel, Benton admitted he'd had other affairs, but that this time he'd fallen in love with her and wanted them to spend the rest of their lives together."

Angela chortled. "What a romantic story this would be if they weren't already married to other people."

"Anyway, they continued to meet and screw and affirm their love for each other. A few days before Benton was killed, they promised each other they'd tell their respective spouses about their love and that they were leaving Clover Ridge."

"Where were they planning to go" Angela asked, downing the last of her wine. "What would they live on?"

"Good questions. Jennifer was vague about the details. She did mention that Benton told her the store wasn't doing that well, but he claimed he had a few irons in the fire and promised he'd take care of her. I imagine he had the stolen gems in mind when he said that."

Angela made a disparaging sound. "And Jennifer fell for it? The way I see it, she was leaving one loser for another."

"You're so much more practical, Angela. And you're forgetting one thing—Jennifer was madly in love with Benton. Why would she doubt what he told her?"

"So, it looks as though both Mariel Parr and Paul Darby knew their spouses were leaving them. Which makes them both murder suspects with a motive."

"Not necessarily," I said. "Jennifer wasn't able to talk to Benton in private those last few days. When she asked if he'd told Mariel, he gave her a vague answer. Which made her suspect he hadn't told her."

"And Jennifer?"

"She admitted that she hadn't told Paul, but he'd found out somehow and shouted at her the day that Benton gave his program at the library."

Angela stretched her arms overhead. "Do you think Benton got cold feet about leaving his life in Clover Ridge?"

"I don't know, but if Jennifer sensed he was having second thoughts—"

"Then she could very well have been the person who killed him."

Angela left shortly afterward. As I put the kitchen in order, I ran through our conversation about what I'd learned from Jennifer. It raised more questions and possibilities. It wasn't unheard of for a murderer to be so upset after killing the person she loved that she'd act grief-stricken as though the loss had been caused by someone other than herself.

Was Jennifer capable of stabbing her lover, given the right provocation?

I puffed up the living room sofa cushions then got ready for bed. Smoky Joe jumped onto the bed to join me. As I stroked his back, I realized it was only Friday night. The entire weekend stretched before me . . . without Dylan.

*　*　*

Saturday morning I pulled myself out of bed at nine o'clock. My mood was as gray as the weather outside. I turned on the radio and switched it off when a silly Christmas song chirped on. I was as grumpy as Scrooge at the start of *A Christmas Carol*. I nibbled on a piece of toast and drank some coffee, then called Jim at the hospital.

"Hi, Caro. Coming to visit me later?"

"Of course. How are you feeling?"

"Pretty good. The doc thinks I can leave in a couple of days."

My heart began to pound. "And you'll be staying with me?"

"Sure thing, if you'll still have me. I have business to see to, don't I?"

Only a few days to find them, and I haven't the slightest idea where the gems might be. "I'm not working today. I'll stop by this afternoon."

"I'd be eternally grateful if you brought me a newspaper and a bunch of grapes. The food here is awful."

I laughed. "Sounds like you're on the mend."

"One more thing, Caro." He sounded wistful.

"What is it?"

"Do you think you could start calling me 'Dad' again?"

"I—I'll think about it."

His request was disconcerting. I'd started calling him Jim when I was fifteen and made myself admit that he didn't take care of me as a father should. I found it hurt less if I thought of him as an adult not attached to me in any special way. I might refer to him as "my dad" or "my father" in conversation, but I hadn't called him "Dad" in half my lifetime. The way I saw it, he no longer deserved the name.

But things had changed recently. Jim was a patient in the hospital and soon would be staying in my home. Though he'd come to Clover Ridge in pursuit of his missing loot, I couldn't deny that he really cared about me. I found it confusing because I could no longer think of him as an insensitive ogre. I smiled as I realized I was actually looking forward to visiting him that afternoon.

However, I had something else to take care of first. I reached for my cell phone and looked up the phone number of the Carlton Manor Nursing Home, where Evelyn's friend Morgan Fuller was residing—if he was still among the living.

"Carlton Manor. Thelma speaking. How can I help you?"

"Could you please tell me if Morgan Fuller is still a resident?"

Thelma laughed, a full-throated happy sound. "He most certainly is. And with whom am I speaking?"

"Carrie Singleton. I'm a friend of a friend. Someone who knew Morgan some years ago."

"I see." After a pause, she said, "Morgan doesn't get many visitors. Are you planning to visit him?"

"I was hoping to stop by now. Is there anything special he likes to eat?"

"Chocolate. Morgan loves chocolate. He'll be thrilled to have a visitor. It's been some time since anyone's come by to see him."

After such a hearty endorsement, I decided to bring him chocolates as well as Evelyn's suggestion of linzer cookies. I asked for directions and slipped into my parka. I felt like a Girl Scout carrying out Evelyn's good deed. I'd spend half an hour with the old gentleman and then be on my way. My own Christmas good deed for the day.

In town I stopped in the gift shop for a copy of *The New York Times* and a small box of Godiva chocolates before walking over to the supermarket on Mercer Street to buy two pounds of grapes and linzer cookies. My gift shopping done, I climbed into my car and drove to the Carlton Manor.

The large white residence set back on a rising lawn was very similar in architectural style to the shops and houses situated around the Green. I parked in the side parking lot and, chocolates and cookies in hand, walked around to the front entrance. A smiling, gray-haired woman greeted me, her hand outstretched.

"Welcome to Carlton Manor."

I recognized her voice. "Hello, Thelma. I'm Carrie Singleton. I'm here to see Morgan Fuller."

"Of course!" Thelma covered my hand in both of hers. "Related to Bosco?"

"His great-niece."

"Ah." Her smile grew wider. "Lovely man, and your Aunt Harriet too. Morgan's in room 107. Through the great room, then turn left. His bed's the one closest to the window. I believe you'll find him reading. He usually reads before lunch, which we serve at eleven forty-five."

Which gives me thirty-five minutes. Just the right amount of time for a visit. "Thank you."

I walked through the pleasant-looking room filled with armchairs and sofas facing a large-screen TV, though most of the eight or ten residents present were in wheelchairs. The place was certainly decorated for the season, with a beautiful Christmas tree in one corner and a silver menorah on the mantel above the fireplace. I continued on down the hall, beset by a twinge of nervousness. As head of P & E, I was getting good at relating to patrons, finding the right words to put someone at ease or resolve a minor problem, but meeting Evelyn's friend was something else entirely. What's more, I wasn't in the library, which had quickly become my safety zone.

Morgan was fast asleep in a lounge chair beside his bed, with a book open facedown on his lap. I hated to wake him, but I hadn't come this far to abort my mission.

"Morgan," I said softly. "Morgan, wake up."

"Shake his shoulder," came the advice from Morgan's roommate. "That's what the nurses do when they have to wake him."

I smiled my thanks, and the man in the next bed returned to his TV program. I stepped closer to Morgan. He wore a blue button-down shirt and jeans. He was thin, almost gaunt, and though his face was well lined, I could tell by his high forehead and even features that he must have been rather handsome in his younger years.

When I touched his shoulder, he let out a rumble of a snore that made me laugh.

"Wha—what it is?" Slowly he opened his blue eyes. "Is it time for lunch?"

"Not yet. My name's Carrie Singleton. Hello, Morgan Fuller."

To my surprise, he thrust out his hand and we shook. His grip was stronger than I'd expect for a man about ninety-five years old.

"Do I know you?"

"No, we've never met."

He grinned. "At my age I'm never sure if I'm talking to someone I used to know years ago or to a stranger."

"A friend of yours asked me to come and visit you."

"Who?"

I glanced over at Morgan's roommate and was happy to see he'd fallen asleep. "Evelyn Havers. She said she used to visit you around Christmas. I've come because she can't."

"Where are my manners? Please sit down." Morgan pointed to his bed.

I sat.

"Evelyn Havers," he mused. "I haven't seen her in years. How is she doing? She and Robert were the nicest neighbors anyone could ask for."

I leaned closer to Morgan. "Actually, Evelyn died about six years ago. I'm one of the few people who can see her when she visits the library where I work." I waited for his reaction, hoping that Evelyn was right about him. "She sends you her love."

"Does she?"

"Yes, she does."

Morgan thought this over and burst out laughing. "And she haunts the library. No big surprise. How she loved that place. Does that sourpuss niece of hers still work there?"

"Oh, yes. Still sour."

This time we both had a good laugh.

"Sorry to hear about Evelyn, though. So she asked you to come visit me. That was mighty nice of her."

"Oh, here. I almost forgot." I handed him the two boxes I was holding. "Merry Christmas. Evelyn said you love linzer cookies, but Thelma said you love chocolate."

"So you brought them both! How sweet of you. I'll sample each after lunch. Thank you, my dear."

"You're welcome," I said. "Enjoy!"

"I certainly will." He looked at me, his eyes narrowing. "You're a pretty lass. Do you have a beau?"

"I'm not sure," I answered, deliberately vague. But I got the sudden urge to say more. "There is someone, except we're on opposite sides of a situation. It's complicated."

Morgan placed a gnarled hand on mine. "Trust me, if you love him and he's good to you, make it work."

"I'll try to."

"Tell me, what do you do in the library?"

I found myself telling Morgan about my job and how much I'd grown to love it. We must have been talking for half an hour when I glanced at my watch. "Here we've been gabbing away, and it's almost time for you to go to lunch."

"It can wait. I'd like to talk to you about something . . . private."

An aide came into the room. "You fellas ready to eat?"

"I am," Morgan's roommate said.

The aide helped him into his wheelchair.

"I'll be there soon," Morgan said.

"Shall I send someone to help you?"

Morgan glanced at me.

"I'll bring him to the dining room in a few minutes," I said.

"All right," the aide said. "Don't dawdle too long."

When I turned back to Morgan, he was shaking his head. "This place is run like an army camp. You'd think something awful would happen if we didn't eat just when they ordered us to."

"What do you want to talk to me about?" I asked, hoping it was neither death nor the afterlife. I hadn't given either subject much thought.

Though no one was in hearing range, Morgan leaned closer to me. When he spoke, he kept his voice soft.

"As I come to the end of my life, I think of the people I knew and how I related to them. I tried to be honest and fair, but things don't always work out the way we want them to."

I nodded, eager to hear his story.

"I was a carpenter all my working life. At first I worked for a large company. The owner wasn't much interested in what kind of a job we did, as long as the article got finished on time. Some of the men I worked with were sloppy. They didn't take pride in their work. They were simply after their paychecks.

"As soon as I'd saved up some money, I opened my own shop and did things my way. Carefully, with attention to detail. My name and my reputation were important to me, and I did the best work I knew how. People got to hear about me. They hired me to build cabinets and chests, bookcases, and whatnot. Soon I had more work than I could handle.

"I took on a helper. Over the years I took on more. I liked to get them young, so I could teach them the trade properly. No short cuts. No sloppy work. Some of them went out on their own. One or two stayed with me." Morgan released a deep sigh.

"I was in my mid-sixties when I hired Bert Crowley. He was a pleasant young man. He had no training as a carpenter, no training of any kind, but he wanted a job so I took him on. At first he was very eager to learn, but after a while the restlessness took over everything he did. He'd be working on a piece—sanding or sawing. Next thing, I'd see him ambling over to one of the other guys for a chat.

"I had a no-smoking policy because of all the wood in the workshop, and simply because I can't stand the smell of nicotine burning. Bert used to ask for coffee breaks, but I smelled the cigarettes on him when he came in from outside.

"I got to thinking it was time to cut him loose. I hated doing it. Hated to give up on someone I figured had the hands to be a good carpenter. But Bert was getting too edgy to make it through the day. Later on I learned he had a drinking problem and it took all his effort not to drink on the job." Morgan shook his head ruefully. "If only I'd picked up on it, I could have helped him.

"Anyway, one day I had to leave early. The three other men working with me were out at customers' homes putting up kitchen cabinets or what-have-you. Bert needed to finish a few things in the shop. I told him to work till five, then lock up. For some reason I'll never understand, he took it to mean he could smoke and work. Later he told me he put the cigarette down for a minute to answer the phone, and before he could do anything, some shavings caught on fire. I understand the fire department came pretty darn fast, but it was too late. The projects we were working on were burned or ruined. Half the shop—the section where I kept the equipment—damaged beyond repair."

"How awful," I said.

"It was. This was my life gone up in smoke. My wife had died two years earlier, and I felt I had nothing to live for." He paused. "And that's when I did something truly awful. I set about making Bert Crowley's life a living hell."

Morgan began to hyperventilate. I looked around. "Where's the call button? You need a nurse."

I finally spotted it and was about to press the button, when he put out a hand. "Please. Don't. I have to finish telling you so you can . . ." He was breathing too strenuously to speak.

Should I ring for help or let him go on with his story that's upsetting him so? "Morgan," I said, "you have to calm down. I'm here to listen to what you want to tell me."

"Water," he managed to croak, pointing to his nightstand.

I poured water into a glass and handed it to him. He gulped down half of it, and I was relieved to see his breathing had slowed to normal. He cleared his throat.

"Sorry. I didn't mean to upset you, but you get the idea how this subject's been weighing on my mind all these years."

"Of course." I waited for Morgan to continue.

"I was furious that someone could be so careless, so thoughtless, and in a matter of minutes destroy what I'd spent years building up. I sued Bert, and since he'd violated a rule I'd steadfastly enforced, I won the case, if you could call it that. He had to pay a few thousand dollars, money I knew he had little of.

"Everyone in town knew what Bert had done. Still, I made

it my business to tell every contractor, carpenter, builder, and plumber just how irresponsible he was. He tried to find work, but no one would hire him. Finally, his brother-in-law got him a job delivering pizza."

"This was what—thirty years ago? Morgan, you can't keep beating yourself up for something you did so long ago."

"How can I forget? The drinking got worse. He crashed his cousin's van and was killed in the accident."

"It wasn't your fault."

"Wasn't it? A young man dead and I helped drive him to it."

I hesitated, then asked, "Did Bert Crowley have any children?"

"His wife Stella was pregnant at the time of the fire. She gave birth to a son. They both still live in Clover Ridge, far as I know."

A son named Chris. "Morgan, what you've just told me is very sad, but you're making yourself sick going over it again and again in your mind. What good does it do? Something terrible happened to you, and you lashed out at the person responsible."

"I did, and I want to make amends."

"How, after all these years?"

"Talking to you has helped me firm up an idea that's been percolating in my mind for some time. I've made some good investments over the years and have no heirs to leave my money to. I want to give Bert's family a check for a substantial amount of money. Two hundred thousand dollars."

I stared at him. "Are you sure?"

Morgan's smile was bittersweet. "I have congestive heart failure, Carrie, along with other medical problems that are getting worse. I doubt I'll still be here come spring. I'd like you to give Stella and her boy the money ASAP. In the Christmas spirit, if you will."

Chapter Thirteen

I left Morgan in the Carlton Manor's dining room and drove home, mulling over the last part of our conversation. I'd tried my best to convince him that he didn't need me to give his very generous check to the Crowleys. His lawyer could mail it to them, along with a very nice letter. But Morgan was adamant. He insisted that a letter wouldn't cut it. The situation required a personal touch. A woman's touch, if that wasn't being sexist. And I was the perfect person to undertake this commission. When he saw that wasn't working, he finally threw at me that if Evelyn Havers trusted me, he knew he could trust me too. Finally, I "cried uncle" and agreed to return on Monday evening, by which time he'd have the check made out so I could present it to Stella and Chris before Christmas Eve.

Smoky Joe twitched his tail repeatedly to show his displeasure at having been left on his own all morning, but started purring the moment I served him his lunch. I made myself an egg salad sandwich. Now that I'd acquired a few more pre-holiday chores—another visit to Morgan and delivering his gift to the Crowleys—I was especially glad I'd ordered Aunt Harriet and Uncle Bosco's gifts online. I had chosen a small food processor for Aunt Harriet, after hearing her complain enough times that the one she had was too large and cumbersome for some of her smaller preps. And I'd bought Uncle Bosco a pair of fur-lined slippers. Having lived with my uncle before moving into the cottage, I knew just how worn and tattered his slippers were. I sighed, envisioning the navy blue, cashmere, V-neck sweater I'd bought for Dylan.

Dylan. I knew he'd come home for the weekend because I'd seen his BMW parked in the mansion's semicircular driveway when I'd passed by a few minutes earlier. But there were no messages on the landline or my cell phone. No texts. No emails.

What do you expect? You drove him away.

I called Jim to let him know I was on my way and hopped back into my car. As I drove to the hospital, I realized I had one more gift to buy—something for my father. What would he like? What could he use? Probably tools to break into a store or a building, but I wasn't about to oblige him with that. Perhaps a pair of gloves or a warm scarf. I'd have to be crazy to face the mobs at the mall. Best to stop in at the men's shop in town. I'd be spending more money but saving valuable time and energy.

The hospital's parking lot was filled with visitors' vehicles. I had to circle twice until I noticed someone backing up and was able to take the vacated space. As it was, a car came speeding toward me from the other direction, its driver clearly annoyed that I'd gotten there before her. I reached for the grapes and newspaper on the passenger seat and headed for the entrance.

I heard voices as I entered my father's room, both of them familiar. Very familiar. I stopped short at the sight of my father laughing and chatting away with none other than Dylan Avery.

"What are you doing here?" I demanded.

"I came to visit your dad. I heard he was hospitalized after someone attacked him."

I glared at Dylan. "And to help convict him of some crime, no doubt. Jim, I don't think you—"

"Now, Caro, there's no need to get upset. Dylan stopped by, and we're having a pleasant little chat. That's all." He grinned when he saw what I was carrying. "Ah, a newspaper and some grapes. Let me have at them."

"Here's the paper, but I have to wash the grapes. And I'll need a bowl. I should have brought one from home."

"There's no need for a bowl. Just—" my father called after me, but I was out of the room and making a dash for the nurse's station. Before I reached it, I felt a tug on my arm. I spun around.

"Dylan! What do you want?"

"To talk to you. Can you manage that?"

"I need to borrow a bowl for my father's grapes."

"Your father won't mind waiting."

I pursed my lips. "Did Jim send you after me?"

Dylan pointed to an empty visitors' room with a wall TV, sofa, and two chairs. "Why don't we sit there and talk?"

"I don't know what there is to talk about," I said, but he didn't hear me. He was heading for the room.

We sat on opposite ends of the sofa and faced each other.

"I'll start," Dylan said, "since I need to explain a few things and apologize."

"Oh? You agree you owe me an apology?"

"I do. When you came to look at the cottage, the case involving your father's possible involvement was farthest from my mind. I'd reached a dead end. He was nowhere to be found."

"What made you go after my father?"

He paused, then said, "A person of interest led me to him."

"Was it Tom Quincy?"

Dylan shot me a look of astonishment, followed by one of admiration. "Yes. How did you know?"

"Someone peered into the cottage window the other night. Later, I realized it was Quincy looking for my father. Eventually he found him and assaulted him."

Dylan whistled. "I wondered about that. Jim refused to say who worked him over."

"Do you think Quincy killed Benton Parr?"

Dylan studied my face before answering. I studied his in return and saw pain and compassion followed by resolve. Part of him wanted to protect me from a discussion about murder and violence, but given all that had transpired, he knew his only chance with me was to be forthright.

"Tom Quincy's a vicious thug, so sure, it's a possibility. Moreover, it's a safe bet he's on John Mathers's list of suspects. Quincy knew Parr. He probably did business with him. They could have had a falling out. Now he's in the wind."

"Strange that something this 'thug' told you about my father made you decide to go after him."

Dylan shrugged. "It's complicated. Quincy claimed to have information about a multimillion dollar theft of uncut gems."

"And he said my father was involved?"

"Could be," he hedged.

"And I'm telling you—my father has nothing to do with Quincy."

"Four months ago this was an open case, a case far from being solved."

"And now?"

Dylan gave a mirthless laugh. "I have doubts those gems will ever be found."

I decided it was time to change the subject. "What were you and my father talking about before, when I came into his room?"

"We were reminiscing about Jordan, how he and I got into a few scrapes when we were kids."

"Like when you picked all those apples in our neighbor's orchard?"

Dylan laughed. "Right. As if there weren't enough apples growing on your own farm. Do you know old Myers came after us with a pitchfork? Your dad managed to calm him down."

"Really?" I said. "I didn't know that part."

"Your father's sorry for a good deal in his life—mostly how he treated his family."

"He said that?"

Dylan shook his head. "Not in so many words, but I read between the lines. And he misses Jordan."

"Me too," I said softly. My brother had died eight years ago in a car accident.

"So, are we good, you and I? Can we still be what we were on our way to becoming?"

"And what exactly is that?" I asked.

"The significant other for each other."

His words set me tingling. Still, I couldn't let the topic go just yet. "What about your case? Are you still going after my father?"

Dylan moved closer to me and took my hand. "Carrie, I'm not the police. I don't arrest people. My job is to recover lost or stolen items the best and most efficient way that I can. I told you—the gems in this case have yet to appear on the market.

The owners have offered an award of half a million dollars to anyone who turns them in to me or the police, no questions asked."

"I see."

"What does that mean?"

"It means I'm sorry I reacted like I did. When you came to the police station to question my father, I was convinced you'd used me to get to Jim."

"Why do you call him Jim?"

I shrugged. "It started when I was fifteen."

Dylan grinned. "About the same time you changed your name from Carolinda."

"Shh! I *hate* it! Don't even say it out loud!"

"Go on."

"I decided that since he was away so much, he wasn't much of a father to Jordan and me. Just another adult who walked in and out of our lives. I began to think of him as Jim, and when he came home for one of his visits, I started calling him that."

"He thinks the world of you, Carrie."

"He asked me to start calling him 'Dad' again," I said.

"Are you going to?"

"I'm considering it."

Dylan stood. "I have to get going. Are we good?"

"I guess."

"Then we're on for tonight?"

I smiled. "We sure are."

"Pick you up at seven. Dress nicely. We're going out in style."

My father was grinning broadly when I returned, bowl in hand, to his room. "Did you and your boyfriend make up?"

"We did, and we're going out tonight." I washed the grapes and put them in the bowl. "Here you go."

Jim popped a few grapes in his mouth and chewed thoughtfully. "He's a good kid, Caro. You could do a lot worse."

I bristled at his paternal comment. "I'm not getting married, you know."

"Maybe you will one of these days. And give me the gift of my first grandchild."

Married? Grandchild? "What did your doctor say when he examined you this morning?"

"He said I'm mending nicely and I can leave here in a few days. Meanwhile, I'm supposed to walk around the hall a few times each day."

"Good idea. Why don't we do a few rounds right now."

After we circled the hall twice, I helped Jim into bed and left him reading the newspaper, subdued and, I suspect, worn out. His injuries and his bout in the hospital had weakened him more than either of us had suspected. For the first time, I admitted to seeing signs that my father was growing old: the graying hair, the wrinkles on his neck. He was approaching sixty, an age when many man were beginning to think about retirement. Certainly not chasing after stolen gems that could be anywhere.

I bent down to kiss his cheek. "Goodbye, Jim."

He surprised me by wrapping his arms around me in a tight hug. "Thanks for coming, Caro. It feels good, being looked after by my grown daughter."

I laughed. "I'll talk to you in the morning. I have work tomorrow, so I won't be back here till five thirty, six o'clock."

"I won't feel bad if you skip a day, Caro. Thanks again for the grapes."

Chapter Fourteen

When I exited the hospital, snowflakes were falling from a dove-gray sky. They wouldn't stick, but served as a vivid reminder that winter was on its way. I shivered as I walked through the parking lot to my car. It was just past three o'clock. In another hour or two, darkness would fall. Today was one of the shortest days of the year. One of the gloomiest too. No wonder Christmas and Chanukah were holidays of light.

I put the car in gear and started for home. My visit to my father had put me in a mellow mood. I was happy that I'd made up with Dylan and that I'd be seeing him tonight. I had a few hours free until I needed to get ready for our date, and decided to stop at some of the gift shops in town in hopes of finding a Christmas gift for Jim and my Secret Santa gift for Dorothy. The library holiday party was Tuesday night, and I didn't expect to have another chance to shop before then.

At first I was too immersed in my thoughts to notice the blue sedan on my tail. A quiver of fear snaked down my spine. It was the same car I'd seen speed away from the cottage the night

Quincy had assaulted Jim. Which meant he hadn't left Clover Ridge, after all.

I made a sharp right turn at the first corner I came to and pulled up behind a parked car. From my rear window I watched the blue car race by. I caught a glimpse of Quincy's furious expression. Why on earth was he following me? Was he out to intimidate me or planning something worse?

I drove on to the center of town. The shops around the Green were in festive mode. Wreaths hung on doors, and strings of lights framed roofs and windows. The sound of Christmas Carols emanated from one of the shops. A large Christmas tree stood in the middle of the Green, bedecked with tinsel and ornaments. Beside it, a vendor was selling roasted chestnuts and other roasted nuts from his truck to a lineup of customers, the delightful aroma perfuming the area. A picture-book scene of Christmas!

I parked behind the library and walked to the men's clothing store on the adjacent side of the Green. I found a blue, tan, and beige cashmere scarf that would accentuate Jim's blue eyes, and stood in line to pay for it. Next door, in the shop for women's clothing, I selected a long silk scarf in muted shades of purple and green I felt would flatter Dorothy's sallow complexion. I headed back to my car, happy with my purchases

"You think you're so smart, don't you?! Just remember, I'm smarter than you."

I spun around and gasped. Tom Quincy stood so close I could smell the pepperoni he must have eaten for lunch on his breath.

"What do you want?" I demanded. "Why can't you leave my father and me alone?"

He sniggered. "I'm here as a reminder. Daddy Jim and I have a business deal. I don't want him to forget it."

A young couple with two laughing children were walking toward us to get to their car. Tom Quincy backed away and seemed to disappear as effectively as Evelyn.

I sank into the front seat of my car, where I remained until my breathing returned to normal. *He only wants to frighten you.* Still, it was unnerving. I didn't like being intimidated by a thug.

I called the police station and Gracie answered. When I asked to speak to John, she said he wasn't in his office.

"Please tell him that—oh, never mind," I ended up saying, suddenly remembering that Jim had asked me not tell John about Tom Quincy. Besides, he hadn't laid a hand on me.

"Are you all right?" Gracie asked, sounded concerned.

"I'm fine, thanks. It's something minor. I'm sure the lieutenant has more pressing matters to attend to."

"I don't know about 'pressing,' but the calls are coming in by the dozen." Gracie laughed. "Sometimes I think the holidays bring out the worst in people."

I drove home slowly, wondering what kind of hold Quincy had over my father if Jim was willing to keep quiet about the attack and pay him a few thousand dollars to boot. As I approached the mansion, I noticed Dylan's car in the driveway. On impulse, I parked behind it and rang the doorbell.

Dylan came to the door in the same jeans and sweater he'd had on earlier. He wore socks, but no shoes. He smiled in delight when he saw me.

"This is a nice surprise." He took me in his arms and kissed me.

I pulled back. "I had a surprise of my own."

"What's wrong, Carrie? What happened?"

"Tom Quincy followed me from the hospital. I made a sudden turn and lost him. I did some shopping in town. When I went to get my car in the library parking lot, he was waiting for me."

His face darkened with worry and anger. "Did he hurt you?"

I shook my head. "No, but he took pleasure in threatening me. For some reason he feels my father owes him, and this was a reminder that he'd better come through."

"What did he say Jim owes him?"

"He didn't say, but my father told me Quincy was shaking him down for a few thousand dollars, which I doubt he has."

Dylan pulled me close, then set me aside as if I were a doll. "Carrie, please go into the kitchen and wait for me there."

"Why? What are you going to do? Call John? He's not at the station. And my father—"

But cell phone in hand, he had already strode into his office and closed the door behind him. I sat down at the round kitchen table to wait. A few minutes later Dylan came to stand before me.

"You can rest easy, Carrie. Tom Quincy won't go near you ever again."

"Why? What did you say to him?"

"It doesn't matter. What matters is he's been told to back off."

Told? Suddenly it all came together. "Quincy's your confidential informant, or whatever they call a snitch in your line of work."

A flush spread across Dylan's face. "I wouldn't call him that."

"But Quincy's the reason you went after my father, right?"

When he didn't answer, I let out an exasperated sigh. "You already told me that much this afternoon."

"He told me your father and Benton Parr stole the gems my company was asked to retrieve."

"Why would he tell you something like that?"

"To get back at them. He said Benton and your father refused to work with him anymore."

I bit back the string of curses running through my mind. "I suppose you pay this stool pigeon."

The flush spread to Dylan's neck. "A few hundred dollars here and there."

"Quincy hurt my father and put him in the hospital. For all I know, he's holding something over Jim's head. Why else would Jim agree to pay him a few thousand dollars, money he doesn't have?"

"I'm sorry about that, Carrie, but I'm not responsible for Tom Quincy's behavior."

"But you are responsible for his being here in Clover Ridge. He's a menace to everyone, and he very well might have killed Benton Parr." I scowled at Dylan. "You said he's on John Mathers's list of murder suspects. Are you going to tell John that Tom Quincy's still in town? Quincy told my father he was leaving, but obviously he means to hang around." *So he can look for the missing gems.*

Dylan hesitated.

"I don't believe it! You're more interested in protecting your snitch than doing what's right." I stood. "Goodbye, Dylan. Clearly we have conflicting agendas. Let me know when you want me to vacate the cottage."

I ran to my car, blinking back tears. I would not cry! Dylan wasn't worth it. That thug Quincy was here because of him! In some ways, Dylan was no better than my father. His end game was retrieving the stolen gems, and he didn't care who got hurt in the process.

Smoky Joe met me at the door, meowing for his dinner. As soon as he cleaned his plate, I picked him up and cuddled him in my arms. The landline phone rang. I ignored it. After seven rings, I lifted the receiver and put it back down. My cell phone began to sound. I turned it on vibrate. I would not talk to Dylan. Nothing he might say could change the way I felt.

The rest of the afternoon dragged on. I finished writing the last of my thank-you notes, then turned on the TV. Nothing but news and Christmas programs. I tried to read but couldn't concentrate. I picked up my cell phone to call Angela but put it down again when I remembered she and Steve were going to a pre-Christmas family party.

Smoky Joe watched as I paced the living room, a puzzled expression on his face. I didn't feel like going to Aunt Harriet and Uncle Bosco's for a bit of sympathy, but I was too restless to stay home. I slipped on my parka and climbed into my car, not sure where I was heading.

I didn't want to run into anyone I knew, so I turned onto the turnpike going west, in a direction I rarely drove. The light snow had stopped, leaving no accumulation. I hadn't gotten very far when I realized I was hungry. I turned off at the next village and followed the signs to the center of town. The pizza parlor appeared to be the only brightly lit shop on Main Street. I stepped inside and breathed in the delicious aroma of baking pies. The front of the shop was filled with customers waiting to place or pick up their orders. Most of the tables in the large eating area in the rear were occupied by families and couples. There were very few single diners. I felt a pang of envy as I observed the young families dining out before settling down to a quiet evening watching TV. I'd probably never marry and raise a family of my own. Not with the emotional baggage I was carrying.

When my order of two slices of veggie pizza and a soda arrived, I carried my tray to one of the small tables along the side wall near the back of the restaurant. Christmas songs played over the public address system, reminding me I was about to have the worst holiday ever. Dylan wouldn't be coming with Jim and me to Aunt Harriet and Uncle Bosco's on Christmas Eve as planned. I shook my head to drive away thoughts of Dylan. It hurt so much, knowing how close I'd come to being part of a couple with a man I was beginning to love.

I never minded eating alone in a restaurant. I'd done it often enough through college and in the following years. To keep my mind occupied, I studied the families at the larger tables a few feet away. A man and a young woman walked past me and sat at the table for two just beyond mine. I recognized Dina Parr and her brother, Richard.

At first they were too busy chomping into their slices to hold a conversation. I was on the verge of leaving when Richard, who faced me, leaned across the small table to address his sister.

"Dee, you're making a huge mistake moving back home. Once again, you're giving our dear mother the power to control you. She'll waste no time telling you how to dress, whom to see. Act Two of everything you hated while we were growing up."

Dina shook her head vehemently. "Not this time, Rich. I'm older. I know who I am, what I want."

His bark of laughter held no humor. "Really? You told me you wanted to run the jewelry store when Dad retired. She's making sure that will never happen."

Dina's voice flattened. "Mom says there's no money to keep the store and buy new merchandise."

"Right. As usual, she does what suits her, and the hell with us. At least someone did us a good deed and got rid of our SOB father."

"Rich, how can you say such a thing?"

"Easily." He stretched across the table and lowered his voice, so I had to strain to hear him. "Ginny and I are having serious money troubles since she was laid off. Danny's medical bills are astronomical; our insurance barely covers half. The other day I went to the store before work and begged our dear father to help us out. A loan, not a gift, mind you. He refused. Claimed he didn't have it."

"I'm sorry, Rich. I wish I had the money to give you. I know what a skinflint Dad could be, but the store *was* losing money these last few months. Probably because he wasn't concentrating on business. Mom said the only way she can pay for my tuition is if I give up my apartment and move back home."

Another bark of laughter. "And you fell for it? Dee, she only wants to control you. Didn't she order you to stop dating Chris?"

"We only went out a few times. Chris is a sweet guy, but he's not my type."

"I'm glad I cut both our parents out of my life," Richard said. "Ginny and the kids are my priority."

Dina sighed. "If only I could find those damn stones! That would solve all my money worries. I could pay for the rest of my college bills and take over the store."

"Yeah, right. The gems you and Chris keep looking for. Maybe they were nothing but the old man's fantasy."

"I tell you they're real, all right! I heard him talking about them on the phone. He said they're worth millions."

Richard laughed. "If you ever find them, please put aside a small portion for me to help pay the mortgage."

"Of course, bro."

"Who was he talking to?" Richard asked, suddenly interested.

"I don't know. Probably his partner."

"You're sure Dad had those gems?"

"He told the person he was speaking to that he was keeping them in a safe place."

I covered my mouth to stifle my excitement.

Richard glanced at his watch. "The Chinese order I called in for Ginny and the kids must be ready. I want to bring it home before it gets cold. It's one of the few joys I can offer them these days."

Brother and sister stood and hugged.

"If you change your mind about moving home, you can camp out in our den until you figure out your next move," Richard said.

"Thanks, Rich, but I'm going to try to make this work—for now."

He nodded. "Just keep on searching for those gems."

"Absolutely. Because once I find them I'll lead my life exactly as I want.

I drove home, mulling over Dina's conversation with her brother. Both Benton and Mariel sounded like extremely selfish parents. Richard was estranged from them, and Dina had chosen to move back home and live with her mother under miserable conditions.

Interesting that Richard had gone to talk to Benton to ask him for a loan. It didn't seem to cross Dina's mind that her brother might have gone to their father's store the morning he'd been murdered. That they might have argued and, in the heat of the moment, Richard killed Benton.

But would Richard have mentioned his visit to the jewelry store if he'd killed Benton? Or was he that certain that Dina would never speak out against him?

As far as I was concerned, Richard Parr was now a solid murder suspect. He had means, motive, and opportunity. It was my duty to tell John Mathers what I'd overheard and let the police take it from there.

Chapter Fifteen

Sunday morning I woke up early, glad that I'd be spending the day at work. The library was a cheerful, bustling place, and helping patrons would keep me too busy to dwell on my unhappy love life.

Jim sounded chipper when I called him at the hospital. "How was your date last night?"

"Tell you when I see you. I'll stop by after work, around five thirty. Did the doctor say when you're being released?" I asked to turn his mind away from Dylan Avery.

"In a few days. He refuses to be more specific than that."

"Okay. Sounds good. Talk to you later."

When I hung up, I realized I was going to have to tell people that Dylan and I were no longer going out. I sighed. Jim, Angela, and my aunt and uncle would be supportive. Still, each time I had to repeat the current status was going to be painful.

Smoky Joe and I had our breakfast, and then he curled up on the living room sofa for a snooze. The library opened at eleven on Sundays. It was eight thirty, so I had a few free hours ahead of me. I called the police station. Someone I didn't know answered the phone.

"Is Lieutenant Mathers there?" I asked.

"No, but he should be in soon. Who is this please?"

"Carrie Singleton."

"Would you like to leave a message, Miss Singleton?"

"Just to say I'll stop by the station later," I said and ended the call.

At a quarter to nine, I carried Smoky Joe to the car and headed for the village center. Such a joyous time of the year! Though the temperature was in the mid-thirties, the sun shone brightly on trees and houses bedecked with holiday and snow-related decorations. And I was miserable. I'd broken up with my boyfriend and would probably have to move out of the cottage I'd grown to love. I needed to track down a bagful of stolen gems before my father left the hospital and started searching for them himself. And figure out who murdered Benton Parr.

Smoky Joe wasn't happy about staying in the car while I went into the police station to talk to John. I placed the few treats I'd remembered to bring along on the passenger seat and left him nibbling away as I headed for the back door of the station. John was talking to the young male officer manning the front desk. He looked up and smiled at me when I entered.

"Good morning, Carrie. Here to confess to a crime?"

I smiled coyly. "Certainly, Lieutenant."

As I followed John into his office, I remembered how reserved and formal he'd been back in October when I'd asked for information about the two murders I eventually helped solve. But now we were friends. He took his seat behind his desk. I closed the door before sitting in one of the two visitors' chairs.

"First off, I want to tell you what I happened to overhear last night."

"I'm listening."

"I'd been out driving and stopped at a pizza parlor, when Dina and Richard Parr came in and sat at a nearby table. I happened to hear their conversation."

"And one of them confessed to their father's murder," he said deadpan.

"Not exactly. Richard told his sister that he'd been to see Benton to ask for a loan. He went to see him one morning last week at the jewelry store."

John nodded. "We know."

"Oh!"

"You sound surprised, Carrie. We talked to everyone in the Parr family. According to Richard, he saw his father the morning before the day he was murdered. We're checking on his story, but so far there are no witnesses to either support it or to say Richard was seen the next morning when Benton was stabbed."

"I'm disappointed that what I told you wasn't much help."

John smiled. "And I appreciate your coming in to share what you heard. Police work is often tedious. What looks like a great lead can turn out to be of no use at all. We have to shift through extraneous, false, and unsubstantiated pieces of information until the real picture presents itself." He stood, ready to see me out.

"I had an unpleasant experience with Tom Quincy yesterday afternoon. Do you know him?"

John sat. "I do. He's a person of interest in my homicide investigation. What happened, Carrie? Did he hurt you in any way?"

"Just frightened me, as was his intention. He followed me from the hospital to the village center. I thought I'd lost him and parked behind the library to do some shopping. When I got back to my car, he was waiting for me."

"What did he say?"

I squirmed, hating to bring my father into the conversation, but there was no getting around it. "He wanted me to remind my father they have a business deal. Not that they do," I quickly added. "Jim wants nothing to do with that man."

"Did Quincy put Jim in the hospital?"

"I'm not supposed to tell you, but yes, he did."

"Are you sure they didn't have some sort of a deal that went south?"

"My father said they didn't, and I believe him."

"Then why would he come after Jim?"

I threw out my hands. "Because he's a psycho and thinks there's easy money to be had when that isn't the case. Maybe he and Benton had a deal that went sour."

"That's possible," John said. "But I think you're not telling me the entire story."

Time to change direction. "Tom Quincy's just out to make trouble! Did you know Dylan pays him for information? Who knows what *information* he makes up to earn his keep."

"That's also possible," John said.

I glared at him. "So what do you plan to do—to keep Quincy away from me and my father?"

"According to Dylan, Tom Quincy left Clover Ridge early this morning for parts unknown."

I felt like a deflated balloon. "Oh. Dylan told you."

"An hour ago. I chewed him out for keeping me in the dark that his info on this case came from a felon—especially someone as erratic and volatile as Tom Quincy."

"Dylan's responsible for bringing that thug to Clover Ridge.

It's partly his fault my father was assaulted. For all we know, Quincy killed Benton Parr."

"I'll put out a be-on-the-lookout alert to bring him back to town when your father's gone. Am I right in thinking he'll be leaving soon?"

I shrugged. "I wouldn't be surprised."

"And I'm thinking he doesn't want to bring charges against Quincy."

"He doesn't."

John gnawed on his lower lip. I got the impression he was struggling with a way to say something that weighed heavily on his mind. He finally spat it out. "I'm truly sorry, Carrie."

"What for?" I asked, astonished.

"For whatever reason Jim Singleton came back here. Somehow he got you involved, and it's not doing you any good."

"I'll survive," I said stoutly.

"You're a good girl, Carrie. You deserve to do more than survive."

Tears sprang to my eyes, and I rubbed them away. Why did any comment that showed someone cared about my welfare make me cry?

John continued. "And I'm gathering from what you've told me that you and Dylan are squabbling."

"I wouldn't call it squabbling. I can't be with a man who's looking to put my father in jail."

"From another perspective, it's unfortunate that Dylan has reason to suspect Jim stole the gems he was hired to retrieve," John said dryly.

"Dylan should have told me he was going after my father

before I signed a lease for the cottage." Saying it aloud sounded childish, but I couldn't help how I felt.

"Maybe he should have, but your father put you in this untenable position. That's not what fathers do."

I sprang to my feet and yanked open the door.

"Don't let Jim Singleton come between you and Dylan," John called after me as I ran into the hall and out of the station.

I sat in my car, trembling and gasping as if I'd run a marathon. I'd gone to see John Mathers about Tom Quincy and hadn't been prepared for a lecture about my father and my love life. What right did he have to tell me how to feel! I didn't want to take my father's side in this matter, but what Dylan had done had cut me to the quick.

No wonder I'd spent most of my post-college years traveling from place to place, never settling down. My dysfunctional family life had left deep scars. I'd learned to avoid emotional entanglements—making solid friendships, falling in love, settling into a community where people cared about me and I cared about them. I'd finally ventured to try that kind of life, and now it was tumbling down!

Smoky Joe rested his head on my lap, and I stroked his back. He'd grown quite a bit since we'd found each other over a month ago.

"You're the one good thing in my life," I murmured. "You and my job."

Smoky Joe purred his agreement.

The library was bustling at a quarter to eleven as members of the staff entered the building via the back entrance. Angela grabbed my arm. "I have something to tell you."

"I have a few things to tell you too."

She studied my face. "Girl, I can see from your face, none of them are good."

Chapter Sixteen

"John's right, you know. Your father brings you nothing but grief. Things will get back to normal once he leaves town."

"Will they?" I frowned at Angela across our bowls of chili at the Cozy Corner Café. "That awful thug that beat up Jim and scared me half to death is Dylan's paid snitch. How can I have a relationship with Dylan after the way he betrayed me? Tracking down my father like he did."

"You mean, like a common criminal?"

"Yes, but . . ."

"I know, he's your father." Angela let out a lungful of exasperation. "You're stuck with a mental tape playing a worn-out message in your brain: 'Family above all else' was drilled into your head. Wipe it out, ASAP."

Her angry tone astonished me. "You're close to your family. What did you have to deal with?"

"My brother."

"You mean—Tommy?"

"When I was little, he used to pinch me or kick me when my parents weren't looking. When I squawked, he always lied, with the most innocent expression on his face. One day when we were both in elementary school, he hit me. I told the principal and he called in my parents."

"So they finally believed you!"

"No, they were angry. They said I was wrong to talk about family business to a stranger like my principal. I told them they never believed me when I told them my brother was hurting me. It wasn't until I asked my aunt if I could come and live with her that they took my complaints seriously."

"What did they do?" Angela's story had shaken me. I always thought she was lucky to have a close-knit, loving family.

"They took my aunt's advice and brought Tommy to a psychiatrist. The doc worked wonders. Tommy still got into trouble, but I didn't care. As long as he wasn't hurting me."

"And now he makes Tarantino-type movies out in Hollywood," I mused.

"I love my brother, but I'm glad he's on the other coast."

We finished our chili and coffee in silence. The emotional level of our conversation had exhausted us both. The waitress brought our check. I reached for my wallet.

"With everything you had to tell me," Angela said, "I almost forgot to tell you about Mom's conversation with Mariel Parr."

"Oh!" I sank back in my chair.

"Mom went over to the Parrs' house yesterday afternoon. Dina wasn't there, and the few neighbors who had been visiting Mariel soon left. Mariel put away the tea they'd been drinking and asked Mom if she'd like a real drink." Angela chuckled. "The strongest alcoholic drink my mother imbibes is a glass of red wine at the holidays. But she didn't say no when Mariel reached for a bottle of scotch."

I laughed. "Sounds like she knew Mariel was about to share a secret or two."

"Of course. Aside from her own curiosity, she knows I'm trying to help you learn as much as you can about the Parrs."

I glanced at my watch. "We'd better get back to work. You can tell me on the way."

We paid the cashier and headed back to the library. The temperature was in the low forties, but the bright sun above made walking a pleasant exercise.

"Mariel downed an entire tumbler of scotch and poured herself a second before she told Mom that things have a way of turning out for the best."

I gripped Angela's arm. "Did she mean Benton? The fact that he was murdered?"

"Sounded that way to me—and it did to Mom too."

"Which makes me wonder if Mariel killed him."

Angela laughed. "She didn't say that, so don't go assuming things."

"How did your mother respond?"

"Tactfully. As you know, I didn't inherit the tactful gene from Mom. She was very sympathetic. Said she gathered that Mariel hadn't been very happy being married to Benton these past few years. Mariel readily agreed."

"That's what she told Jim when they spoke briefly at the wake. Did Mariel mention anything about the jewelry store?"

"She said it hasn't been making enough money these past few years." Angela lowered her voice, though no one was in hearing range. "And that's why she didn't file for divorce."

"Ah!" I thought a moment. "Did she know that Benton was carrying on with Jennifer Darby?"

"She alluded to 'one or two dalliances.'"

I laughed. "Very proper, isn't she?"

"Always," Angela agreed. "Mariel told Mom that she planned to sell the jewelry store. It's in a desirable location and can be used to house a variety of retail businesses. This way she can sell the merchandise separately and at least have some money to live on."

I nodded. "Dina was upset about that. She was hoping to manage the store."

"Mariel had plenty to say about Dina after she downed her second scotch and poured herself a third."

My eyes widened. "Wow! She was really letting loose. I hope your mother didn't match her drink for drink."

"Not my mom—not Rosemary Vecchio! And Mariel didn't seem to notice she was drinking alone. Mom said the words poured out of her. She thought Mariel had bottled up her feelings for a very long time and simply had to tell someone."

"Dina," I reminded Angela.

"It turns out Mariel's very disappointed with her daughter. She's twenty-three and still doesn't have her degree. She takes no pride in her appearance. She's not like her brother, who has a family and a good job."

"And doesn't speak to his mother." I said. "But getting back to Dina—why did she agree to move back home?"

"Mariel said she'll continue to pay for Dina's college education, but not for her apartment. And she'd only pay for her tuition if she stopped seeing Chris Crowley."

"Manipulative, isn't she?" I was beginning to thoroughly dislike Mariel Parr.

"Mariel told my mother the Crowleys come from the other side of the tracks. Chris's father was a drunkard and his mother cleaned houses, and if Dina didn't have such an inferiority complex, she'd realize that she and Chris came from two different worlds, and she never would have gone out with him in the first place."

" 'The other side of the tracks,' " I repeated. "Do people actually use that expression in the twenty-first century?"

"Mariel does."

I tried to absorb everything Angela had told me as we crossed the library parking lot. I pulled open the back door and was about to enter the building, when Angela touched my arm.

"One last thing. Though she was three sheets to the wind, Mariel was very cagey when she told Mom she hoped to come into some money. She'd hired a man to track down some merchandise Benton had hidden away."

"The gems!" we both exclaimed.

Then it hit me. "Oh, no! Mariel hired Quincy to find them."

Chapter Seventeen

I unlocked my office door and found Trish feeding Smoky Joe. Happiness coursed through me when he left his dish to greet me with a head butt. The little devil was everyone's favorite, but he knew I was his mama.

"He's had quite a time while you were gone," Trish said. "Dashed through the reading room to chase after a mouse. Caused quite an uproar."

"Oh, no! Maybe someone will complain to Sally, and she'll decide that having a library cat isn't a good idea after all."

Trish dismissed that worry with a wave of her hand. "Sally adores Smoky Joe. Besides, didn't she say she's glad we have a mouse catcher on the premises?"

"Does the library often get mice? I know they tend to move into buildings when the weather turns cold."

"I don't remember the library having a problem with mice in past years. Could be Jennifer's not keeping the coffee shop as clean as she should. I've seen debris left on tables quite a few times in the past month. Once someone left a plastic container with some tuna in it. She tossed it when she caught me staring at it. I didn't comment or anything, just ordered my coffee, but still."

"Ugh! Remind me not to eat anything there," I said.

Trish opened the door for an impatient Smoky Joe. How he loved the patrons' attention! "I'm off to man the hospitality desk," she said, following him out.

"I'll relieve you at three thirty," I said. "I'll introduce the choral singers at two and stay awhile to listen and take photos."

"They're really wonderful. We've been lucky to have them these past three years."

"And you were smart enough to remind me to book them for next December."

Trish grinned. "That's what I'm here for."

"I don't know what I'd do without you," I said.

"Yeah. Right," she joshed and was gone.

I went through the list of phone calls Trish had answered that required a callback, then glanced through my emails. So many matters to attend to! I had no time to dwell on John and Angela's comments about my relationships with Jim and Dylan or to analyze what I'd learned about Mariel, Dina, and Chris in the past two days. I shuddered to think that Mariel had hired Tom Quincy to find the gems. It meant he'd be back in Clover Ridge, regardless of Dylan's instructions.

"And what are you daydreaming about, pray tell?"

I gave a start. "Hello, Evelyn."

"That's not a very welcoming greeting." She perched on the edge of Trish's desk. Today she wore a white silk blouse under a red cardigan, a gray skirt, and sensible black shoes. Christmas tree earrings dangled from her earlobes.

"I've often wondered—where do you keep all your many outfits?" I asked.

"No need to concern yourself about my clothes. They're in a safe place. Now tell me, how did your visit with Morgan go?"

Once again, the queen of deflection ducks my questions. "We got along fine. He sends you his greetings and didn't seem at all surprised that you're haunting the library."

Evelyn smiled. "Such a lovely man. Thank you so much for paying him a visit."

"I'm going back to the Carlton Manor tomorrow night. Morgan's asked me to deliver a very large check to Stella and Chris Crowley."

"Did he? Bert Crowley started the fire that burned down his shop. Tragic. Morgan was never the same after that."

"Morgan feels awful for the way he treated Bert Crowley. He feels responsible for his early death."

Evelyn frowned. "Bert Crowley was a weak, sniveling excuse of a man. Morgan gave him a job and training that offered the promise of a good future. And what did he do? Continued to drink and disregarded Morgan's no-smoking rule."

I stared at her, taken aback by her vehement tone. I'd never seen Evelyn so angry. "I told Morgan that his lawyer could just as easily send them a check, but he wants the gift to have a personal touch. Of course I agreed to do it. I'm afraid he doesn't have much time left."

"That's what I sensed," Evelyn said softly. She treated me to a tender smile. "You're a good girl, Carrie."

"Thank you."

Her manner became brisk as she leaned toward me. "Now tell me what's been happening in your life."

I grimaced. "I never realized what a peaceful life I'd been leading until Jim came to town."

"How's he doing?"

"He's improving and should be leaving the hospital soon. But the man who attacked him followed me into town on Saturday and gave me a message for my father."

"Oh no! Did you tell John Mathers?"

"I did. The man's name is Tom Quincy. He's a criminal and he's Dylan's snitch."

"Oh." Evelyn nodded her head. "Could be that's how Dylan knew your father and Benton had stolen those stones. Are you back on good terms with Dylan?"

"I'd rather not talk about Dylan. What do you know about Mariel Parr?"

"I knew her mother better. Mariel always struck me as a cold fish. Someone who cares too much about appearances. Why do you ask? Do you think she might have killed Benton?"

"I'm beginning to wonder," I said. "According to Angela's mother, Mariel was fed up with Benton and his affairs. Somehow she found out about the stolen gems."

"Really? Clever Mariel."

"She hired Tom Quincy to find them."

Evelyn laughed. "Not very clever, after all."

"I wonder if she knew about Jennifer and Benton," I mused.

"One morning about two months ago, I happened to overhear two women talking in the coffee shop," Evelyn said. "The tone of the conversation struck me as strange at the time, so I hovered about for a few minutes. Mariel was asking Jennifer question after question, about nothing more important than coffee and where she bought supplies for the shop. Jennifer answered so softly, I could hardly hear her. That very afternoon Benton showed up at the coffee shop. I listened to *that* conversation and put two and two together."

"So, Mariel knew about the affair early on," I said. "She could have been planning Benton's murder all this time."

"Let's not jump to any conclusions," Evelyn said.

"Or course not. We need proof. Evidence." *And I have to find those gems!*

I glanced at my watch. "The choral group's due to arrive soon. I have to hand out programs and make the introduction."

"Mustn't be late," Evelyn agreed and began to fade.

I thought about what she'd just told me as I started down the stairs to the meeting room. Since Evelyn was invisible to everyone but little Tacey and me, she could listen in on any conversation in the library. Was it possible she'd seen or heard other conversations relevant to Benton's murder?

My cell phone pinged when I was halfway down the stairs. *A text!* My heart leaped to my throat as I retrieved my phone from my pocket. I hoped it wasn't from Dylan.

It was.

Leaving 4 the airport. Back in CR the 24. Sorry u r upset. Let's talk when I'm home. I care about you.

He cares about me! Exhilaration swept over me because, for once, someone worthwhile, someone *I* cared for, wanted me enough to pursue me after I'd told him off. Then I remembered he'd been tracking my father for months and hadn't had the decency to tell me. But maybe—

"Hello, Carrie. Quite a crowd today! I bet every seat will be taken."

I smiled at Doris Johnson, a white-haired woman in her early eighties, and her friend Tessie Williamson. They always arrived at programs extra early in order to nab front-row seats. "Sure looks that way. I'm glad you both could make it."

"Oh, we wouldn't miss the choral group!" Tessie said.

I stood outside the entrance and handed out copies of the afternoon's musical program. The room was quickly filling up. I greeted the singers gathered in our small utility room and gave each a bottle of water. At two o'clock I walked to the front of the room and greeted the audience. They settled down in their seats in quiet anticipation. The chorale entered the room. I introduced Roger Leighton, the music director, and then presented the group of twenty singers, saying how happy we were to have them return to our library. The audience gave them a rousing round of applause. I stood to the side and snapped a few photos before taking my seat.

Their voices and harmonies were truly beautiful as they offered up renditions of old English Christmas carols and popular holiday songs, including a few in French and German. The melodies stirred up memories of past Christmas seasons—shopping in the mall with friends; the one year Jim drove Jordan, my mother, and me into Manhattan on Christmas Eve to see the tree in Rockefeller Center and then have dinner in a French restaurant.

I chatted with patrons during the break, then went upstairs to relieve Trish at the hospitality desk so she could listen to the rest of the concert. Smoky Joe came bounding toward me as I walked through the reading room.

"And what have you been up to?" I picked him up and held him in my arms. He licked my nose, then struggled to be free and ran to my office, so I knew either he was hungry or needed to use his litter box. Turned out he wanted both.

I enjoyed the time I spent at the hospitality desk. Mostly, I collected checks for programs and trips, though I often found myself giving advice and recommendations regarding movies and books. I liked chatting with the library's patrons—getting to know about their lives and their families, which programs they loved and which they didn't much care for. When I glanced at my watch, I was surprised to see it was already twenty to five.

This is my home! No matter what happens with Jim or with Dylan, Clover Ridge is where I live and work, where I have my roots and my people.

I reached for my cell phone and speed-dialed Aunt Harriet and Uncle Bosco's number. Aunt Harriet answered. "Carrie, dear, we were just talking about you."

"Care to have a dinner guest tonight?"

"We'd love it."

"I hope you don't mind if I bring Smoky Joe. If it's a problem, he'll stay in the car."

"No problem at all. We even have an old litter box somewhere in the garage. I'll send your uncle out for a bag of kitty litter."

"I can bring some. There's plenty here in the library."

Aunt Harriet laughed. "Don't bother, Carrie. I expect Smoky Joe will be a frequent visitor." She lowered her voice. "Besides, it will be a good excuse to get your uncle out and about. He fell asleep in front of the TV an hour ago."

When five o'clock arrived, I went searching for Smoky Joe. Usually he sensed when it was time to go home and came looking for me. But today I checked out every nook and cranny on the library's main level as I called his name. I peered into the computer room, the room where we held our meetings, the children's area. No sign of him. I hoped he hadn't ventured downstairs or up into the attic.

When I circled the reading room for the second time, I noticed that the door to the coffee shop was closed. As I approached the closed door, I heard voices raised in anger.

"I told you, I don't know who he is! Why can't you believe me?"

"How can I, Jennifer? You swore you weren't sleeping with that jeweler, didn't you? Now he's gone, and I catch you with some stranger!"

"Catch me? He was threatening me, Paul. I was terrified."

"It sure didn't look that way. I better never see you with him again."

"I hope I never see him again!"

The Darbys were arguing. I didn't mean to eavesdrop, but my feet remained glued to the floor.

Jennifer let out a deep sigh. "I've had enough of your badgering. I'll move out and stay at my sister's."

"You can't leave me! I need you. You're my wife."

"You smother me!" Jennifer cried.

There were sounds of scuffling, and then she shouted, "Let go of me!"

The door flung open and Paul Darby stormed out of the coffee shop. He glared at me as he passed. "What are you doing here?"

"Looking for my—"

I heard a meow as Smoky Joe came running toward me. But instead of stopping, he raced into the coffee shop and scurried behind the counter.

"I didn't mean to intrude," I said to Jennifer as she sank into a chair at one of the small tables, holding her head in her hands.

"It doesn't matter. He won't believe a word I say." She released an unhappy bark of laughter. "That man was harassing me, and Paul thought he was my new lover."

My pulse quickened. "What man?"

Jennifer looked up, astonished by my curiosity. "I don't know his name, but I saw him leaving the jewelry store late one night when I was going to meet Benton. I think it was a day or two before Benton was murdered."

"Was he older? Fierce looking?"

"Yes. Why?"

"I bet it's the same guy who hassled me yesterday."

"You're kidding!"

"Where did you see him? What did he say?" I asked.

"I went home for lunch today because I wanted to take care of a few things. Paul wasn't there. The man was waiting for me when I came out of the house to drive back to the library."

Jennifer looked down at her feet. "He asked me if I knew where Benton kept his merchandise. I told him he kept it in the safe, of course, but that answer didn't suit him. He got this crazy look and grabbed my arm. 'You'll have to do better than that,' he said. I tried to break free, but he held on tight." She looked up at me, fear in her eyes. "He kissed my forehead and said we'd be talking again soon. It really creeped me out. He took off when Paul came walking toward us."

"Tom Quincy," I said. *So much for Dylan getting him to leave Clover Ridge.*

"Who's Tom Quincy?" Jennifer asked.

"A thief who was doing business with Benton," I said more forcefully than was probably necessary. "Benton never told you about him?"

She shook her head. "I didn't know anything involving the store."

"It turns out Benton had some illegally gotten gems in his possession. And lots of people are after them."

"Including your father."

I nodded. "So you know that much."

"I don't have any idea where they are!"

"Nobody does. Mariel hired Quincy to find the gems."

"I suppose she'll claim them for herself."

I laughed. "No chance of that happening. If Quincy finds them, he'll fence them and pocket the money." I watched Jennifer slowly get to her feet as if she were in a daze. "Are you all right?"

She nodded. "I'm going to stay at my sister's house for a few days. Eventually, Paul will come get me, and it will start all over again."

"So why do you stay with him?" I realized what I'd just said and began apologizing. "I'm sorry. I don't have any business asking you that. Your marriage is none of my business. It's just that you seem to be under such a terrible strain."

There were tears in her eyes when she answered. "I can't abandon Paul now, no matter how awful things are between us. We've been together since high school. Losing his job did terrible things to his ego. Then Benton came along, and we fell in love. But Benton's gone now."

Smoky Joe suddenly appeared. I reached down to pet him. "What on earth does he find so interesting behind the counter?" I asked.

"Probably the mouse. Or mice. There's probably more than one."

My mouth fell open. "You've seen it?"

Jennifer nodded. "I've been so upset lately, I've let things slide. I'll do a thorough cleaning tomorrow. Hopefully, the mouse family will move on."

"I sure hope so." I stood. "If you ever need someone to talk to, I'd be happy to be your sounding board. But right now I better get over to my aunt and uncle's."

Chapter Eighteen

It's amazing how one's mood and outlook can change in twenty-four hours, I mused as I slipped under the covers and reached for the novel I'd been reading. Last night I'd gone to sleep feeling that nothing was going right in my life. I certainly had a different slant on things tonight. I'd just spent the most wonderful evening with Aunt Harriet and Uncle Bosco, laughing and chatting over a delicious meatloaf dinner. They were my family, my go-to people who sustained me when I was feeling blue. I appreciated having them in my life, especially since I never could depend on my parents for emotional support.

Somehow Aunt Harriet and Uncle Bosco managed to make me see that dumping Dylan was the dumbest thing I could possibly do. Yes, he should have told me he was tracking my father as a suspect in the heist he'd been investigating. But, more importantly, Dylan and I cared about each other. The fact that he'd texted me to say how much he cared was proof that he was steadfast and already committed to our relationship—two qualities, they insisted, I'd appreciate more and more as time went on.

Knowing he'd been chasing after Jim still rankled. But as

Aunt Harriet said when I was helping her put the kitchen back in order, in real life people sometimes hurt the person they love. The important thing is to learn from the experience and move on. I hoped to be able to do that. At least that's what I texted Dylan. He wrote back to say he had a good feeling about us.

My concentration was shot. I found myself reading the same paragraph again and again. No surprise there. I had my own mystery to solve. Who had killed Benton and where had he hidden the gems? Wherever I turned, Tom Quincy showed his face—confronting my father, menacing Jennifer and me, searching for the gems on Mariel's behalf, though it was clear to me he was after them for himself.

I yawned as it occurred to me that I ought to tell John Mathers that Quincy had never left Clover Ridge. I should tell Dylan as well. And my father. I sighed. He wasn't going to be happy that John now knew Quincy had been the person who'd assaulted him. Well, I'd told John and there was no way to undo it now.

My thoughts, which were beginning to dovetail, one into another, veered to musings about the Darbys. Jennifer was a pretty woman in her mid-thirties. I had no idea if she'd attended college or had trained for a career, but she seemed content to run the library's coffee shop. Though it couldn't be paying much of a salary. And Paul was out of work, had been for some time. Had Jennifer tried to get a better-paying job? Was she too emotionally fragile to hold one? Did she love Paul?

Paul had a volatile temper, which was probably exacerbated by being unemployed and knowing his wife had taken a lover. Did Paul kill Benton? He'd attacked him the night Benton had presented his program. Paul knew exactly where he'd be, where to wait for him. The only thing he hadn't counted on was my presence on the scene.

Jennifer was harder to figure out. She'd fallen for Benton in a big way and claimed that he loved her too. Was she being naïve and merely the last in a long line of adulterous affairs, or had Benton been telling her the truth about wanting to go away with her and start a new life, improbable as it sounded?

If that was so, Benton was counting on fencing the gems he and Jim had stolen to start a new life with Jennifer. Which meant he'd hidden the gems somewhere close by. Somewhere in Clover Ridge, I was willing to bet. Somewhere safe.

I turned on my side and wondered about Jennifer and Paul's troubled marriage. If she'd been so enamored of Benton, and Paul found out and was driving her crazy as she claimed, why didn't she leave him? Did she still love him despite their problems? Or did she feel obligated to take care of him? Not having a single answer to my many questions, I finally drifted off to sleep.

* * *

I turned away from the furry face rubbing mine. A minute later, a paw worked its way under the covers and patted my arm.

"I'm getting up," I mumbled. I glanced at the clock. "No, I'm not, Smoky Joe. It's not even six o'clock."

But he was persistent. Five minutes later, after stopping in the bathroom, I fed him his breakfast. "You're waking me up much too early," I told him as he guzzled down his food. "If you keep it up, I'll have to put you in the laundry room for the night."

I showered, got dressed, and ate my own breakfast, then figured I had enough time to visit Jim before going in to work. As I drove to the hospital, I called the police station to tell John what I'd learned the day before. This time Gracie, the dispatcher, answered my call. I heard voices in the background. *Surprising,* I thought, *for a small-town police station at seven fifteen in the morning.*

"Yes, the lieutenant's in his office. I have a feeling he'll want to talk to you," she said.

Why? A shiver of fear chased down my spine. *What could Jim have done this time? Nothing,* I told myself. He was still in the hospital. Unless Quincy had gone after him a second time and managed to—

"Carrie, can you stop by the station?" John asked. "I'd like us to have a chat."

A chat? "Is this about my father? Is he all right?"

"Jim's fine, Carrie. Still in the hospital, far as I know."

"Oh, good." I released a gallon of air. "I'll be there in a few minutes."

As soon as I walked through the station door, Gracie buzzed me into the section past the main waiting area, where several police officers were conversing in quiet tones. They stopped to watch her escort me to John's office. *What's going on? What does it have to do with me?*

Gracie knocked on the closed door. Officer Danny Brower opened it. He and John exchanged glances. Danny nodded to me as he left with Gracie. Suddenly alarmed, I wondered if I'd done something illegal, something that I wasn't aware of.

"Carrie, thanks for coming," John said. "Please shut the door and have a seat."

"Sure." I did as requested. John's eyes were bleary, and his usually smoothly shaven face had a day's growth. It looked as if he hadn't been to bed at all last night.

"Carrie, Tom Quincy's dead."

I stared across the desk at John. "Really? When did this happen?"

"Late last night. We found his body on the street. He's been murdered."

I blinked furiously as the news sank it. I disliked the man. In truth, he terrified me because I knew of his capability for violence. Still, hearing that he'd been murdered was a shock to my system.

"Why do you want to talk to *me*? Do you think I might have killed him because he bullied me the other night?"

John gave me a half smile. "No, Carrie. You're not here as a person of interest. I want to hear once again what transpired between you and Quincy Saturday afternoon. I hope you don't mind if I record it so I can go over it at my leisure."

So much had happened since then; Saturday afternoon's incident seemed to have occurred ages ago. "As I told you, he tailed me in a blue car when I left the hospital after visiting my father. I made a sudden turn and thought I'd lost him, but when I finished shopping in the village center, he came up to me in the library parking lot and said I needed to remember he was smarter than I was and that he and my father had a business arrangement and my father had better not forget it."

"Anything else?"

I shook my head. "No."

"Do you know what he meant by 'a business arrangement' with your father?"

I decided to go for the truth. "Jim said Quincy shook him down for three thousand dollars. He told Quincy he didn't have it, but he'd get it for him."

"Do you know why Tom Quincy thought your father would give him the money if they had no deal going?"

"I don't. I think Jim decided it would be the best way to get rid of him. I mean, get Quincy off his back," I quickly added.

John's laugh held no humor. "It seems someone else wanted to get rid of Quincy."

"He lied to Dylan. He never left Clover Ridge."

John's head jerked up, suddenly at attention. "You're right. How did you know?"

"For one thing, Angela's mother is friendly with Benton's widow. Mariel told Rosemary Vecchio she'd hired someone to find some missing gems. I think the person she hired was Tom Quincy."

"Interesting," John said calmly. But the way his eyes flashed, I gathered this was news to him. "What gems was she talking about?"

I shrugged. "I couldn't say—or how she knew Benton had hidden them."

Oops! John will wonder how I knew Benton had hidden the gems. He didn't press me.

Though I knew he would have loved to drill me on the subject. Time to redirect John's attention.

"I heard Jennifer and her husband arguing in the coffee shop. He'd come upon Quincy talking to Jennifer outside their house. He thought there was something romantic going on because Quincy kissed Jennifer on the forehead, when in fact he was menacing her."

"Why would he do that?"

"Could be he thinks she might know where Benton hid the gems that Mariel wanted him to find for her."

John eyed me thoughtfully. "How many people are after those gems, do you think?"

I felt my cheeks grow warm. Instead of answering, I asked, "Who do you think killed Tom Quincy?"

John sat back in his chair and stretched his arms overhead. "The million-dollar question. He was found on a deserted street a few blocks from the Darbys' home. Knifed in the back."

"Knifed? Like Benton. Do you think he was killed by the same person?"

"Very likely, though no weapon was found, just as in Benton's case. The medical examiner should be able to tell us if the same knife was used on both victims."

I hesitated before asking, "Do you think Paul Darby killed Quincy?"

"We're questioning him now."

I left John, promising to call if I remembered anything else I'd heard when Jennifer and Paul were arguing. I climbed into my car and drove slowly to the hospital.

Once again, all arrows pointed to Paul Darby. He was strong enough to attack Quincy, and he had motive as well. Besides, Quincy's body was found near his home. But wouldn't he have moved the body to avoid suspicion?

Certainly Jennifer wasn't strong enough to take on Quincy. But what if he'd come to her house to hassle her again? Her nerves were strung out, and she was unable to take any more stress. In fact, I wouldn't be surprised if, given all she'd been exposed to, she was suffering from post-traumatic stress disorder. If Quincy had come and upset her again, she might have followed him and stabbed him in the back to be rid of him once and for all.

Chapter Nineteen

I found Jim at the nurses' station, chatting away with an attractive nurse in her forties. Her name tag said "Vicki."

"Here she is! My daughter's come to visit." He hugged me. I tried to break his hold, but he squeezed tighter.

"Hello, Carrie," Vicki said. "Your father's been waiting anxiously for your arrival."

"I had to stop at the police station first," I said.

Vicki's eyebrows shot up, but Jim nodded. "John called. He'll be by to talk to me sometime this afternoon."

A buzzer sounded. "Catch you later, Jim." Vicki waved over her shoulder as she strode off to a patient's room. "I want to hear all about it."

When we got to Jim's room, I nodded to his roommate, who was watching TV, and then closed the curtain to give us some privacy. My father sat in his chair. I perched on the foot edge of his bed.

"So, Tom Quincy's bit the dust," he mused.

I nodded. "Knifed in the back near Benton's girlfriend's house."

He guffawed. "This time they can't try to pin it on me. I was here in the hospital. Nurses and aides come in often enough to give me an alibi for the night."

"Speaking of which, when are they letting you out?"

"Wednesday morning. The doctor wants to make sure there's no internal bleeding. Can you pick me up around eleven?"

"Sure. I'll be here," I said. "Any idea how long you'll be staying with me?"

Jim shot me a look of exaggerated hurt. "Don't tell me you can't bear to put up with your old dad for a while."

"You're only hanging around in hopes of finding those gems you and Benton stole."

"That's cold, Carrie. Very cold. I want to spend Christmas with you."

"In that case, you'll come with me to Aunt Harriet and Uncle Bosco's on Christmas Eve."

Jim grimaced. "Of course. Christmas and family go together. Now tell me what you know about Quincy being offed."

"For one thing, he followed me from here on Saturday afternoon. I thought I lost him, but he was waiting for me in the library parking lot, where he told me you needed to remember your agreement with him."

Jim's face went red with fury. "Why the SO—"

"I told John what happened. And Dylan. Did you know Quincy was Dylan's snitch?"

"I'm not surprised. He was going to get a share of those gems any way he could."

"And your friend Mariel hired him to find the gems."

My father burst out laughing. "So Mariel knew about the gems! Clever girl. I wonder how she found out they existed. I doubt Benton ever told her. On second thought, not such a clever girl to hire that crook."

I ignored the irony of my father calling someone else a crook. "It seems everyone knew about the gems one way or another," I said. "According to Benton's girlfriend, Jennifer Darby, Benton had access to secret funds he planned to use to whisk the two of them far, far away from Clover Ridge."

"Hah!" Jim rolled his eyes. "I can't see old Benton giving up his plush life here to go off with some young chick."

"I think John likes Jennifer's husband for Quincy's murder. Paul Darcy saw Jennifer with Quincy and mistook it for a lovers' meeting."

Jim narrowed his eyes as he met my gaze. "I hope you didn't tell our policeman friend I had anything to do with Quincy."

"He wanted to know why Quincy was following me from the hospital. And what kind of business arrangement you had with him. I said there was no arrangement but that it was Quincy who'd assaulted you."

His lips pressed together like a machine-sewn seam. "I wish you hadn't done that, Carrie."

I glared back at him. "And I wish you'd never brought Quincy into my life!" I stood. "I'll pick you up Wednesday morning."

Jim put out a hand to stop me. "I'm sorry, Carrie. I know this has been hard for you."

"You have no idea how difficult. We live by different values, you and I, and yours keep on jabbing me in the ribs."

He called after me, but I strode out of the room and down the hall. When would I get it through my head that Jim Singleton's first order of business was robbing some poor mark and not getting caught? Good thing I hadn't ended my relationship with Dylan on his account.

I drove back to the cottage for Smoky Joe and then on to the library. On the way, I made a phone call to Carlton Manor and asked to speak to the director. When a Mrs. Harrington got on the line, I introduced myself and explained that I'd be stopping by that evening to see Morgan Fuller and asked if I could bring my cat to the facility. When she hesitated, I quickly added, "Smoky Joe's the library cat at the Clover Ridge Library, where I work. He's very well behaved and used to being with people."

"Smoky Joe!" she exclaimed. "I've heard about him, but things have been so hectic here lately, I haven't had a moment to stop by the library."

A cat lover! "Of course I won't let him out of Morgan's room, and I don't plan to be there more than a few minutes. But Morgan had a cat he loved, and with Christmas coming, I thought he'd enjoy the treat."

"I suppose it will be okay since his roommate has no allergies." She laughed. "In fact, Ralph makes sure that Cindy, the service dog that visits occasionally, stops by his room every time she's here."

I said goodbye and stroked Smoky Joe's flank. "You're getting quite a reputation, my furry friend."

With only four days till Christmas, the library was brimming with holiday spirit. The lights on the tree blinked on and off, and all nine candles on the large electric Chanukah menorah were lit. We were holding our staff party the next evening in a nearby restaurant. The library would be closing early, an unusual occurrence, so everyone could attend. Of course the library board was invited, though my uncle wasn't planning to attend.

As soon as Smoky Joe was free, he tore through the reading room to get to the coffee shop. Was Jennifer feeding him despite my strict orders that no one was to give him anything to eat? Or was he still hunting down that mouse?

Whatever the reason, it offered me a good excuse to follow him into the shop and chat with Jennifer again in hopes of learning anything I could. Of course there was a good possibility she'd be furious with me for telling John her husband had made comments about Tom Quincy, and she might consider me the reason Paul was being questioned about Quincy's murder.

It was interesting that Paul Darby was one of the last people to have seen both murder victims.

But the door to the coffee shop was closed, and there was no sign of Jennifer. I turned away and nearly bumped into Sally.

"Oh, here you are," she said. "I've been looking for you!"

I stared at her flushed face. "Why? What's wrong?" My heart plummeted. It had been weeks since Sally had called me into her office to reprimand me for something I'd done or failed to do.

She patted my shoulder. "Don't worry. It's nothing very demanding, and I *know* you'll handle it with aplomb—the way you deal with everything your job requires."

I grabbed her hand—tight. "Sally, what are you trying to tell me?"

"Rico called me this morning."

I thought a moment. "Rico Benedetti? Why did he call you and not me? He's coming this afternoon to lead our holiday singers."

Sally cleared her throat.

"Well, isn't he?"

"The poor guy has the flu and has been instructed by his doctor to stay in bed. He called me at seven thirty to apologize profusely for—"

"He can't come." Panic rushed over me like a tsunami. In the past two months since I'd become head of Programs and Events, two scheduled activities had needed to be canceled. But this! The Holiday Singers Present was an annual presentation, one of the library's favorites. Patrons signed up in early November to take part in a concert of holiday and seasonal songs. Twenty were chosen by lottery. Each year a different music director was invited to lead the singers. He or she came to the library twice, along with an accompanying pianist. The first time was a rehearsal in late November, when the director brought along the lyrics of each of the songs chosen for the program. The second time was the day of the performance.

This afternoon was the day Rico Benedetti was to lead the Holiday Singers Present!

"I hate the idea of cancelling!" I exclaimed. "Everyone's been looking forward to it! And I can't possibly schedule it later in the week. The room's busy with programs every day from morning till night until Christmas Day."

"I agree, cancelling's out of the question," Sally said.

My spirits brightened. "Of course! Someone can come in his place. Rico must know several musicians who can substitute for him."

"That was the first thing I asked. Unfortunately, everyone he knows is busy this afternoon. Which is why I *knew* you'd be willing to take his place." Sally's glowing smile was as phony as a nine-dollar bill.

"Me?! What makes you think I could lead a group of singers in a program almost an hour and a half long?"

"I remembered having read in your job application form that you were in the chorus in high school and college."

"That was a long time ago, Sally. I first joined the chorus in junior high because my music teacher said I had a good voice. Since I wanted to belong to something where I didn't stand out, I always joined the chorus after that. I don't have any experience *leading* a chorus."

Sally waved her hand. "But you know what a chorus is all about. Rico's sending over his pianist—I think you met Celindra when she came with him a few weeks ago."

"Yes, I—"

"And Rico's emailing you a recording of most of the songs on the Holiday Singers program, as well as extensive program notes regarding each song. Why don't you spend the rest of the morning going over this so we can have a successful program?"

It was a command, not a suggestion.

Sally winked. "I wouldn't be surprised if we have a few board members stopping by, as well as Terry Egan, that cute young fellow from the local paper."

"Terry Egan! Why is he coming?"

"He thought it would make a great human interest story for the Sunday edition."

Just what I needed. "I have several phone calls to make, and—"

"I asked Trish to come in early today." Sally looked at her

wristwatch. "She should be here in fifteen minutes. I'm sure you have a copy of the concert's program."

Nervousness, high anxiety, and anger at Sally for putting me in this situation stirred up my pulse as I returned to my office. Having sung in a chorus throughout my school years, I knew that conducting one wasn't easy. Forget conducting—I hadn't even *sung* in a chorus for quite some time.

I tried to look on the positive side. I was very familiar with the songs that Rico had chosen for our library's program. And having a pianist would be a huge help. Then too, the singers were motivated, and I wouldn't have any discipline problems like my teachers used to have to deal with in high school. The bottom line was I had no choice in the matter. Sally decreed and I had to obey. I could only hope I made no serious faux pas in the hour and a half I'd be conducting the chorus.

Chapter Twenty

"And what exactly are you doing that's so engrossing?"

I gave a start, then grimaced when I noticed Evelyn perched on the edge of Trish's desk.

"Trish will be here in five minutes," I said. "Besides, I can't talk."

"Why? What's up?"

"Sally's got me conducting the Holiday Singers Present this afternoon! Can you imagine? The musical director who's supposed to do it is home, sick with the flu. I'm listening to his musical arrangements so I won't screw up."

"I'm sure you'll do a great job."

"I hope so."

Evelyn giggled. "At least you can't do a worse muck-up than Sally did some years ago. The director couldn't make it, and she thought she could replace him, easy as pie. Trouble is, she's tone deaf."

"No wonder she looked so—frantic. And insisted I could do a great job because I've been in choruses all throughout school."

"You will," Evelyn said airily. "Anything new on the murder investigation? Finding the gems?"

"There's been another murder—Tom Quincy."

When Evelyn sent me a puzzled look, I explained. "I told you about him. Quincy's the thug that beat up Jim and followed me from the hospital on Saturday—I suppose to show us he meant business. He threatened Jennifer Darby, Benton Parr's girlfriend."

"Why her?"

"He must have thought she knew where Benton had hidden the gems." Which got me thinking.

"Did you happen to hear what Benton and Jennifer discussed when he visited her at the coffee shop?"

She drew back, affronted. "Of course not! I don't listen in on private conversations. If I happen to overhear something, that's a different matter. But I didn't hear what they were talking about."

So much for that! Time to change the subject. "Guess what I have planned for Morgan tonight?"

"What?"

"You told me he once had a cat. I got permission to bring Smoky Joe to the nursing home to visit Morgan."

"God bless you, Carrie." And with that, Evelyn disappeared.

A moment later I knew why. Trish walked through the door. "Hi, Carrie. Were you on the phone just now?"

"No," I said, putting on a puzzled expression.

"I thought I heard you talking to someone."

"More likely I was talking to myself," I fibbed. "Sally has me leading the Holiday Singers Present program! The director who was supposed to can't make it."

Trish rolled her eyes. "Don't I know it. She's so nervous

about this afternoon. She must have great faith in you if she's asked you to handle this."

"I wouldn't say 'asked' is the right word in this case. Can't talk any more. I have to finish listening to the way he led each song and then read over his notes."

"I promise to be as silent as . . ." Trish thought a moment. "I refuse to say 'silent as the dead' or 'silent as a grave.'"

"You might say 'silent as a non-purring cat.'"

"Or 'silent as a non-snoring man.'"

We both burst out laughing.

"Okay, I'll be as quiet as I can," she said. And she was.

I put my earbuds back in and listened to the rest of the songs Rico had sent me, and then read over his notes. I liked his arrangements and was starting to feel confident that I could lead the group to sing these familiar songs without too much difficulty.

Smoky Joe scratched at the door to be let into the office, and I fed him. After a bit of grooming and using the litter box, he was off again. Trish and I ordered in sandwiches from the Cozy Corner Café. There was no time to venture out for lunch. Then I listened for a third time to the songs Rico had sent me.

Suddenly, Trish was waving her hands in my face. "Enough!" she said when I removed my earbuds so I could hear her. "You're overdoing it."

"You think? I just want to get it right."

"You *will* get it right. Time to go. It's a quarter to two."

I grabbed the program on which I'd scratched a few notes and hurried downstairs to the meeting room. Patrons sat in chairs outside the room. Inside, every seat was occupied, and Sally was telling the last few arrivals to stand against the back wall. The piano was in place at the front of the room beside the area, now empty, where the singers would stand. Once again, I wished the library extension had already been built, so many more people could sit comfortably in the room to enjoy our programs and events.

Celindra Grayson, the pianist, stood tapping her foot impatiently, no doubt expecting me to have shown up earlier. She wore what appeared to be a long dress made up of several colorful scarfs, and a ring on every finger.

"Hello, Celindra," I greeted her, suddenly overcome by what lay before me. A jolt of pure terror zipped through my body, and I considered making a break for it.

"I thought you'd want to go over today's program," she said gruffly.

"Sorry. I was in my office going over the tape Rico sent me, and lost track of time."

She grunted something, then sat down at the piano and said I didn't have much to worry about since each song had a brief introduction, and she'd nod when it was time to start them singing.

With that, she played an introduction to "Silent Night," and the hum of conversation stopped abruptly.

She's good! I thought. My fear slipped away like an unnecessary coat. I greeted the chorus of twenty as they walked from our small utility room onto the stage and stood ready to perform.

"Good afternoon. I'm sorry to have to tell you I've been recruited to fill in for Maestro Benedetti, who's home sick with the flu."

"We have faith in you, Carrie," Fred Whistler, a retiree, called out.

There were sounds of agreement from other choristers.

I smiled. "Thanks for your vote of confidence." I turned to

the audience. "Good afternoon, everyone. Welcome to this year's concert by the Holiday Singers Present! I want to thank you all for attending. Unfortunately, music master Enrico Benedetti is too sick to be with us, but Celindra Grayson, his wonderful pianist, is here to make sure we present a program that you'll enjoy."

Snap! went a flash, and I caught sight of Terry Egan, the reporter, standing next to his photographer. But it was too late to worry if I'd squinted, because once again Celindra had begun to play the opening notes of "Silent Night." *Pay attention!* I told myself as I met her gaze and then turned to face the chorus. *Now!* My arm came down and twenty voices began to sing. I merely maintained the tempo, they were so good.

And so it went with the rest of the program. The singers sang beautifully and in unison. Each rendition was greeted with a hearty burst of applause that I sensed came from true appreciation of a well-sung performance. We stopped for a short intermission when we were two-thirds through the program. Most of us took the opportunity to drink from the water bottles Trish and Sally were handing out.

Sally beamed as she gave me mine. "You're a natural, Carrie."

"Did you take photos?" I asked.

"Of course."

Aunt Harriet and Uncle Bosco came over to compliment me on my new role as chorus director, when Celindra sent me a look I'd already learned to respect. I nodded to Max and he flipped the lights a few times. But instead of turning to the singers, I cleared my throat and addressed the audience.

"Before we resume our concert, I want to take this moment to thank you all for coming and making this year's Holiday Singers Present program such a success! I was terrified when asked to lead the chorus, but they're so professional, they hardly needed me."

The audience burst into loud applause. Quickly, I added, "And we were fortunate to have a wonderful pianist to accompany us—Celindra Grayson."

Celindra half-rose from the piano as the applause began again. I continued hastily before she started playing.

"I want to take this opportunity to tell you how happy I am to be a part of the Clover Ridge Library community. It's hard to believe I became the head of Programs and Events in October. Only two months, and it seems like I've been here for years. I love my job, and I hope to create many new programs for you to enjoy."

Instead of applause, a ripple of laughter ran through the audience. My face grew warm. *Are they laughing at me?* Humiliated, I nodded to Celindra to start playing, which she did, the introduction to a rollicking Chanukah song.

"Look, Carrie, look," a few of the choristers said.

Reluctantly, I turned around. Smoky Joe was strolling down the aisle with all eyes on him. What was he doing here? He never ventured downstairs.

I went to pick him up, and the applause became deafening. I blinked back tears of happiness. "Smoky Joe came down to say he's happy to be your library cat," I announced.

When the applause died down, I said, "Let's get on with the second part of our concert."

Chapter
Twenty-One

I didn't get much work done the rest of the afternoon, and for once I wasn't concerned. The concert had been a huge success, and that was wonderful publicity for the library. Terry's photographer had managed to get a great shot of me holding Smoky Joe in my arms.

Sally was ecstatic. "See? I told you you could do it," she said as we made our way upstairs amid congratulations and hugs.

"Still, I don't like being put in that position," I told her.

She blinked. After a second she said, "Understood."

"Good."

I never would have dared to assert myself like that just a month before. I never would have addressed the audience as I had, telling them how happy I was to be a part of the library. I was miles away from the unhappy girl who had come to stay with her great-aunt and -uncle because she had nowhere else to go.

At five o'clock I gathered Smoky Joe in my arms and stopped by the circulation desk to say hi to Angela, whom I hadn't seen all day.

"We were mobbed from nine till now, or I would have come

by. I heard you were a big hit this afternoon," she told me as she ran her hand down Smoky Joe's back.

"Thank goodness it worked out. I can't believe Sally, making me lead a chorus with no rehearsal."

Angela laughed. "She has good instincts. By now she knows you'll come through, no matter what she throws your way."

"You think?"

"I know."

*   *   *

I thought about Angela's words as I headed to the Carlton Manor, taking bites of my tuna salad sandwich as I drove along. Sally had apparently been a dud leading the chorus years ago. She wouldn't have ordered me to do the same if she had thought I might also screw up.

She depended on me, and she knew I'd come through!

It gave me a warm feeling.

The feeling quickly faded when I thought of Jim. He was my parent and should have been looking out for me. Instead, he'd tried to drag me into his dirty business. And tomorrow I was picking him up from the hospital. That meant he'd start nosing around again in search of the gems. And here I was, doing nothing to find them before he did.

The parking lot at the nursing home was crowded. I figured many visitors also stopped in on their way home from work. Made sense. I gathered Smoky Joe in my arms, telling myself I needed to buy him a carrier. Marion Marshall told me the sooner I got him used to it, the easier it would be for me, since cats not used to carriers often fought like anything not to be enclosed in one.

For the first time, Smoky Joe was tense. His nails dug into my shoulder through my parka. Because he'd immediately taken to roaming the library, making friendly overtures to patrons, it hadn't occurred to me that he might find another place alarming. Maybe bringing him with me wasn't such a wise idea.

I stroked his back. "Nothing to be afraid of," I murmured in his ear. A minute later, I felt the vibrations as he began to purr.

I greeted Morgan's roommate as we entered the room. His eyes widened when he saw Smoky Joe. He gave a little chuckle and went back to watching TV. Morgan sat dozing in his chair. I called his name softly, then louder. A tremor ran down his body as he woke up.

"Sorry, Carrie. I tend to fall asleep after dinner. So glad to see you."

"I brought you Smoky Joe, our library cat."

I set Smoky Joe on the bed. He jumped off and sniffed Morgan's leg. Then he jumped onto Morgan's lap."

We both chuckled. "He likes you," I said. "He's very friendly, but he rarely gets in people's laps, unless he knows them."

"I like him too, don't I, fella?" Morgan stroked his back. Smoky Joe's purr grew louder. Morgan turned to me. There were tears in his eyes. "Thanks for bringing him tonight."

"Evelyn told me you had a cat you were fond of."

"Snuggles. Had to give her up when I came here. Evelyn and Robert were kind enough to take her. I would have been beside myself if she'd had to go to the animal shelter."

"Are they having any holiday celebrations here in the Carlton Manor?" I asked, to change the subject from sad memories.

"All week, and it's not even Christmas yet. Carolers come through the halls, and we have entertainers every afternoon.

They told us we're getting a special treat for dinner on Saturday." He shrugged. "Not that any of it interests me anymore."

We sat in silence, with no need for words. Though Morgan's eyes closed, he continued to stroke Smoky Joe. *He knows he's going to die soon.*

After a few minutes, I spoke his name.

"I know. The check for the Crowleys. After all, that's what you came for."

"And to visit you," I said with feeling.

Morgan reached over to pat my shoulder. "Don't think I don't appreciate it." He pointed to his night table. "It's in an envelope in the top drawer."

Smoky Joe jumped off his lap as I handed Morgan a white envelope with Chris's and his mother's names on it. His long, slender fingers opened the flap to check the contents, then licked the envelope to seal it. "I should have looked up their address."

"I'll get it on my cell phone," I said.

Morgan smiled. "I never did get comfortable with those smartphones."

I stood and hugged him. "I'll take care of this for you."

"Thank you. I know you will."

"I'll try to stop by again."

Morgan waved his hand. "If you find the time."

I looked around for Smoky Joe. "Smoky Joe, where are you?"

Morgan's roommate pointed to the now open door I'd closed behind me when I came into the room. "He dashed out when an aide stopped by with my meds."

"Oh!" I ran into the hall, frantic to find my half-grown kitten. I stopped two visitors walking toward me.

"Did you see a gray cat with a bushy tail run by?"

"A cat?" the man asked in disbelief while the woman shook her head.

Where could he have gone? The hall was long and veered off in three directions. Most doors were closed, but a few stood open. I turned to my left and peered into the first open door I came to.

"Did you see a gray cat?" I asked the man lying on his side.

He shook his head.

Should I go in and check? I hated to invade someone's privacy, but I had to find Smoky Joe.

Three rooms down the hall, I peered into the half-open door. A woman draped in a mink coat was bending down and stroking Smoky Joe while a white-haired woman beamed at them from her bed.

"Sweet, isn't he?" the older woman said. "I remember how you used to bring home every stray kitten that crossed your path."

I was about to knock on the door, when her visitor said, "And now that Benton's gone, I can keep as many as I like."

Benton!

The older woman lowered her voice, so I was unable to hear her comment, but whatever she'd said made her companion laugh.

"You have no idea *how* many benefits there are to not having him around any longer."

The woman had to be Mariel Parr, speaking to her mother. I paused a minute, then knocked on the door.

"Come in," the two women called out together.

"Have you seen—" I began, then pretended to be astonished by the sight of Smoky Joe enjoying Mariel's attention. "Here you are!" I scooped him up in my arms.

Mariel frowned. "Such a lovely surprise, finding a cat in this

Allison Brook

place. But must you take him? My mother and I were just reminiscing about cats we used to have when I was growing up."

"I'm afraid it's time we left. I brought Smoky Joe to the Carlton Manor to visit someone, and the little devil escaped."

The woman peered at me. "Aren't you Carrie Singleton—Jim's girl?"

"I am." I pretended to suddenly recognize her. "And you're Mariel Parr. I met you at Benton's funeral service. How are you doing?"

"As well as can be expected, considering the police aren't making any headway finding Benton's killer."

"I'm so sorry," I murmured.

"This is my mother, Mrs. Bennett," Mariel said.

"Dorie. Pleased to meet you, Carrie." The older woman put out her right hand. I freed mine and we shook.

"I was visiting Morgan Fuller," I said, tightening my hold on Smoky Joe, who saw this as an opportunity to wriggle free. "Well, I'd better go before he takes off again."

"Nice meeting you, Carrie. Please say hello to your dad for me," Mariel said.

"Get him a carrier," Dorie called after me. "He won't like it, but you'll be glad you did."

That was interesting, I thought as I hurried out to the parking lot. Now Smoky Joe was squirming big time, and the last thing I wanted was to have to spend my evening searching for him. I breathed a sigh of relief when I finally opened the car door and slid both of us inside.

"This is where you're staying when I visit the Crowleys," I told him.

Smoky Joe jumped to the back seat and peered out the side

166

window. I put the Crowleys' address into my GPS and drove slowly back toward the village center. Mariel's words rang in my ears. Clearly, she was enjoying her role as the merry widow—soaking up everyone's sympathy, yet free to do as she pleased. She had plans to sell the jewelry store, and she had her daughter back under her thumb. I hoped John had thoroughly investigated her alibi for the time of her husband's murder. Mariel had everything to gain and nothing to lose with Benton gone. She'd known he was running around, perhaps had even known that he was planning to elope with Jennifer for parts unknown.

And she'd hired Tom Quincy to find the gems, which could solve all of her financial problems.

There was good reason the spouse was always the first suspect.

Chapter Twenty-Two

Chris Crowley and his mother lived a few blocks from where Tom Quincy's body had been discovered. I found this out when I had to detour around the crime scene, which still had yellow tape marking off the area.

The small, wooden-framed house had been painted white several years ago and was sadly in need of a new coat. Lights shone through the curtains from what I assumed was the living room or den and from a room upstairs, most likely a bedroom. Good. Someone was home, which meant I could carry out my obligation. It was starting to snow as the weatherman had predicted, and I looked forward to arriving home at my cottage within the hour.

I parked on the street, behind a Camry with a dented rear fender, and started up the cement walk. The wooden steps leading to the closed-in porch dipped in the center from years of use. A ratty-looking wreath hung on the front door.

"Be right there!" a strong woman's voice called out in response to my knock. I imagined she looked through the peephole because a minute later the door swung open.

"Yes? Can I help you?"

Stella Crowley was a handsome woman in her mid-fifties. She stood close to six feet tall in her jeans and sweatshirt. Her manner was pleasant, assured, and a trifle wary.

"Hello, Mrs. Crowley. My name is Carrie Singleton. I need to talk to you about a rather delicate subject. May I come in?"

I must have appeared harmless and not too much of a crackpot, because she opened the door wider and I stepped inside. "We can talk here," she said, leading me to the living room to the right of the small entrance. A three-foot Christmas tree devoid of any ornaments stood in the corner. I could tell it was artificial and, like the wreath outside, was shabby and should have been thrown out a year or two ago.

"We haven't gotten around to putting up the lights and ornaments," she commented. "Hopefully, we'll get to it by Friday. Can I get you something to drink?"

"No, thanks. I'm fine."

We sat down on two loveseats and faced one another across a scratched wooden cocktail table.

"Now, what is this about?" Mrs. Crowley asked.

I opened my mouth to explain, when we heard footsteps tramping down the staircase. I turned as Chris came to stand at the entrance to the living room, followed by Dina Parr.

"Mom, Dina and I are going out for some pizza." His eyes widened when he saw me. "We thought we heard the doorbell. Carrie from the library, right? What are you doing here?"

Dina made a semicircular gesture of greeting with her open palm. I was surprised to see her here in Chris's home after what I'd overheard her telling her brother Saturday night.

"Hello, Chris. I came to talk to you and your mom on behalf of a man who's—well, approaching the end of his life."

Chris strode into the living room. "Who? What are you talking about?"

I glanced at Dina. "It's a private matter."

"I'll wait in the kitchen," Dina said.

"Don't be silly," Mrs. Crowley said. "Sit down, Dina. I have no idea what this is about, but it shouldn't take very long."

Dina dropped into a wing chair. Chris leaned against the wall. Three sets of eyes fixed on me. Nervous as I was, I couldn't help noting from what I'd observed that Dina was a frequent and welcome visitor to the Crowleys' home.

I cleared my throat. "I've just come from the Carlton Manor, where Morgan Fuller's a resident."

"My grandmother's there," Dina said.

I stifled my impulse to tell her I'd just seen Dorie and Mariel as well. Now was not the time to deviate from the reason for my visit. I stared at Mrs. Crowley. Her face had turned white.

"Morgan Fuller. That awful man!"

Chris smacked a fist into his hand. "He's the reason my father died so young. Why we live in this dump. Why I couldn't go away to college."

"I'm sorry to have upset you both," I said, "but as I said, Morgan is dying."

"Good!" Chris said.

"Chris, please hear her out," his mother admonished.

I pressed on. "He's very sorry for the way he treated your father."

"And saw to it he never got another job in this town," Chris said.

"He was upset because of the fire that burned down his shop," I said lamely, though I could well understand Morgan's anger.

"That was an accident," Chris spit out.

"Accident or not, Morgan has asked me to give you a rather substantial check."

"To pay us off?" Mrs. Crowley said, her tone one of amazement. "Does he think that makes up for all the miserable years since that damn accident?"

Their spin of the "accident" was infuriating. I felt like running out of that house and taking the check with me. But it wasn't mine to withhold. Chris and his mother hadn't caused the fire. It wasn't their fault they had an alcoholic for a husband and a father. A man who refused to obey the one simple but crucial work rule: no smoking in the shop. But I supposed they needed to see him as the aggrieved party in order to rationalize his downfall to themselves. It wasn't my place to strip them of their illusion.

"I don't imagine Mr. Fuller believes that for one minute. He was extremely upset because—" I met Mrs. Crowley's gaze straight on. "I think you know very well why he was upset. But he regrets his behavior afterward. He can't make up for what's happened, but he can make your lives a little easier." I opened my pocketbook and withdrew the envelope Morgan had given me. "Here's a check for two hundred thousand dollars."

Silence. Dina burst out laughing. "Hey, Chris. Now you can buy the jewelry store from my mom."

Chris's face lit up. "Now *we* can buy it, Dina, like we talked about."

"Come on, Chris—that was all a fantasy."

"A fantasy that can come true," he said.

171

"Not for me," Dina said bitterly. "No one's gifted me a hefty check for Christmas."

"I don't care whose money it is," Chris said. "We can still be partners."

Stella Crowley touched her son's forearm. "It's a bit early to decide what you'll be doing with your half of the money."

"Your mother's right," Dina said. "I should be going and let you two discuss things."

"I'll call you later," Chris called after Dina as I followed her to the front door.

When we were outside I said, "By the way, I ran into your mother and grandmother tonight."

"Did you?" Dina's voice was flat.

"Uh-huh. I brought my cat to the Carlton Manor for Morgan's sake. He used to have a cat. We got to talking and Smoky Joe escaped. I found him in your grandmother's room. Your mother was petting him."

Dina let out a bark of a laugh. "I'm not surprised. Mother prefers cats to people. Dad always claimed he was allergic to cats, so we never had any. Who knows if that was true."

I didn't know how to respond, so I said nothing.

"Grandma's sweet," Dina said. "I should visit her."

"Well, good night." I started walking toward my car, when Dina put a hand on my shoulder.

"Carrie, would you like to go for a drink or something?" She saw my startled expression and laughed. "Or a cup of coffee, if you don't drink."

"I'm really in the mood for a few slices of pizza, but I have Smoky Joe in the car." I thought a moment. "It's a mild night and he is wearing his fur coat. If we stop someplace, I won't be able to stay long."

"We'll order, eat, and run. How does that sound?" Dina smiled—the first time I'd seen her really smile—and it transformed her face. She was really very pretty.

Now, if she got a good haircut and wore some makeup and got rid of those drab, shapeless tops and pants—

"What's so funny?"

Suddenly I'm the fashion police. "I was thinking how much I've changed these past few months," I said. "No more Goth clothes, Doc Martens, or purple hair."

Dina studied my brown slacks, the tailored beige sweater under my open parka. She had a quizzical expression on her face. "You? For real?"

"For real."

"Antonio's has better pies, but Raimo's is closer and won't be as crowded. Follow me."

"Raimo's it is," I said and headed for my car.

I found Smoky Joe asleep in the passenger's seat. I covered him with the extra jacket I kept on the back seat, and he snuggled down deeper into feline slumber.

"We'll be home soon," I whispered, patting his head.

Raimo's was far from crowded, though it was only seven thirty. Dina and I staked out the table in the far corner by tossing our jackets on the chairs, then went up to the counter to place our orders.

"Mothers bring their kids here for an early dinner," she said. "The high school kids start coming in around nine thirty."

I carried my two slices of veggie pizza, a large coke, and a small salad to the table. I took my first bite. "Not bad," I said, "but not as good as Antonio's."

"They're the best," Dina agreed.

I was hungry and finished the first slice before asking my first question. "Are you and Chris going out?"

Dina rolled her eyes. "Absolutely not, though he likes to think we're soul mates. I mean, we're good friends, but that's it."

I wasn't ready to let her off the hook. "Funny, when you and Chris helped your father with his library program, I got the impression you guys were dating."

She shrugged as if she was conceding a point. "Yeah, we did—for a very short while. He's a good guy, but he's so clingy. He has no self-confidence."

"Growing up without a father must have been difficult."

"Stella couldn't bear to think her husband was a loser, so she filled Chris's head with fantasies—that Bert was misunderstood and victimized, when the truth is he was too drunk to keep a job." She looked sheepish when she added, "Chris only found out recently that his father started the fire where he'd been working."

"How do you know all this?"

"I thought he should know the truth, so I told him." Dina bit her lip. "I think I made an awful mistake. It left him more confused than ever. Now he feels he has to prove to me and to the world that he's not a bum like his father."

"Your father must have seen something in Chris, or he wouldn't have hired him."

Dina snorted. "My mother tried to talk my father out of hiring Chris because he came from the wrong side of the tracks— like anyone but her would use that stupid expression—and because he'd dropped out of college. It's not like he failed or couldn't do the work. He left because he didn't find the courses relevant, and he'd run out of money. Turned out Chris loved learning the jewelry business, so he took a course in gemology. We both did. He's on the shy side, but when he worked at the store, he was amazingly good with the customers."

"I understand your mother wants to sell the jewelry store."

"She does. I wish she'd keep it and let me run it, but she'll do what she wants."

I bit into my second slice of pizza.

"Of course, everything would be different if I knew where my father had stashed the gems."

I gasped, then coughed as a piece of crust caught in my throat. Dina leaned over to pound my back. Miraculously, the piece was dislodged. I sipped my soda.

"Just as I thought," she said softly. "You know about them too."

I nodded. There was no point in playing dumb. Not that I expected to learn anything from her.

Dina cackled. "Here we sit in a pizza parlor, the daughters of two thieves."

"I grew up ashamed and embarrassed, knowing my father was a thief," I said. "Jim was away most of the time, and I missed him a lot. Now I'm glad he wasn't around."

"I only found out a few months ago," Dina said, "when I started spending more time helping out in the store. My father would occasionally get calls that he'd take in the back room. The parts I managed to overhear were about merchandise, but he sounded furtive. He made sure Chris and I were out in front when he took those calls." She snorted. "Of course, some of the time he was probably talking to his latest babe."

"Jennifer Darby," I said. "She seemed to think your father was in love with her. They were planning to leave town."

"I doubt that very much," Dina scoffed. "Jennifer was only the last of a long parade of women. I've known about them for the past eight years."

"Do you think your mother knew?"

"I think she did but pretended she didn't. My mother likes to act like everything's all right. She lives by the code that appearances rule. If you pretend all is well, then everything will look just fine, and people won't know anything's wrong. But people always know, don't they?"

"They do," I agreed.

Dina stood suddenly and gathered up her debris to toss in the nearby garbage can. When she sat down again, she cocked her head at me.

"So, I've been thinking."

"Yes?" I sipped the last of my soda and gathered up my rubbish.

"I bet your father came to Clover Ridge to get his share of the heist."

Startled, I gaped at her. "How—I mean, where did you get that idea?"

Dina grinned. "I'm a pretty good detective when I want to be. I made it my business to listen in on conversations and check out my father's texts when he left his phone in his jacket."

"Clever," I said.

"Did you ever think how your life could change if you recovered those stones?"

"Frankly, no. I wish my father would forget about those damn gems and go off somewhere far away."

Dina stared at me in disbelief. "Come on, Carrie. You must have given it some thought."

"I've wondered where your father hid them," I admitted.

"So have I," Dina said. "And I have an idea where they might be. The thing is, I need a partner. Someone with a car."

Don't be too eager. Play dumb. "What about Chris? You may not be dating, but you guys struck me as BFFs."

She let loose a derisive snort. "Are you kidding? Let him in on it, and I'll have him around for the rest of my life. I want to start out on my own, with no one but me in charge." She shot me a sly look. "And I suspect you wouldn't interfere with that."

"I certainly wouldn't. But are you sure you want to share the loot?"

"Seventy–thirty."

"Whoa! This is a fifty–fifty deal. Our fathers were in on it together."

"And mine was smart enough to keep it all."

"Look where it got him," I pointed out. "Fifty-five–forty-five is the best I can do."

"Sixty–forty, and that's my final offer."

I stuck out my hand. "Deal. When do we get started?"

"Is tomorrow soon enough?"

"Sorry. I have to bring my father home from the hospital in the morning, and after work I have the library holiday party."

"Thursday morning, then. I'll call you at eight, eight fifteen, and we'll go over the details. Figure on a little excursion that should take three, four hours tops."

"Very good. Talk to you then." I gathered up my things to leave.

Dina grinned. "If I'm as right as I think I am, we'll be treating ourselves to an early Christmas present."

Chapter
Twenty-Three

Smoky Joe meowed his greeting, along with forceful head butts to tell me in no uncertain terms that he was seriously annoyed to have been kept waiting.

"I know, Furry Face. You're hungry and you don't like being confined to a car."

I turned on the motor and started for home. Satisfied with my apology, Smoky Joe bumped against my hip and settled down beside me.

What was I thinking? I drove home, stunned by what I'd gotten myself into. But I had to seize the only opportunity that had come my way. By some warped ethical line of reasoning, Dina trusted me to have the same morals she did simply because both our fathers were thieves. The way I saw it, her father had duped mine. Now was my chance to turn the tables—find the gems and hand them over to Dylan.

I gnawed at my lip as I considered how many people I'd be pissing off by returning the gems to their rightful owner: my father, Dina, Mariel, Richard, and Chris Crowley.

I shuddered as I factored in one more detail: one of them

might be a murderer. Even if Quincy had murdered Benton, someone had done away with Quincy and wouldn't hesitate to kill again.

Rush hour was over, and the traffic had eased up. I drove on autopilot, not paying too much attention to the vehicles around me. There weren't many on the road. But after traveling two miles, I realized that a car had remained about four car lengths behind me. No biggie, I thought as I changed lanes, until the other driver did the same.

Anxiety tingled along my neck as I approached the private road leading to Dylan's mansion-sized home and, farther on, my cottage. Dylan was away in another city and not expected home until the weekend. I drove past my turnoff and slowed down. The other car slowed down too.

My heart pounded as I made a quick U-turn and pulled over to the side of the road. A passing car honked angrily. In my rear-view mirror I watched as the car that had been following me slowed down. Was the driver planning to dash across the road to talk to me? Shoot me dead?

I stomped on the pedal and took off. The other car made a U-turn and, though I was speeding, zipped past me. It was a gray Honda, but I couldn't make out the driver's face. My hands shook as I turned onto the private road to my cottage.

My first impulse was to call John Mathers to tell him someone had been tailing me. But how could I, after making a deal with Dina to retrieve the gems our fathers had stolen? Even though I had no intention of keeping them, John's questions were bound to probe areas I couldn't talk about. He'd know I was deflecting and holding back information, and would throw up his hands in frustration. No, it wasn't fair to turn to John for help.

I assumed that the driver who had been following me was after the gems. It could be Chris, Mariel, or Richard. Not Dina, since she didn't own a car—or so she said. I'd have to find out who drove a gray Honda.

And then what? I supposed remain on my guard.

When I arrived home, I made sure all of the doors and windows were securely locked. I fed Smoky Joe then called my father at the hospital.

"Hi, Jim. Is your doctor still planning on letting you go home tomorrow?"

"So I've been told. What's wrong, Caro?"

"Nothing," I said, wondering how he'd picked up on the residual nervousness I still felt from having been followed home.

"You sound troubled."

"Just frazzled. It's a busy time of the year. What time should I come by?

"Dr. B usually does rounds at eight, eight thirty. After the paperwork, I should be good to go at nine, nine-thirty. I figure no later than ten."

"Okay. We can stop off on the way home for whatever you might need, then I have to go to work. And the library holiday party is tomorrow night. Sorry to abandon you."

Jim's deep laugh came over the wire. "Don't you worry a thing about me, Caro. I appreciate your taking me in until I'm steady on my feet. That should be very soon. I feel stronger every day."

You can't wait to go after those gems. And then you'll be on your way. "At least we'll be together over Christmas."

"Looking forward to it, honey."

Tears welled up as I disconnected. Damn it, why was I still

so vulnerable and in need of my father's love? I was thirty years old, for God's sake! When was I going to realize I couldn't depend on Jim Singleton in the way other people took it for granted that their dads were a part of their lives? Besides, I told myself as I scrubbed away the tears, I was an adult now. I didn't need my father to protect me from the evils of the world. I had to look after myself and not rely on anyone else.

I woke up the following morning determined to be strong. I'd do what I had to: drive Jim home from the hospital, find the gems, turn them in, and get on with my life.

And there was Dylan. I smiled as I reminisced about one of our romantic moments. He'd be home for the weekend. All the turmoil in my life these past few days couldn't distract me from missing him. I couldn't wait to see him. I'd felt betrayed and wounded when I first realized he'd been hunting Jim, spurred on by my loyalty to my father, who was my flesh and blood. But I no longer felt conflicted. My father's criminal actions had led to consequences that had nothing to do with me. Dylan and I cared for each other. We could resume our relationship, if I wanted. It was something, I realized, that I wanted very much.

I entered my father's hospital room and found Jim chatting with his roommate, a man in his mid-sixties. He had a full head of white hair; a round, red face; and, from what I could tell, since he was under a blanket, a rather round body. Not a healthy specimen, though he'd make a perfect Santa.

"Ah, Caro! I was just telling Ernie about you. Ernie Pfeiffer, my daughter, Carrie Singleton. Ernie, here, is gonna have his gall bladder removed sometime today."

"The sooner, the better. Your dad's been bragging about you—how proud he is of you."

I rolled my eyes, but I couldn't help feeling pleased. "Is that so?"

"I understand you work in the library. My neighbor works there too."

"Really? Who's that?"

"Dorothy Hawkins. You know. The Dragon Lady."

I couldn't help it—I burst out laughing.

Ernie grinned. "You work with her, but try living next door to the woman. She's tried to sue me four times in the past twelve years. Got nowhere, in any event. The last time was over one of my trees that has branches extending over her property."

"What's her husband like?" I asked, to stop him from going into a long story. But I was curious as well.

"Freddy Hawkins? He's an okay guy. Doesn't say much. I guess she has him pretty well cowed. But he put his foot down the time my dog ran loose and she called the police, demanding that they put Old Barney to sleep."

"Oh, no!" I exclaimed.

Ernie waved a hand. "Don't worry. The police told her they weren't in the exterminating business. Barney died in his sleep a year later."

"I'm all packed," my father said.

"So we can go?"

"Soon as the nurse comes with the necessary papers to sign."

I wondered if thieves had a medical plan covering hospital stays, but remained silent on the subject. I didn't want to get involved. My father must have read my mind because he laughed. "Good thing I got health insurance a few years ago. It's covered almost all my expenses here."

"I'm glad," I said.

A few minutes later, a nurse entered the room with the necessary papers. Jim signed them. She asked if he wanted a wheelchair to transport him down to the exit.

"No way. I can walk fine."

I grabbed his small suitcase, said goodbye to Ernie Pfeiffer, and we started walking slowly down the hall.

"I have some food in the house and a casserole you can warm up for dinner tonight. Would you like to stop at a drugstore for anything?"

"Yes, to fill my latest prescription."

We stopped at the CVS drive-thru window and picked up Jim's medicine. When we arrived at the cottage, I carried his suitcase into his room. Instead of following me, he plopped down on the den sofa and turned on the TV.

"Are you hungry? I'll make you a sandwich, if you like, before I go to work."

"I'll eat later. You've done enough."

"You'll find plenty of cold cuts in the fridge. For dinner, heat up the casserole on the middle oven rack for twenty minutes at three hundred and twenty-five degrees. There are greens for salad in the refrigerator bins."

Jim waved away my concerns. "Don't worry, Caro. I'll figure it out."

I made myself a tuna salad sandwich and wrapped it in tinfoil to eat later on in my office. Then, since I'd be going directly to the party from work, I changed into a sleek black dress with a plunging neckline and a hemline a few inches above my knees. I slipped into a pair of suede sling-back heels and put eye makeup in my pocketbook to apply later on at work.

Jim whistled. "Wow! Don't you look gorgeous!"

"Thanks. I'll be back from the party around nine thirty," I said, scooping up Smoky Joe. "Stay out of trouble."

"Of course, daughter dear. I'll be fine."

I felt a sense of relief as I headed off to work. My father was safely ensconced in my cottage and, judging by his faltering pace when we'd stopped in the drugstore, he wasn't strong enough to wander off and get into mischief. I was beginning to understand why someone grieving or beset by problems would find her workplace a haven of solace. My responsibilities as head of P and E gave me no time to think about my father or the gems, or to wonder who had followed me last night.

An incoming text pinged as I approached the library parking lot. I drove into an empty space and pulled out my phone to read the message.

Home Thursday night. Talk 2 u then. Can't wait.

Dylan! My heart thumped against my ribs. Two days from now I'd be back in his arms.

I grinned as I imagined the surprised look on his face when I handed over the gems—if Dina was right and her father had hidden them where she suspected. Of course I needed to figure out how to get them away from her, but that was on tomorrow's agenda. First I had to get through today.

The cheerful holiday spirit overtook me the moment I entered the library. Somehow Sally had managed to infuse the entire main floor with the delicious aroma of potpourri.

"Like it?" she asked, coming to stand beside me.

"Smells yummy."

"Jennifer made a huge batch of potpourri with cinnamon, orange, and cranberries. She brought it in this morning, along with several pine cones which we set beside the bowls."

"Oh! Is she all right then?"

"Jennifer?" Sally wrinkled her brow. "As far as I know. Why?"

"Marital problems," I said.

"Of course. The police questioned her husband about the murders, but they let him go."

The lights on the large Christmas tree in the main reading room caught my attention.

"Lovely, isn't it?" Sally said.

"Beautiful. I could stare at it all day." We walked closer to the tree, where a small crowd of patrons had gathered. Smoky Joe stared at the lights, his little black nose inches from the lowest branch.

"Don't get any ideas about climbing that tree," I admonished him.

"I don't think any of us will get much work done these next few days," Sally said. "I still have a few gifts to wrap and place under my tree at home."

"Don't forget your Secret Santa gift," I said, suddenly remembering my gift for Dorothy, which I'd had the foresight to place in the trunk of my car.

Sally patted my arm. "Thanks for reminding me. I'll have to stop home for that little item."

She left and, not for the first time, I marveled at how we'd become friends after our very rough beginning back in October.

I knew Trish was minding the office, so I decided to stop in at the library coffee shop to see how Jennifer was coping. I admit, I had an ulterior motive too. Jennifer was the *one* link, if a very tenuous one, to the missing gems and the two murders. Not that tenuous, though, when one considered that her husband, Paul, had been brought in for questioning regarding both murders.

I found her serving coffee and scones to two patrons chatting at one of the tables. I waited until she was back behind the counter before addressing her. "How are you doing, Jennifer? I stopped by the other day, but the coffee shop was closed."

"Yes, I had a few personal errands that required immediate attention." She appeared calm and self-possessed. No sign of the grieving, frantic woman I'd spoken to last week.

"You seem to be feeling much . . . better," I said, hoping my adverb didn't offend.

"I *am* much better," Jennifer said, "now that I have a plan."

"Oh. Well, that's good."

"I've made up my mind to leave Paul. I'm going to put some distance between me and this place."

"Oh," I said again, sounding like the village idiot. *What on earth was responsible for the change in Jennifer?*

"I sense that I can trust you, Carrie, not to say a word to anyone."

"Of course I won't."

"I haven't told anyone, not even Sally." She gave a self-deprecating laugh. "She'll easily find someone to take over the coffee shop. But it's time I moved on with my life. Finally said goodbye to my life in Clover Ridge."

"Why, Jennifer? What made you suddenly decide?"

She clamped her mouth shut as one of the women came to the counter and plucked a few napkins from the holder. Jennifer waited until the woman sat down again and spoke to her companion.

"The police questioned Paul about that man's murder. He came home in a lousy mood. Yes, he happened to see the man, Tom Quincy. Yes, he went over to talk to him, to tell him to keep far away from me. Yes, someone might have seen them talking, but he never laid a finger on him. The police must have believed him because they brought him home hours later."

"I still don't understand."

"Paul lashed into me, claimed all this was happening to him because I had an affair with Benton. He went on and on. I tried to escape to our bedroom, but he followed me there and ranted some more. Finally, he went downstairs and started drinking. He fell asleep on the living room couch. I packed a bag and went to my sister's. I needed to make a clean break from everything bad in my life."

"Where will you go? What will you live on?" I asked.

She smiled. "I'll manage. I'll get a job somewhere. Start off fresh in a new town."

I nodded, but something wasn't adding up. Something made me ask, "Are you sorry you got involved with Benton Parr?"

"No, but last night it hit me. I was never in love with Benton. I turned to him because my marriage was over, only I wasn't strong enough to leave Paul."

"And now you're strong enough?"

Her smile had something of the Cheshire Cat about it. "Strong enough to move on."

Chapter
Twenty-Four

I felt perplexed as I walked to my office. Why the sudden change in Jennifer? Was she involved with another man? It didn't sound like she was, but something had radically altered her thinking. What could it be? Not only had she finally decided to end her marriage to Paul, but she'd done a complete one-eighty regarding Benton Parr who, only a week ago, she'd told me was her one true love.

As the king says in *The King and I*: " 'Tis a puzzlement." And I had no way of solving that mystery right now.

As I passed through the reading room, I caught sight of an elderly male patron ignoring the newspaper in his lap to stroke a tranquil Smoky Joe sitting at the side of his chair. I smiled to think that my little feline was proving to be a wonderful addition to the Clover Ridge Library.

I greeted Trish, went over a few items with her, then settled down at my desk to tackle the pile of paperwork I hoped to wade through before leaving for the holiday party.

My library phone rang and I answered it. "Good morning,

Carrie Singleton of Programs and Events speaking. How may I help you?"

"Hi, Carrie. It's Dina Parr."

"Oh, hello."

My tone of voice must have conveyed the fact that I wasn't alone because she said, "Sounds like you have company."

"That's true."

"I'm calling to see if we're still on for our excursion tomorrow morning."

"We are. Want to tell me more about it?"

"We'll be going to my father's cabin in the woods about an hour's drive from here. Pick me up at eight fifteen."

"Will do."

"See you then."

She disconnected and I did too. Trish shot me a questioning look, and I waved my hand as if it wasn't a matter of importance.

The day passed slowly. I called home to see how my father was managing. He must have been sleeping because he didn't answer the phone. I hoped he wasn't out searching for the gems. There was nothing I could do if he was. I sighed. On the one hand, I was glad to have him with me over the holidays. On the other hand, I worried how he would react after I turned over the gems to Dylan. I sighed again. He was bound to leave town as soon as he felt better and the matter of the stolen gems was settled. Until then, I expected to be on the alert and too tense to relax.

I ate my sandwich at one when Trish left the office to man the hospitality desk. Minutes later, Evelyn made an appearance. She beamed at me.

"Don't you look gorgeous!"

"Thank you. So do you." I admired her navy silk dress and short matching jacket. Instead of her usual low-heeled, practical shoes, today Evelyn wore navy sling-back heels. Her gray hair looked as though it had been styled.

"Who did your hair?—which looks lovely today. I mean, I had no idea there were beauty salons for ghosts."

Evelyn brushed my curiosity aside. "Not now, Carrie. Concentrate on what's important. The matter of two murders and a small fortune of missing gems requires your attention."

I stared at her as she perched on her favorite place—Trish's desk. "I don't know who committed the murders. I only know they must be linked to the missing gems."

"Who knows about the gems?" Evelyn asked.

"Lots of people." I started ticking them off on my fingers. "My father; Dina Parr and her brother, Richard; their mother, Mariel; Chris Crowley; and maybe Jennifer Darby."

"That's quite a list. Any idea where they might be?"

I told Evelyn about my plans to drive to Benton's cabin in the woods with Dina.

"And if you find them there, how do you plan on taking them from Dina?"

"I'll think of something."

Evelyn pursed her lips. "I don't like this, Carrie. For all you know, Dina killed her father and Tom Quincy to get her hands on these gems. She doesn't have a car, so she's roped you into helping her."

"You're right. She could be the killer, but she trusts me. I could offer to hide the gems until we can fence them. After all, she's living at home now and wouldn't want her mother to find them."

"You're taking a big risk. I think you ought to tell Lieutenant Mathers. Let him search the cabin instead of you going there."

To change the subject, I told her that I'd stopped by Morgan's nursing home to pick up the check last night and delivered it to Stella and Chris Crowley.

"They must have appreciated that."

"I think they did. In their own way. That's where I ran into Dina."

"Really? That surprises me."

"I got the feeling she spends a lot of her free time there. Dina claims there's nothing romantic between her and Chris, but I sense he doesn't see it that way. Anyway, we left mother and son discussing how they might spend the money. We went out for pizza, and she told me a few things about the Crowleys. Stella's done a number on Chris, leading him to believe his father was a victim all his life and not a drunkard that started a fire. Dina said she got sick of hearing that from Chris, so she told him the truth."

"Dina sounds like a gem," Evelyn said sarcastically.

I laughed. "I kind of like her, despite her larcenous tendencies. She doesn't have it easy. Her father was a thief and a hypocrite, and her mother's a snob."

"Your parents were far from ideal, yet you turned out all right."

"Thank you, Evelyn. Speaking of which, I brought Jim home from the hospital this morning. And he didn't answer the phone when I called a few minutes ago."

Evelyn looked worried. "Let's hope he didn't go off hunting for those troublesome gems. He's weak, and the murderer has already killed two people."

I suddenly remembered. "Jim's roommate in the hospital was Dorothy's neighbor."

Evelyn looked frightened. "Not Ernie Pfeiffer!"

"That's his name. He's none too fond of your niece. Said she's tried to sue him a few times."

"He's not someone you want to mess with, Carrie. I told Dorothy not to get involved with him in any way, shape, or form. And certainly not to set out to sue him. But did she listen to me? Of course not!"

"Why?"

"We, Robert and I, had the misfortune of investing with Ernie Pfeiffer. We trusted him and handed over most of our savings. Robert soon realized he was running a Ponzi scheme and demanded our money back. Only after we threatened to go to the authorities did he return about two-thirds of what we'd invested with him." She paused. "Then the nasty incidents began, incidents I know were his doing."

"I'm sorry, Evelyn."

She began to fade. "I'm too upset to talk about it anymore. Take care, my girl. Don't do anything foolish. Your life is more valuable than all the gems in the world."

I stared at the empty space where Evelyn had been only moments before. I'd never seen her so distraught, not even when she was afraid that her niece Dorothy had murdered two people. I called the cottage landline again and got a busy signal. Relieved that my father was back from wherever he'd gone, I was able to settle down to do paperwork until the library closed at five.

A light snow was falling when I carried Smoky Joe out to the car. I wished I'd been smart enough to wear boots instead of exposing my favorite black heels to the elements. All of the patrons had exited the library minutes earlier, and those of us on staff were leaving in groups of twos and threes to head for the restaurant half a mile outside of town. Angela had offered to drive me there, but I had to drop Smoky Joe off at my aunt and uncle's house and pick him up later, so I thought it would be best if I drove to the restaurant myself.

"Don't tell me you're bringing that cat to our Christmas party!"

I stared at Dorothy, noting the expression of indignation on her face.

"Don't worry, Dorothy. I'm—" I stopped short, having decided it was none of her business where Smoky Joe would be for the next few hours.

"Yes?" she encouraged, her eyes alight with interest. Or was it malice?

"No need to worry. *That cat*, as you put it, will be well taken care of."

"I wasn't worried." She expelled a loud huff and moved on.

Sourpuss. I was surprised Dorothy was coming to the holiday party since she had no friends among the library staff. Even Sally, who used to be her friend, steered clear of her these days. And I had the unfortunate honor of being her Secret Santa! I thought of the pretty scarf I'd bought for her, tucked away in the trunk of my car. *She doesn't deserve it.*

At the restaurant, the maître d' showed me to a private room where piped-in Christmas music played softly. I dropped Dorothy's Secret Santa gift on the small table set up for the presents and approached the dining table. There were fifteen of us, which I thought was a nice jolly number. I was sorry Trish and Susan couldn't make it, but they both had family commitments. Angela called my name, and I scooted along the wall to the empty chair between her and Sally. Marion, her assistant Gayle, and Harvey Kirk, the computer librarian, greeted me from across the table. I was sitting amid friends, exactly where I wanted to be! Dorothy, I was glad to see, was at the far end of the table.

We chatted easily through our salad and main course. I enjoyed my stuffed flounder and was looking forward to dessert. As the two servers cleared our dishes, Sally stood to make some announcements. Soon we were being served coffee or tea, chocolate mousse or cheesecake. Angela ordered one dessert, and I ordered the other so we could have a bit of both. Both the mousse and the cake were delicious.

"And now for our Secret Santa presents," Marion announced.

She walked over to the small table piled with gifts. I knew it was the library's tradition to keep the giver and receiver a secret until this moment, when they were distributed at the holiday dinner. I felt a bit anxious, hoping that Dorothy would like what I'd bought her. I'd paid a few dollars more than the prearranged amount for her silk scarf because it included two of the colors she wore most often—violet and hunter green.

The gifts were lovely. Angela received a large mug, Sally a beautiful serving dish. I went up when my name was called and lifted the largest box on the table. "Wow!" I said as my colleagues laughed and made speculative comments about what might be inside.

I tore through the wrapping paper and opened the box. Inside was a statue of a gray cat with green eyes. I held it up and everyone applauded. I glanced at the card, which I should have done first and smiled at Sally's message.

"Thank you, Sally. This takes the place of honor in my living room."

Sally grinned. "Check out the bottom of the box."

I felt inside the box. There was a cat toy filled with catnip. I held it up and said, "Smoky Joe thanks you."

Everyone applauded. Everyone but Dorothy. She stared balefully at me. Oh, no! I hope she wasn't about to start another campaign against me because Sally was my friend and no longer hers.

I threw back my shoulders and smiled as I carried my gifts to my seat. I would *not* let myself be cowed by that unhappy woman! I was no longer the vulnerable newcomer to the library. If Dorothy started causing trouble again, I was ready for her.

I watched carefully as she unwrapped my gift. Her pursed lips relaxed into a genuine smile when she lifted the scarf from the box. "Thank you, Carrie. I love the colors."

"I know you do," I said.

She nodded, and I felt as if I'd passed a test. Dorothy wouldn't be pulling her shenanigans on me, at least not in the immediate future.

Chapter Twenty-Five

I was the first to leave the party. I hugged my friends goodbye, and carried my Secret Santa gifts out to the rear parking lot. The snow had stopped, leaving a light covering on the ground so that I made a trail of footprints to my car. After clearing off the windows with the snow brush and ice scraper gadget Uncle Bosco had bought for me, I drove to my aunt and uncle's house. Uncle Bosco greeted me at the door. Smoky Joe meowed loudly to let me know he was seriously annoyed at having been left behind.

"He spent most of the time staring out the window, looking for you," my uncle said.

I stroked Smoky Joe's head. "Sorry, pal, but you can't go everywhere I go."

I thanked Uncle Bosco and kissed him goodbye, then carried Smoky Joe out to the car. I gave him Sally's toy, and he settled down to chew on it.

"We're homeward bound, Smoky Joe!" I announced and started the car. He head-butted me, then curled up on the passenger's seat. I exhaled loudly, glad that I hadn't left him in the car while I was at the holiday party, as I'd first considered doing.

Read and Gone

The killer could very well have taken Smoky Joe or hurt him while I was inside the restaurant, as a warning to stop me from chasing after the gems.

I drove slowly, on the alert to spot anyone who might be following me, but no one was. When I reached the cottage, I was startled to see a gray Lexus parked next to my father's car. I carried the box into the house, letting Smoky Joe follow me on his own. My father and Mariel Parr were sitting in the living room, drinking coffee.

They didn't hear me come in because they were laughing over something one of them had said. Smoky Joe ran to Mariel, and she bent down to pet him.

"Evening, Caro," my father called to me. "Say hello to Mariel Parr."

Mariel and I greeted each other. She looked lovely in a navy pant suit and white turtleneck sweater. "I told your father we'd met at my mother's nursing home last night. Quite a coincidence."

"Yes, quite a coincidence," I echoed, wishing she weren't constantly popping up in my life.

"What do you have there?" my father asked.

"A statue of a cat," I said, opening the box to show them. "My Secret Santa gift."

My father and Mariel made a fuss about it, saying it was lovely. "And there's the perfect spot for it," Mariel said, pointing to the long low table against the window. I put it down and had to agree she was right.

"How are you feeling?" I asked Jim.

"Not bad."

"I called you earlier today, but you didn't answer," I told him.

"I went out for a short while." He laughed, sounding

embarrassed. "I felt a bit dizzy, so I came right back. Decided I'd better take it easy the next few days."

"Did you need something? There's plenty to eat in the refrigerator."

"I needed a breath of fresh air. And to buy a newspaper."

"I brought dinner over," Mariel said.

I sniffed the fragrant aroma of Chinese food. "Smells good."

"There's some left in the fridge," Jim said.

I laughed. "Thanks, but I had plenty to eat at the party."

Mariel stood and gathered up her cup and Jim's. "It's time I started for home," she said.

"Thanks for looking after my—Jim," I said, hoping for some explanation. *Who had called whom? What was going on here?*

Mariel smiled. "My pleasure. I'm glad he's well enough to have left the hospital."

I walked her to the door, then stopped in the kitchen to feed Smoky Joe. That accomplished, I rejoined Jim in the living room.

I plopped down on the sofa and put my feet up on the coffee table. "Are you two an item?" I asked, more to hear his response than because I imagined there was anything between them.

"Not yet, but things may be heading in that direction."

I stared at him.

He laughed. "Shocked? Older people have relationships, you know."

My brain knew they did, but this was my father! "I wouldn't think she's your type—not that I'd know what your type might be," I said archly.

Jim shrugged. "Actually, in our case, it's mostly a business deal."

I grimaced. "Oh, no! Don't tell me."

"I'm afraid so. Mariel and I are both after the gems that Benton hid. We agreed to go fifty–fifty."

My heart pounded when I asked, "Does she know where they are?"

"No, but now that she's given it some thought, she has a good idea where they might be. She'd hired Tom Quincy to find them, but he managed to get himself knocked off. Mariel's glad he's out of the picture, especially after I filled her in on his background. She realizes she was a fool to trust him."

"Why did she?"

"Quincy introduced himself at the wake, pretending to be Benton's good pal and confidante. He told her about the gems, which she had no idea existed. He offered to find them for her for a fee. She agreed, but after talking to him a few times, she began to suspect he'd only pumped her for information about her husband and planned to keep the gems for himself."

I thought this over carefully. "Maybe Mariel killed Quincy when she realized he was using her."

Jim looked at me in disbelief. "Are you kidding? Mariel would never hurt a fly. Though someone did us both a favor by knocking him off. Can you imagine the nerve of the guy—out to steal what some of us worked so hard to get."

I burst out laughing. "Poor, Jim. I can't believe you're first discovering there's no honor among thieves."

He sighed. "Caro, won't you consider calling me 'Dad'? You used to call me 'Daddy.'"

"Sure, when I was little, but even when you weren't in prison, you were hardly ever around. I missed you so much, it hurt less when I thought of you as just another adult. I'll need some time to consider calling you 'Dad.'"

"Fair enough."

"How long are you planning to stay?" *This time,* I added silently.

"Too early to say, but I'll be here through the holidays."

"Sure, while you search for the gems," I said bitterly.

He turned up his palms. "I won't lie to you, Caro. I came here to get back my share—and to see you, of course."

Smoky Joe chose that minute to jump on the sofa beside me and do his after-dinner cleaning. "Where does Mariel think Benton hid them?" I asked casually, as if I were taking nothing more than a polite interest.

"She mentioned a cabin in the woods where he used to go fishing."

"Oh, no!"

Jim eyed me sharply.

"Sorry. Smoky Joe's nail caught on my hand," I fibbed.

"Is it bleeding? Let me take a look."

I put the back of my hand to my mouth, pretending to lick imaginary blood from my imaginary wound. "It's nothing." I got up. "I'd better wash it and put some bacitracin on it."

Jim stood too. "I'm tired. I'm going to lie down. Good night, honey. See you in the morning."

He embraced me in a bear hug, making me feel even more guilty for what I was about to do. "And thanks again for letting me stay here. It means a lot to me."

I closed my bedroom door behind me and called Dina on my cell phone. She answered on the third ring.

"Dina, it's Carrie."

"Hi, Carrie. I thought you had a party this evening."

"I just got in. Your mother was here visiting my dad."

"So that's where she went. She wouldn't tell me when I asked."

"They've joined forces to look for the gems. Your mother wants to check out the cabin."

"She can't!" Dina's cry was heartfelt, which made me realize just how desperate she was to find the gems before her mother did. "Did your father say when they planned to check out the cabin?"

"I know he's not strong enough to take that kind of trip, at least for the next few days. Though your mother might go searching on her own."

"I have to stop her."

"But how?" I asked.

"Let me think." After a minute she said, "My mother's been after me to go to her hair stylist and let her have her way with me—hair-wise, that is. Oh! She's calling me. Gotta go. Talk to you later."

Twenty minutes later, my cell phone jingled.

"Done!" Dina announced triumphantly. "I told her I was willing to go for a complete makeover—hair, clothes, and makeup. I acted as if I was wavering, that if we didn't do it ASAP, I might change my mind. And she fell for it—hook, line, and sinker."

"That's great, Dina, only we were planning to drive up to your father's cabin tomorrow morning."

"That's the great part! You still can go there! The cabin's just south of Litchfield, about an hour's drive from here—less if there's no traffic. I'll text you the directions. The key's under one of the big stones near the back door."

Chapter
Twenty-Six

"And where are you off to so early in the morning?" my father asked as I was slipping into my parka.

I spun around and pasted a smile on my face. "I—I'm meeting a friend for breakfast, and then I've got some errands to run before I go into work—with the holidays and everything," I finished lamely. "Can I get you something, Jim? I'll be swinging by later to pick up Smoky Joe."

"No, thanks. I plan to run a few errands myself." He crossed the small hall to hug me.

"Are you okay to drive?"

"I'm feeling stronger today." He shot me a rueful smile. "I wish you'd go ahead and do it."

"Do what?"

"Start calling me 'Dad.'" He winked. "It would be a nice Christmas present."

"I said I'd think about it."

Smoky Joe heard me unlock the front door and came running. I bent down to pet him. "Stay here and be a good boy. I'll be back for you before you know it."

Inside my car, I glanced down at my cell phone to reread Dina's directions to the cabin. It was mostly parkway driving until I turned onto a curvy two-lane road and then onto the narrow country road that led to the cottage.

Check out the master bedroom and the built-ins in the living room. I don't think he ever installed a safe, but who knows. Text me THE SECOND you find anything. Good luck.

I headed for Route 95 and joined the heavy flow of traffic driving to New Haven. For the twentieth time I considered texting Dina to say I'd decided not to go. I had a slew of reasons: it wasn't my cabin; we were partners and should be doing this together. But for each reason, I offered up a counter reason: I had Dina's permission to enter her family's cabin on my own. She was doing her part by keeping Mariel occupied so *she* wouldn't drive to the cabin.

Still, it worried me that I was doing something illegal—semi-trespassing, if there were such a thing—by entering the premises under murky conditions, like searching for stolen gems. And what did Dina expect me to do if I discovered her father had installed a safe? Figure out the combination somehow? Take a hammer and smash it in?

Finding the gems was just as problematic as not finding them. I planned to hand them over to Dylan, which was bound to infuriate my father and Dina. She'd see it as an act of betrayal and might come after me to take revenge.

The murderer would be furious as well.

Who was the murderer? I should have spent more time trying to identify the man or woman who had killed Benton and Quincy. It was someone desperate or callous enough to have killed two people while searching for the stolen gems.

I felt a tremor of fear. What if Dina was the killer? She claimed she didn't have a car, but her mother did. What if the two of them were in on it together and were planning to drive to the cottage that morning? I shook my head vehemently. That was a ridiculous idea! They certainly wouldn't want me going there on my own. They wouldn't want me involved, at all—unless they were afraid I was helping my father and wanted to keep an eye on me. Besides, I doubted that Dina was that good an actress—able to pretend she resented Mariel when all this time they were searching for the gems together.

I refused to consider the possibility that Jim was the murderer. A thief, yes, but never a killer. Besides, he'd been laid up in the hospital when Quincy was murdered.

I had to admit it gave me a warm and fuzzy feeling, knowing how much he wanted me to start calling him "Dad." The man was evasive and as slippery as an eel, but I was getting used to spending time with him. I *liked* spending time with him. Lately, except for his criminal proclivities, he'd been doing things a father was supposed to do, like making breakfast and buying Christmas decorations.

But those weren't among the most important fatherly duties and responsibilities. I couldn't depend on him the way I depended on my aunt and uncle—trusting him to be around when I needed him. I had to be content with knowing that Jim loved me and was proud of me, and for some reason that still meant a lot.

When I turned onto the two-lane road, the traffic eased up. Soon I was the only car in sight. I passed stately homes, their properties bordered by low fences or walls made of stones. They reminded me of Robert Frost's poem "Mending Wall" and the famous "Good fences make good neighbors" line. I pictured myself living in one of these houses with my husband and children and working in a nearby library. A fantasy, surely, if the complications and problems in my life right now were any indication of my chance to have a typically normal future.

I made the right turn onto the narrower road and reached my destination without getting lost. For which I was grateful because the trip had taken longer than I'd expected, and I had to be at the library at one o'clock. The cabin was situated on a rise about twenty feet above the road, surrounded by trees on three sides. I pulled onto the snow-covered driveway and tramped around to the rear of the small dwelling. After fumbling under a few large rocks, I found the key and unlocked the back door, which opened onto a small mudroom. A musty smell greeted me, along with a clammy, gripping chill. No heat, of course. Another reason to work as quickly as possible.

Several fishing rods were propped against one wall. I soon discovered that the two tackle boxes on the only shelf were filled with fishing hooks and flies and weren't concealing a bag full of gems.

It took me a few minutes to examine the kitchen shelves, fridge, and oven carefully. No gems, not even in the half-filled jar of flour. A narrow hall led to a bathroom and two small bedrooms. Dina had told me that when she and her brother were young, the family used to come up to the cabin for two weeks in July, when the jewelry story was closed for vacation, and occasionally on holidays and weekends. Eventually, only their father would come here to fish and swim in the lake below, on the other side of the road.

I pulled up the hood of my parka as I went into the first bedroom that Dina and Richard must have shared when they were small. I opened drawers, looked under mattresses, ran my gloved hand over the shelf in the small closet. Nothing. Searching the master bedroom took a bit longer as I explored the two bureaus and larger closet, but it offered the same results.

The bathroom medicine chest had several bottles of outdated pills. I opened them all but only found pills inside. There was a small breakfront in the dining room area filled with dishes and nothing else. The only item of interest in the living room was a ledger, its pages covered with figures that might be of interest to Benton's heirs. I examined the built-in bookcases along one wall, pulling out several books at a time to feel behind for a secret panel or safe, but found nothing. No books with cutout spaces in which to hide anything either.

I took down the two paintings hanging above the sofa and felt along the back of each. Nothing. Frustrated, I let out a loud sigh. As far as I could tell, Benton Parr hadn't hidden the gems in his getaway cabin. Of course, he might have dug a hole in the backyard and buried them there, but I wasn't about to find out.

As I cast a final glance around the living room to make sure I hadn't missed anything, the sound of a passing car startled me. I told myself to relax. The Parrs had used the cabin as a weekend and summer vacation home, but there were probably people who lived in the area year-round. Communities changed. Now the Hamptons out on Long Island had many year-round residents. Even Clover Ridge, with its population of close to twenty thousand, was both a year-round and summer community.

I retrieved the key I'd left on the kitchen table and slammed the door shut. I tried the handle. The lock held fast. Once outside, I knelt down to place the key under the same rock where I'd found it. I sensed someone was nearby. Before I could look behind me, I felt an excruciating pain as someone struck my head with a heavy object. I shut my eyes in pain and collapsed on my side. Another blow hammered my skull. Barely conscious, I was aware of hands rummaging through my pockets, then a muttering of curses as he or she ransacked my pocketbook. I heard footsteps running off, the start-up of a car. Then nothing.

The jingle of my cell phone roused me. Someone was calling! I shook my head and immediately regretted having done so when a shooting pain immediately followed. I grabbed the handle of my pocketbook to draw it closer and fumbled for my phone.

"Hello," I croaked.

"Carrie, what's wrong?" It was Dylan, sounding more worried than I'd ever heard.

"He hit me over the head. Twice." I dropped the phone and threw up part of my breakfast.

I could hardly make out his words. "Where are you! I called you at work and at home over an hour ago. Your father said you were out running errands."

I managed to retrieve the phone. "I'm near Litchfield. At Benton Parr's cabin."

"What the hell are you doing there?"

"Looking for—" I stopped when I realized what I was saying.

"Don't tell me your father asked you to suss out those gems."

"Of course he didn't! Jim doesn't know where I went, and don't you tell him."

"Then why on earth are you looking for them? People have gotten killed over those damn gems."

"They're not here." I tried to laugh and found myself wincing in pain. "The person who hit me was out of luck."

"The killer, you mean. You're lucky you're still alive."

A tremor racked my body as the truth of his words sank in. "I know. I'm leaving."

"Are you sure you can drive? You shouldn't if you're dizzy or your head hurts a lot."

"I'm okay," I lied. "I just want to get back to Clover Ridge ASAP."

"Don't speed," he admonished. "And call me on my cell if you find you're feeling woozy or have to stop for any reason. I'll come and get you."

Despite my throbbing head, I found myself smiling. "That's sweet of you, but I'll be fine. I'm heading for home now. I'll take some aspirin, then go to the library."

"Carrie, I don't think—"

I ended the call. Slowly and gracelessly, I rose to my feet and stumbled to my car. I took several deep breaths before setting out for home. I drove slowly and carefully as various thoughts raged through my aching head. I winced as I realized I hadn't had the slightest inkling that someone had followed me to the cabin. Dylan was right. My assailant might have been the killer—or someone else who was after the gems.

I called Sally to tell her I'd be coming in later than scheduled because I'd had an accident.

"Oh, no! Were you driving?"

"I hurt my head and may stop off at an urgent care facility," I said to buy time. I didn't intend to stop for medical attention.

"Poor Carrie. Don't bother coming in if you're not up to it."

"I want to," I said fervently. I meant it too. Right now I'd feel safest in the library. Surely no one would try to attack me there.

Next, I called Dina. She didn't answer and my call went straight to voicemail. A minute later she called me back. I heard people speaking in the background.

"Hello, Carrie. Any luck?"

"Nope. No sign of the gems at your father's cabin. Even worse, I was followed and attacked."

"Oh, no! Poor you."

I heard a burst of laughter in the background. "Where are you?" I asked.

"At a pub just outside of town."

"With your mother?" I asked.

"She's not here."

I felt my anger rising. "Why not? I thought you were going to spend the day with her to make sure she didn't drive out to the cottage."

"Sorry, Carrie," Dina said, not sounding sorry at all. "She begged off at the last minute. Said something came up that needed her immediate attention and we'd have our mother–daughter day very soon."

I bit back my response. There was no point in making Dina my enemy.

"Though we did have a rather long chat over breakfast. Mom said that Dad used to rent a self-storage unit years ago and wondered if he'd kept it all these years. If there was stuff in it, she said we should clean it out and cancel the rental."

"Wouldn't she know?"

Dina laughed. "I think she was pumping me to see if I knew anything about it since I'd been working part-time in the store. She asked—ever so casually—if I'd ever come upon a rental agreement for the storage unit. Dad kept lots of papers in his store office."

"What did you tell her?"

"That I'd never come across anything like that—which is true enough."

"A storage unit would be a great hiding place, if he still rented it. What on earth did he need one for?"

"Years ago, he often bought old furniture at yard sales and auctions. He read up on antique furniture and insisted that some of the pieces people were selling for a song had to be worth something. Kind of like *Antiques Roadshow*."

"But you don't know if he still has this unit or where it's located."

"Uh-uh. Which got me wondering—with your library background, you'd probably know the fastest way to go about finding this unit."

"Sorry, Dina. After what happened to me, my gem-searching days are over. You're on your own."

"Thanks a lot, Carrie. Some partner you turned out to be!"

Chapter
Twenty-Seven

I drove home, my irritation with Dina simmering like a tomato sauce over a low flame. Had she deliberately sent me off on a wild goose chase while she had other fish to fry? Despite my bad mood, I giggled at my visit to the Land of Mixed Metaphors and Trite Expressions. Still, I couldn't shake the feeling that, after finding out her mother had other plans for the day, Dina could have called to say she'd go to the cottage with me. Of course Mariel might have canceled after Dina knew I'd be starting out, and Dina hadn't seen any point in calling. At least she'd learned there was one more possible place where Benton might have socked away the gems. But as I'd told Dina, I was no longer her partner in crime.

I wondered if Mariel was the person who had followed me to the cabin and hit me over the head. It was plausible. But how did she get wind that I'd be going there? And if it wasn't Mariel, how did my assailant, whoever he was, know to follow me there?

My thoughts led me back to Dina. She was the only person who knew when and where I was going. Was this her way of ensuring that she'd get the gems in the end—letting me do the leg work, then stealing them from me when I was out of commission?

It was the perfect plan. Better than if we'd found the gems together and had to divvy them up.

Or had she sent her brother after me? Richard would know how to get to the cabin without having to tail me.

Now that my trust in Dina had hit rock bottom, I was glad I'd ended our so-called "partnership." When I got to the library, I'd make a list of the self-storage places within a twenty-mile radius of Clover Ridge and figure out what to say to the receptionist when I called, so she'd give me the necessary information. I sighed. They probably didn't hand out information to just anyone and certainly not over the phone. I wondered if I'd come to a dead end regarding this possible lead since I had no intention of traipsing from one storage place to another. I sighed again. There had to be another way of approaching this problem. I just hadn't figured it out yet.

I arrived home, relieved to discover that Jim had gone out. But I'd just had time to take Smoky Joe in my arms and give him a few smooches, when the doorbell rang. I went to answer it.

"Dylan!" I set Smoky Joe down.

We stared at each other for a moment before I rushed into his open arms. He pressed me tight against his chest.

"I didn't expect to see you," I mumbled into his jacket.

"I had to make sure you were all right."

Hand in hand, we walked into the living room and sat on the sofa.

"I'm okay." I winced. "Or I will be after I have a cup of tea and a couple of aspirins."

"Can I take a look?" he asked.

"Yes."

Gingerly, he lifted my hair in sections to examine my scalp.

When he was done, he patted my shoulder. "I don't see a break in the skin, so there's no need for any salve. But an ice pack will help the swelling. Be right back."

He returned with a bag of frozen vegetables and a dish towel. I giggled but held the bag against my head.

"Would you like a doctor to check you over? I have a good friend who's an internist. His office is a few blocks from the library."

"Thank you, but I'm feeling better."

"In that case, come into the kitchen and I'll make you some tea."

"I will, right after I stop in the bathroom."

A few minutes later, I found Dylan setting down a plate of cat food for Smoky Joe.

"He was hungry," he said, almost apologetically.

I bit back my grin. "Smoky Joe's a growing cat. He's always hungry."

When the kettle whistled, Dylan poured water into a mug that held a teabag. A minute later, he placed it in front of me, along with the bottle of aspirin.

"Would you like to eat something?" he asked. "A piece of toast? An English muffin? I see you're well stocked with a variety of choices."

"No, thanks. Tea is fine. But I'd like some cold water for my aspirin."

I downed two tablets with water, then tried to sip my tea. Still too hot. I glanced up and found Dylan staring at me.

"You look worried," I said. "I'm okay, really. I'll finish my tea, then leave for the library. I'm running late."

"I look worried because you frightened me, Carrie. You can't imagine what ran through my head when you told me you were at Benton's cabin and someone attacked you. I nearly called the police in the area and would have if I'd thought they'd get there in time to do any good."

I was touched by his concern but also found myself bristling under his unspoken criticism that I'd put myself in harm's way.

"I was vigilant as I drove to the cabin. As far as I could tell, no one tailed me."

"Who knew you were going there?"

I told Dylan about my "partnership" with Dina and why I'd ended up going there alone, as well as the sudden alliance between her mother and my father. "Though it turns out Dina didn't spend the day with Mariel, after all."

"So Dina knew you'd be there, and possibly so did her mother and your father."

I stared at Dylan. "I've considered the possibility of Dina and Mariel, but you can't imagine my own father would want to hurt me."

He frowned. "I can imagine a whole slew of possibilities, which I won't go into right now. Forget about those damn gems! I'll do my best to retrieve them for their owner. It's my job. Not yours."

Dylan left and I rested awhile on the living room sofa. I washed my face and slipped the bottle of aspirin into my pocketbook. Then I picked up Smoky Joe and drove to the library. My head still throbbed, and I wondered if I was making a mistake by going into work today. Dylan thought I should have stayed home. I loved that he cared about me, because I sure cared a lot about him. But I wasn't used to having a boyfriend criticizing my behavior, even if he thought it was for my own good.

It is for your own good, dummy! I giggled because Dylan was right—at least in this case. I was an idiot to have gone off alone to a place I'd never been to. I should have been suspicious when Dina suddenly couldn't go with me.

And where was Jim? Dylan had spoken to him early that morning. Had my father gone with Mariel to check out the storage unit Benton may or may not have kept all these years? I was back to first base without any idea where Benton had hidden the gems or who had killed him and Tom Quincy.

Trish instructed me to sit at my desk, doing a bare minimum of work, while she oversaw whatever programs were in progress.

"Are you hungry?" she asked, all motherly concern.

"Actually, I am," I said. "I think I forgot to eat lunch."

"A bunch of us ordered in lunch, and I have half a sandwich left over in the fridge. Turkey with guacamole on rye."

"Sounds yummy, but you were probably saving it to bring home."

Trish waved her hand. "With all the food I'm making for Christmas, I'd end up tossing it. Be right back."

While she was gone, Angela stopped by.

"I heard you hurt your head. How are you feeling?"

"Actually, someone hit me—hard."

Angela's mouth fell open. "Don't tell me you were looking for those gems."

"I was."

"Carrie! It might have been the murderer."

"I know, but for some reason he didn't want to kill me."

"I wonder why. Where did this happen?"

Before I could answer, my office door flung open.

"Here you go!" Trish placed the tinfoil-wrapped half sandwich on my desk. "Would you like something to drink?" she asked.

"Tea. Anything."

"I'll get some nice tea from the coffee shop, instead of the stuff in our lounge. You deserve it."

She was off again. Angela laughed. "What service! Maybe I'll come in injured and pale to see what Fran does for me. Where were you that the killer came after you in broad daylight?"

I started telling her about my pact with Dina and the ride out to Benton's cabin, when someone knocked and entered the office.

"How are you feeling?" Sally asked. "Here's some chocolate mousse I ordered and couldn't finish."

Trish returned with my tea and a scone. "Jennifer said they're fresh. She baked them this morning."

I smiled at my friends. "Thank you for all this food. I'll try to eat most of it."

I wondered what time Jennifer had arrived at work today. But my head was throbbing and my friends were chattering, and I couldn't ask what they—except for Angela—would consider a very silly question.

They finally left me alone—Trish to staff the hospitality desk, Angela and Sally back to their posts. I managed to eat almost everything and to drink all of my tea. My gait was unsteady as I made my way to the ladies' room. When I returned to my office, I realized I was exhausted. I laid my head on my desk and promptly fell asleep.

"So this is how our library dollars are being spent," a male voice said. "On well-fed, sleeping librarians."

I raised my head too quickly. "Ouch!" I said.

"Sorry to disturb you," John Mathers said as he folded his rangy frame into Trish's chair. "I heard you got walloped on the noggin."

I frowned. "Dylan told you."

"He sure did. And I'm here to tell you both officially and as a friend to stop looking for those damn gems."

I burst out laughing. "Dylan's words exactly. Do lawmen and investigators study the same script?"

John's face took on a grim expression. "It's not funny, Carrie. Two people have been murdered because of those gems. I don't want you to be victim number three." His face grew thunderously angry. "And if I had the authority to do it, I'd order your father to leave town. He's brought us nothing but grief."

Like the old-time sheriffs in Westerns, I thought but didn't dare say aloud. "Sorry, John. There's nothing funny about getting hit on the head." I rubbed my scalp gingerly. "It still hurts."

"Keep on icing it."

"Right. I should."

"Did you see anything of the person who struck you? Notice his shoes? Smell a cologne or aftershave lotion?"

"Nothing. I was crouched down, putting the key under the rock where I'd found it, when he hit me. It was totally unexpected."

"Did you notice anyone following you on your drive to the cabin? See a parked vehicle when you were ready to leave?"

"No to both, though I remember hearing a car passing when I was inside the cabin. He must have doubled back and parked out of sight."

John threw up his hands and gave a snort of frustration. "We have nothing to follow up on. Either this perp is extremely smart or extremely lucky."

"Dina said her mother mentioned a storage unit Benton used to have. Mariel wasn't sure if he still rented it."

"For once we got there first. Danny Brower and I searched it the day after Benton was killed."

"I'm surprised Mariel gave you permission. Or maybe she didn't know about the gems then."

John's smile was humorless. "Could be, since she gave us sweeping permission to search the house, the store, and any and all possessions and locations."

"Interesting how many people knew about the gems," I mused. "Dina, her mother, her brother, Chris Crowley, Jennifer Darby, perhaps her husband, the deceased Mr. Quincy."

"Quite a list there, not to mention your father," John said, rising to his six feet plus inches. "Remember, Carrie. No more sleuthing. Your aunt and uncle would be devastated if anything were to happen to you."

"No more sleuthing," I promised. "To be honest, I haven't the slightest idea where those gems might be."

Trish entered the office, along with Smoky Joe carrying a streamer of crepe paper in his mouth. It trailed behind him like a banner.

"Where did he get that?" I asked Trish after she'd greeted John.

"From the children's party." She handed me a cup filled with candy.

"Thank you."

John shook his head when I held out the cup. I popped a chocolate candy in my mouth. *When was I going to stop eating?*

"Merry Christmas to you both," he said on his way out. "Carrie, I'll see you Christmas Eve at your aunt and uncle's. Try to stay out of trouble till then."

Chapter
Twenty-Eight

I turned on my computer to check on any emails I might have received in the past hour. Trish left for the day, and Susan arrived, rosy-cheeked from the cold. She went to work at the hospitality desk while I attended to the paperwork that never stopped piling up. Though Sally had told me to go home early, I decided to stay. Still, I found myself glancing at the clock, like a bored high school senior waiting for the dismissal bell to ring, as it moved to five o'clock. Though I'd only been there a few hours, I was bushed.

Jim called to say he'd be making dinner. "Pasta, meatballs, and sausages. And a nice, crisp green salad. I'm afraid I went overboard. We'll have enough leftovers to feed an army."

Now was the perfect time to tell the little white lie I'd invented to explain why my head was throbbing. "That's the best news I've heard all day. I'm looking forward to a meal I don't have to prepare. I banged my head on a cabinet door someone left open in the staff room, and it's still feeling tender."

"Oh, no, Caro!"

"I'll be okay. The aspirin I took seem to be working."

He was about to disconnect when I asked, "Were you out

running errands this morning? I stopped by the cottage before going to work, and you weren't there."

"That's true enough," he answered, enigmatic as ever.

"Did that include spending time with Mariel Parr?" I asked.

"An hour or so."

"Any luck regarding your joint project?"

"None whatsoever."

I grinned, imagining them sorting through old pieces of furniture in Benton's storage facility in search of the ever-elusive gems, and was glad to have skipped that chore. "I'll be home around five thirty, depending on traffic."

"Drive carefully, Caro."

I stopped in the ladies' room. Dorothy was there, combing her hair.

"Do you have special plans to celebrate Christmas?" I asked, to be polite.

She frowned. "The usual. My husband and I are going to my sister's house. My brother's noisy brood will be there. Last year his two youngest were horsing around and almost knocked over the tree. I told my dumb sister-in-law they needed to be taught proper manners. She just laughed and said kids were bursting with energy and needed to let it out."

"Oh," I said, not certain how to respond. "I'll be going to my aunt and uncle's Christmas Eve."

"Will your father and your boyfriend be going there too?"

"Yes," I answered, startled that she knew about Dylan and me and that my father was in town. But on second thought, it wasn't all that surprising. My life wasn't exactly tranquil, and people talked. Everyone knew what went on in Clover Ridge.

Besides, Dorothy was known to make it her business to find out everything she could about people so she could hold it over their heads.

"Your cat's been running around like crazy today," Dorothy said. "I had to shoo him away from the reference area."

"With all the parties going on, the mice have been venturing out in search of food."

"I wish he'd kill them all and be done with it!" She spun on her heel and took off.

I used the facilities then scoured the library in search of Smoky Joe. I found him in the coffee shop, where Jennifer was setting down half a muffin on a paper plate before him.

"Please don't do that!" I snatched up the plate and tossed it in the garbage pail. Smoky Joe meowed his complaint.

"Sorry, Carrie. He was sniffing around my work area. I thought he was hungry."

He was after the mice, but I didn't want to upset her about them. "Smoky Joe gets fed on a schedule. I've told everyone in the library, verbally and in flyers, that he's not to be fed." *Hint, hint.*

"You must have forgotten to tell me," she said stiffly. "All these rules and regulations! I can't wait to leave this place."

I opened my mouth to apologize, but Jennifer brushed past me. I lifted Smoky Joe. It was time to go home.

I was putting him in the car and settling into my own seat when someone knocked on the window. My body jerked like a marionette. I banged my head on the car roof, something I didn't need. I rubbed the two bumps as I lowered the car window.

"Chris, what are you doing here?"

"Sorry—didn't mean to frighten you. I stopped by to return a few books as the library was closing. I have to talk to you. Figured maybe I'd catch you out here before you left."

I looked behind us at the many cars backing up to exit the lot. "You took your life in your hands. Everyone's eager to get home. What's so important it couldn't wait?"

Chris gazed down at the ground. "I thought you'd want to know. Morgan Fuller died."

"He did?" A lump rose in my throat. "I'm sorry to hear that. He was a lovely man. When did it happen?"

"Earlier today. Yesterday Mom went to the nursing home to thank him for the check you brought us. They let her see him even though his nurse said he was barely conscious. Mom left him a note. She asked to be called when he died."

I should have called him! "Morgan knew he was dying, but first he needed to make amends to you and your mother. Once that was done, he allowed himself to go."

"Mom and I appreciate it. We sure could use the money," Chris said.

"I was glad to help Morgan carry out his wish. Good-night, Chris, and Merry Christmas."

"Wait!" he yelled as I started to close the window.

"What is it?" I rubbed the left side of my face that was beginning to freeze.

"I was wondering—did you get to talk to Dina the other night?"

"We went out for pizza. We talked."

"Did she say anything about me?"

"Please, Chris! I'm not in the habit of repeating my private conversations to a third party."

222

"I'm not after gossip, Carrie. I love Dina, but her mother's forbidden her to go out with me."

"That's hard to believe," I said, to avoid telling him the truth. "Dina's over twenty-one, isn't she?"

"Yeah, but she doesn't have a penny to her name. The only way that bitch Mariel will pay for her tuition is if Dina does whatever she says."

"And she doesn't want Dina to go out with you?"

"You got it. Mariel tells her I have no future. But now I have half the money Morgan gave me and Mom. More, if I can convince Mom to lend me some of her portion. Then I can take out a bank loan. Find a store in a good location and with low rent, and Dina and I can open up our own jewelry store."

I eyed him warily. "Don't you need lots of cash to buy merchandise?"

Chris waved away my concern. "If I have enough of a down payment, I can borrow the rest. I know how to make things work. Besides . . ."

You're hoping to find the gems like everyone else who knows about them. "What about Dina?" I asked, knowing the answer to my question. "Is Dina on board with your plans? Does she feel the same way you do?"

"I know she does, only she's not a risk taker. Dina's afraid of screwing things up with her mother. She wants to get her degree before anything else. Probably because she wasted those years partying and not being focused." He eyed me closely. "Did she talk about any of this to you? I have to know."

I swallowed, worried how'd he'd react if I told him the truth. I didn't want to find out, so I took the easy way out.

"Chris, I'm afraid I can't help you. Dina didn't say much

about you except that the two of you were good friends. I told her how sorry I was that her father had been murdered, and we mostly talked about Benton."

"Yeah," he said sourly. "Good old Benton. What a shit he turned out to be."

"I suppose you got to know him pretty well, working for him all that time."

"He promised to teach me about diamonds, rubies, and emeralds, but instead had me do mostly paperwork and sales. Believe me, he was far from the nice person he pretended to be."

"He was a thief," I said, to observe his reaction.

Chris laughed. "Yeah. A thief who fleeces his partner. Your father must be sorely pissed."

"He's not happy about it," I admitted.

"And who would blame him if he decided to knock off old Benton?"

"Good night, Chris." I shut the window and started the car.

Chapter
Twenty-Nine

My cell phone rang when I was halfway home. It was Dylan.

"Hiya, babe. Where are you?"

I smiled. It was the first time he'd called me "babe" or any other endearment. "On the road driving home."

"I know it's late notice, but I didn't know if I'd finish my work, and it looks like I'll be done in half an hour or so. Would you like to go out for dinner around seven?"

"I'd love to, but I can't. Jim's making dinner tonight."

"Oh, okay. I understand."

The disappointment in his voice caught me in my solar plexus. "In which case I'd like you to come to dinner with us tonight. Jim said he made lots of food. Much more than the two of us can possibly eat."

"I don't know, Carrie. I hate to intrude. Your dad just got out of the hospital. He'll probably want to enjoy a quiet evening at home with you."

I laughed. "I doubt it. He was out today searching for those damn gems. Besides, I'd like you to come." I paused before adding, "He has to get used to spending time with both of us together."

Dylan hesitated, then said, "Good point. I accept your kind offer. I'll bring a nice merlot for our dinner." He laughed.

"What's so funny?"

"Socializing with Jim Singleton, my number-one suspect. Maybe I'll get lucky and he'll share a confidence or two."

"If you're referring to the stolen gems, forget it. Jim has no idea where Benton's stashed them. I don't think anyone does. You may have to accept that they're gone forever."

"I doubt it, Carrie. I have the feeling they'll turn up sooner or later under the most surprising circumstances."

"Come by in about an hour, or whenever you're finished working," I said.

"Will do. I can't wait to see you."

I changed stations, from a discussion of the depressing international news to one playing soft rock, and sang along with every selection the rest of the way home. I was happy, I realized, and my fatigue had all but evaporated.

I heard Jim whistling in the kitchen as soon as I unlocked the front door and set Smoky Joe down. "I'm home," I called out. "Mmm—smells scrumptious." I breathed in the rich aroma of a well-seasoned tomato sauce as I hung up my parka.

He came into the hall, wearing an apron over his jeans and a spatula in hand, to buss my cheek. "You're just in time to cut up the salad."

I grinned. "I see you're pawning off the boring work on me."

"Why not, since you're my sous chef?"

"But not the scullery maid. You're in charge of cleaning the pots and pans."

"Ouch. You really know how to hurt a guy."

"I'll set the table," I offered, about to mention we'd be three for dinner.

"Already taken care of. I thought we'd eat in the dining room tonight."

"Okay." I glanced at the dining room table and was surprised to see it was set for four."

"Who's coming?" I asked.

"Mariel and her daughter. I hope you don't mind. When I realized how much food I was preparing, I thought it would be a sin not to have more people share it."

A sin? Isn't stealing a sin? "Actually, we'll be five," I said. "Dylan invited me out. I asked him to join us for dinner instead."

After a pause, Jim asked, "Do you think that was wise? Dylan would like nothing more then to ship me off to the slammer."

"What he'd really like is to find those gems so he could hand them back to their rightful owner."

"That's not going to happen if I can help it," he mumbled.

"You know there's a reward for finding the gems," I reminded him. "Half a million dollars is nothing to sneeze at."

My father sent me a look I couldn't interpret. "Why don't I open up a bottle of wine? We'll imbibe as we cook."

"I don't think that's a good idea," I said. "You just had a concussion."

"True. And you banged your head on a cabinet."

We stared at each other for a moment.

"Maybe it we only drink half a glass each . . ."

"Good idea," Jim agreed and went to open a bottle of red wine.

We worked in silence. I added a fifth place setting to the

dining room table and switched on the Christmas tree lights. I stood there a minute, watching them twinkle off and on, breathing in the pine aroma that made me nostalgic for—for what? Certainly not for the Christmases of my childhood. They were usually sad affairs.

"Meow!"

I gazed down at Smoky Joe weaving in between my ankles. "Hungry, are you? Let's go into the kitchen, and I'll give you your dinner."

"What time did you tell Mariel and Dina to be here?" I asked.

"Six thirty."

"Good. Dylan should be arriving then too."

The three of them met at the front door and poured into the hall. Dylan waited while Mariel and Dina hugged me, and Dina handed me a cake box. Then he kissed me and gave me a dozen red roses.

"Thank you. These are beautiful!" No one had ever given me a dozen roses before.

My father joined in the greetings. Dylan handed him the bottle of wine he'd been holding. Jim led Dylan and Mariel into the living room while Dina followed me into the kitchen. "How's your head?"

I touched the bumps gingerly. "Still hurts, but not as much."

"I'm really sorry that someone attacked you."

"Not as sorry as I am." I opened the fridge and got out a bottle of seltzer and a pitcher of water. "Could you please put these on the dining room table?"

"Of course." Dina took the seltzer and water from me. "What's Dylan Avery doing here?"

"I invited him. He's my boyfriend."

"Oh."

"I had no idea you and your mother were coming for dinner," I said.

"Your father invited us." She grinned. "I think he has a thing for my mother."

I suppressed my shudder. "Did she tell you they checked out your father's storage bin today?"

"Of course not. Your father said they did?"

"Not exactly, but he said they'd spent some time together, so I'm assuming it was at the storage unit. Anyway, the gems are still missing."

Dina snorted. "I can't think where else Dad might have put them."

"Me neither. Lieutenant Mathers came to see me today. He asked me to stop looking for them, and I have."

Dina left and Jim came into the kitchen. He peered into the oven to see how the three different kinds of hors d'oeuvres he'd put in earlier were doing. "Perfect! We don't want them to burn." He slipped mitts on his hands and drew out the hot trays.

I pointed to the platters I'd taken down from the cabinet above the sink. "Why don't you do the mushrooms? I'll see to the other two trays."

"Oh, no, Caro. Go join our guests. I'll take care of everything."

He used a spatula to transfer the stuffed mushrooms onto a platter and followed me into the living room. When had my father gotten so skillful in the kitchen? When had he learned how to be a good host? I'd never seen this side of him. But then he must have entertained guests in the many years he'd lived away from us. There were so many things I didn't know about Jim Singleton, things I doubted he'd ever share with me.

Dylan, Dina, and Mariel were deep in conversation when Jim and I joined them. Our guests appeared very much at their ease as they sipped the wine my father had served them and selected mushrooms from the platter he held before them. They were talking about diamonds and their various colors. Dylan, of course, knew gems, and Dina had learned about them from her father, but I was surprised that Mariel also appeared well informed. As far as I knew, she'd never worked in the store with Benton.

My father set the almost-empty platter of mushrooms on the coffee table and minutes later carried out the other two platters of appetizers. We noshed and opened the bottle of wine that Dylan had brought. Our conversation covered a variety of topics but never touched on the two murders or the missing gems.

Finally, my father nodded to me. I followed him into the kitchen to help him serve dinner.

"Need any help?" Dina asked, joining us.

"Of course," Jim and I said in unison. We burst out laughing, and at that moment I felt as close to him as I ever had.

Jim drained the pasta and poured it into a bowl. He spooned the sauce, filled with meatballs and sausage, into another bowl while I dressed the salad with oil and vinegar and then handed Dina the large bowl to carry to the table. I followed closely behind, a dish of grated cheese in one hand and a plate of vegetables in the other.

"Chris came to talk to me as I was leaving work," I told her.

She stopped and I nearly walked into her. "Really? What did he want?"

"He wanted to know what you had said to me about him.

He really loves you and doesn't think very highly of either of your parents."

Dina bit her lip as she thought about this. "What did you tell him?"

"I did my best to avoid saying you're not interested in him. He thinks you care about him and you're only obeying your mother's wishes not to see him because she's supporting you now."

Dina exhaled loudly. "Did he say anything else?"

"He plans to open a jewelry store—with you. With his share of the money Morgan left him, he thinks he can raise enough capital to find a store and buy enough merchandise to get started."

"Our dream was to run Dad's store. Any store," Dina said, sounding dreamy herself.

I stared at her. "Are you interested in Chris?"

She bit her lip. "Maybe. I'm not sure."

How can she not know what she thinks? What she feels? But maybe that's what happens when your parents control you and don't let you decide things for yourself.

For the first time I was glad that ever since I was in my teens, neither one of my parents had told me what to do. Perhaps it was out of negligence, but I'd been free to make my own decisions and my own mistakes.

I called Dylan and Mariel to the table, and the five of us sat down—my father at the head, Dylan next to me on the side closest to the kitchen, with Mariel and Dina across from us and Mariel closer to Jim.

Were they interested in each other? I found it difficult to tell since they both made it their business to be social and to chat with everyone. When Mariel heard I'd hurt my head, she was all sweetness and sympathy. I doubted she knew the circumstances of my attack since Jim didn't know and I didn't think Dina would have told her. Unless she was the one who had clobbered me.

We all praised Jim's delicious dinner. No one brought up the subject of the gems, which had to be on everyone's mind. All of us present knew the story behind them, and each of us wanted to find them for a different reason. But I'd promised to have nothing more to do with the gems, and instead I found myself ruminating about the two homicides.

I turned to Dylan. "It's frightening to think a murderer's running loose in Clover Ridge. Have the police made any headway in their investigation?"

He shot me a warning glance before answering. "Not as far as I know."

Time to stir the pot. "Strange that they never found the knife the killer used . . ." My flustered gaze went from Dina to Mariel. "Sorry. I shouldn't be talking like this. Benton was your father and your husband."

"Frankly, it's a relief to talk about it," Mariel said. "Everyone else pussyfoots around the topic, when it's uppermost on their minds."

"Did they say what kind of knife was used?" I asked. "Anything special?"

"According to the police report, it was an ordinary kitchen knife you'd find in any home."

"Years ago Dad took one from the house and used it to open envelopes and small boxes," Dina said. "He often left it out on the counter. I don't know how many times Chris and I told him to put it away in a drawer or some safe place."

I doubted Mariel was going to find what I was about to say

any kind of relief. "Dina, did your brother know your father left that knife lying around?"

Mother and daughter gaped open-mouthed at me. Dina found her voice. "That's a terrible thing to say! My brother would never hurt our father."

"I got the impression that they weren't on good terms," I said.

"Where did you hear that?" Mariel asked indignantly. "It couldn't be further from the truth."

I persisted. "What about your own relationship with Richard? How often did you see your son and his family?"

"Carrie!" Dylan warned, his voice low and ominous.

I ignored him and spoke in a solemn tone. "I'm sorry to be saying some truths you might find painful, but Benton was murdered. Whoever did it has to pay the price."

Jim scraped back his chair. "Will you look at that? The Santa on top of the tree appears to be tilting." He walked into the living room.

"I'm not saying Richard murdered his father," I said, "but he did ask Benton for a loan and was refused."

"How the hell do you know that?" Dina demanded.

"I have my ways," I said.

"That's enough, Carrie." Dylan gripped my arm.

I shook free as a thumping noise and a cry of pain sounded from the other room. My father had fallen! I raced into the living room and crouched beside him. He lay still on his back, one leg sprawled on a toppled-over present. I took his hand and felt his wrist for a pulse. It seemed erratic. "Daddy! Daddy! Are you okay? Can you speak?"

Nothing. His hand remained limp in mine. Tears welled up

in my eyes. He was dead because of me. Because I didn't have the sense not to taunt Mariel and Dina.

"Talk to me! Please talk to me, Daddy," I cried.

Dylan set me aside so he could listen to my father's chest. "He's breathing."

"Will he be all right?"

"I think so. He knocked himself out when his head hit the floor."

"I'll call nine-one-one."

I jerked around to stare at Mariel. "Thank you."

"Have them send an ambulance," Dylan said.

"I was planning to," Mariel said wryly, returning to the dining room where she'd left her cell phone.

My father stirred. "I was reaching for the Santa when I got dizzy. Ouch! My head aches."

"Of course it hurts," I said. "You fell backward and landed on your head. You could have another concussion."

A minute or two later, Mariel returned. "The ambulance is on its way."

Jim made an effort to sit up, but slid back down to the floor. "This is ridiculous! I'm fine."

"Lie still," Dylan said.

My father pushed him away and struggled unsuccessfully to raise his head. "I'm not going back to any damn hospital!"

"Daddy, you need to have a doctor look at you."

Mariel knelt beside my father. "Jim, I hope you feel better soon. I'm sorry the evening ended this way. We'll talk tomorrow." She stood and turned to me. "Carrie, Dina and I are leaving. Please get our jackets."

I blinked back tears as I went to the hall closet. What had I hoped to accomplish by saying those hurtful things to Dina and her mother? My father had gone to straighten out the Santa on the tree—if it was even necessary—in an attempt to change the subject. To get me to shut up.

No one spoke as I handed Dina and Mariel their jackets. They left and I returned to my father. Dylan had brought him a glass of water that he sipped slowly.

"I can't see how two glasses of wine made me dizzy," my father was saying.

"By my count, you had three at least," Dylan said. "Neither you nor Carrie should have been drinking tonight."

I knelt beside my father and squeezed his hand. "I'm sorry I riled up your guests."

He tried to laugh. "What the hell did you hope to achieve? Hearing one of them confess she offed Benton? Really, Caro. You make a lousy detective."

"Or was it your way of paying them back?" Dylan asked.

His words stung, but I forced myself to answer honestly. "Partly. I wanted to see their reactions regarding Richard—if they suspected he might have killed his father. But I was angry at Dina for sending me off to the cabin alone, supposedly so she could spend the morning with her mother, then not bothering to let me know her mother had canceled their plans. And at Mariel for being the worst kind of hypocrite."

"And you're worried Mariel Parr has her hooks in your father."

His bull's-eye made me blush. I felt my ears grow warm. "That too," I mumbled. I finally managed to look him in the eye. "Are you mad at me?"

"Not mad. Disappointed is more like it."

"Oh." I curled up into a ball beside my father.

A siren blasted the silence as an ambulance approached the cottage. Smoky Joe, who had come to sniff my father and me, no doubt wondering why we were lying on the living room floor, scurried into my bedroom and hid under the bed. Minutes later, three emergency medical technicians—two men and a young woman—were at the door with a gurney. One asked me what had happened while the other two gently lifted my father onto the stretcher.

"Caro, my wallet's on my bureau. We'll need to bring it to the hospital. My insurance information's inside."

I went to get his wallet and my parka. "Can I ride with him in the ambulance?" I asked.

"Sure," the older of the two men answered.

"Go ahead," Dylan said. "I'll follow in my car."

"You don't have to come," I said, still smarting from his earlier comments.

"Please don't argue, Caro," my father said.

"All right." I turned to Dylan. "You can meet us at the hospital. Thanks," I said none too graciously.

He shot me a grin. "Don't mention it."

Inside the ambulance, I held my father's hand as we rode to the hospital.

"Thanks, honey," he said, giving me a lopsided grin.

"For ruining dinner? You're welcome."

"For calling me 'Daddy' instead of 'Jim.'"

I bent down to kiss his cheek. "Now that I'm thirty, I think I'll change it to 'Dad.'"

Chapter Thirty

When Dylan arrived at the hospital, my father was already in triage. We sat outside in the nearly empty waiting room while he provided a hospital worker with the necessary information.

"The ER doesn't appear to be very busy tonight," Dylan said.

"Good. The sooner a doctor checks him out, the better."

"They'll probably want to do a CT scan and other tests. After all, he only left here a day ago."

"Don't I know it." I buried my face in my hands, trying not to cry.

Dylan put his arm around me. "Stop beating yourself up. Jim knew he shouldn't have been drinking."

"He was trying to get me to stop asking those dumb questions. As if they got us anywhere."

Dylan let out a sigh. "I'm beginning to wonder if those gems are gone for good. Nobody seems to know where Benton hid them. I'll wait until after Christmas to write up my report."

A few minutes later, my father was wheeled into a cubicle.

Dylan and I sat with him until a young Indian doctor arrived. She examined him and questioned him about his fall. Then she turned to me.

"Are you his daughter?"

"I am."

"We're going to take a CT scan as soon as the machine is free. Given your dad's history, we'll be keeping him overnight."

My father tried to sit up. "I'm not staying here! I just got out of this place."

"Mr. Singleton, we're doing what's best for you," the doctor said with more authority than I'd have expected. "You got dizzy, fell and hit your head, and lost consciousness for a few minutes. Please don't make it any more difficult. We should have an available room within the hour."

"How long will he be staying?" I asked, concerned because I was scheduled to work the next day. I couldn't keep on taking time off to bring him home from the hospital.

"I can't say for sure, but if he's not concussed, he can probably leave some time tomorrow." the doctor said.

Dylan must have read my mind, because he said, "I don't have anything scheduled tomorrow. I'll pick him up and drive him to the cottage when he's discharged."

"Thank you so much!"

Dylan winked. "I can tell you mean it this time."

A technician arrived to escort my father to the radiology department in the basement.

"That was fast," the doctor said.

"Go home, Caro," my father said. "There's no point in you waiting around. The CT scan will take awhile."

"I think I should—"

"Dylan, please take her home and see that she gets some rest. She's suffered her own share of blows today."

I rubbed my head. With all that had transpired in the past hour, I'd forgotten the assault at the cabin earlier in the day. It seemed to have happened a long time ago.

"We're leaving," Dylan said, taking hold of my upper arm.

"All right, Dad. I'm going. I'll talk to you in the morning."

"Sorry to leave you with the cleaning up. I meant to take care of it."

"You'll do the cleaning up next meal we make," I said.

Dylan and I didn't speak as we headed to the parking lot and started for home. At the first traffic light, he reached for my hand. "I've learned a lot about you these past few days."

"Really? Like what? That I'm impulsive and say things I'm better off not saying?"

"Like being a loving daughter under the most trying circumstances. And wanting to help your father the best way you know how."

"I've come to accept that I love my father, warts and all, but I refuse to aid or abet him in his criminal activities. Nor will I allow him to destroy my relationship with you."

"I was wrong to stay on his case. I should have asked to be taken off it once I—"

He stopped suddenly.

"Once you what?" I prodded.

"Once I realized I was falling in love with you."

"Oh." A wave of happiness swept over me. I closed my eyes and saw fireworks. Or at least a very bright moon shining down on me and warming my heart on this cold December night. "You really mean it?"

239

"I do."

I hesitated, then forged ahead. "You're not just saying that because Jordan's my brother and I'm a link to your happy childhood?"

"My happy childhood." Daryl let out a bark of laughter that held no humor. "I'll fill you in on that mistaken notion some day. You don't need to worry that I care about you for some convoluted reason. I love you because you're you. I know the kind of life you led before you moved to Clover Ridge. How you tackled your new job and solved two murders. You're a strong, competent, beautiful, sexy woman, Carolinda Singleton, and I adore you."

I punched his thigh none too gently. "I told you not to call me that. My name is Carrie. I changed it officially."

Dylan laughed. "I'll try to keep that in mind."

We held hands the rest of the way home. As we turned onto the private road where we both lived, I knew I didn't want to let him go.

"Will you stay with me tonight?" I asked.

"I was going to suggest it."

*   *   *

That night, we lay, side by side, holding hands. I had no idea what time I fell asleep, but a furry face butting against my cheek woke me up. I glanced at the clock. It was seven, the time I usually awoke when I had to be at work at nine.

I turned to Dylan and found him smiling down at me.

"Good morning," I said, as though his presence in my bed was a usual occurrence.

"Looks like a nice morning."

"You've been up," I said.

"For the past hour, but I wanted to be here when you woke up." Dylan stroked my cheek with the back of his hand as he gazed into my eyes. "Tell you what. I'm going home to shower and dress. I'll be back for some morning sustenance."

"You're welcome, as long as you know it's just toast and coffee." I padded off to the bathroom.

"That's okay with me."

I showered and brushed my teeth, then called the hospital. The operator connected me to my father's room, where his phone rang and rang. I figured he was either in the bathroom or having another test or scan. I got dressed and called again. Still no answer.

Dylan returned half an hour later, a copy of *The Wall Street Journal* in hand, as I was finally connecting with my father.

"Where have you been?" I asked.

"Getting another CT scan. They're doing them early today because of the holiday."

"Did the doctor say when you can go home?"

"He wants to keep me until midafternoon."

"I'll be at work, so Dylan has offered to pick you up. Here's his cell number." I rattled it off.

"Tell Dylan thanks for me—for looking after you and for everything else."

"I will." We disconnected and I burst out laughing.

"What's so funny?" Dylan asked, glancing up from the newspaper.

"My father. I think he knew you were here with me. And he thanks you—for everything."

"He's welcome," Dylan said with a broad grin.

I poured out cups of coffee and asked Dylan if he wanted a roll, an English muffin, or a few slices of multigrain toast.

"Toast," he said. "Well done."

I put two slices and my English muffin in the toaster oven and sat down to sip my coffee. It felt so normal and right to be having breakfast with Dylan. I smiled, thinking that this could happen day after day—until he left on another assignment.

"I have a few things to take care of this morning. I'll call the hospital around noon to find out when they want Jim to vacate his room," Dylan said as he spooned a healthy amount of apricot jelly onto his toast. "I suppose you'll want to have a quiet dinner at home with him tonight."

"And with you. There are plenty of leftovers."

"Or I was thinking of making one of my Moroccan dinners."

"I had no idea you knew Moroccan cuisine."

"Ah, Miss Singleton. There are many things you've yet to learn about me."

I grabbed him around the waist and planted a kiss on his cheek. "Beware, I intend to find out each and every one of them."

Dylan's cell phone rang. "Maybe they're letting Jim out earlier than he thought," he said as he put it to his ear.

"Really?!" he said a moment later. The tight seam of his lips told me it was bad news. "Carrie's here with me. I'd like to share this with her." He listened, then said, "Sure, I'll put her on."

"What's wrong?" I asked. "Did something happen to Uncle Bosco? Aunt Harriet?"

Dylan shook his head as he handed me his phone.

"Hello, Carrie. It's John Mathers. Mariel Parr has been murdered."

Chapter
Thirty-One

I swallowed, but no words came. Moments passed before I could speak. "John, I—I can hardly believe Mariel's dead! She and Dina were here last night, having dinner with my father, Dylan, and me."

"So Dina's told us. I'm at the crime scene with the medical examiner and two investigators from the forensics lab. As soon as I'm finished, I'll want to talk to everyone who came into contact with Mariel in the past forty-eight hours."

"I'm about to leave for work. I'll be at the library until it closes at three. Then I'm off for the weekend."

"I'll catch up with you, one place or another." John let out a rueful chuckle. "I knew I shouldn't have left my Christmas shopping this late. Tell your dad I'll be stopping by the cottage for a chat."

"Jim's in the hospital. Dylan's bringing him home later today, and we'll be in all evening. Dad took a tumble last night and lost consciousness. They kept him overnight to monitor him since he'd just been concussed."

"Sorry about that. Dina mentioned he'd fallen. Don't you

worry. I'll catch up with you both. It's merely a formality as far as you, Jim, and Dylan are concerned."

"Did someone break into the house? Is Dina all right?"

"This was no break-in, and Dina's fine. Mariel was stabbed—the ME estimates between three and six this morning. There's no sign of the weapon."

"Oh, no! Do you think it's the same person that killed Benton and Tom Quincy?"

"I have to go, Carrie. Please put Dylan back on the line."

I handed the phone to Dylan. He and John conversed in low tones as I forced myself to finish my breakfast. Mariel was dead! Murdered! It sounded to me that the killer had used the same knife he'd used to kill Benton. But why kill Mariel? Was it over the gems, or had she managed to piss off the killer about something else? And where had this happened? John didn't—or wouldn't—say.

I cleared the table, stepping around Dylan as he continued to speak to John in low tones. What was he finding out? Would he share it with me? I used the bathroom, shrugged into my winter parka, then gathered Smoky Joe in my arms. When I returned to the kitchen, Dylan was ending the conversation. He looked up at me as he slipped his phone in his pocket.

"John asked what we talked about over dinner."

I grimaced. "So he joins the ranks of those who know I tried to provoke Mariel and Dina into talking about Richard."

"I'm afraid so. John intends to question Dina and her brother as soon as the ME and techs finish up. They've been notified of Mariel's death and have been asked to wait at home to be interviewed."

"At least he doesn't consider us suspects."

Dylan laughed. "You and I can vouch for one another, and your father spent the night in the hospital."

"I just realized, this makes John privy to . . . er . . . aspects of our relationship."

"I suppose you're right. Does it bother you?"

I thought a moment. "Not in the least."

Smoky Joe began to squirm, so I set him down.

Dylan grinned. "I'm glad, because word's bound to get out that we're a couple."

A couple! I drew in a deep breath. "Oh," was all I could manage. *Time to change the subject.* "Where was Mariel found? John didn't say."

"A few feet from the spot where they found Tom Quincy's body. Near Jennifer and Paul Darby's house."

"Oh, no! What was she doing there?"

"That's what John intends to find out."

"Who discovered the body?"

"You won't believe it."

I stared at him. "Not Paul Darby."

"He claimed he was out taking a walk because he couldn't sleep. Despite the fact that early this morning the temperature was down in the twenties."

"Paul Darby had no reason to kill Mariel. But Dina resented her mother, and so did her brother."

"They'll all be questioned in time." Dylan kissed me soundly on the lips. "Now leave, woman, or you'll be late to work."

I picked up the remote control to the small TV on the kitchen wall. "I will as soon as I find out if the media has the news about Mariel's murder."

I clicked to the local channel and had to wait through three commercials. First, a newscaster interviewed shoppers waiting to enter the mall, followed by a snippet of an accident involving two cars. I turned off the TV.

"No mention of the murder."

"It will be all over the news within the hour," Dylan predicted.

I went into the living room and scooped up Smoky Joe. He'd been sitting at the window, watching the antics of two squirrels on the back lawn. "Talk to you later." I dropped a kiss on Dylan's head and stepped outside. The cold weather chilled my nose and cheeks.

I buried my face in Smoky Joe's neck as I strode out to my car. "What a morning, eh, Smoky Joe?"

My thoughts jostled against one another as I tried to absorb all that had transpired in the past twenty-four hours. I'd driven to Benton's cabin to search for the gems and had been struck on the head for my troubles. I'd riled up Dina and Mariel, hoping to force one of them to admit Richard might have killed Benton, but instead my father ended up unconscious on the living room floor. I had been forced to admit to myself that I loved my father. Dylan had told me he loved me, and we had taken our relationship to the next level. Last but not least, Mariel Parr had been murdered.

I was glad the traffic was light enough to allow me to ruminate about the events that had impacted my recent life.

Dylan loved me! How I adored hearing him say it, knowing that he really meant it. Because I loved him and had probably fallen in love with him the morning I had gone to see the cottage for the first time. Still, giving my heart so completely was scary. Now I was vulnerable to another person's words and actions.

Dylan could stop loving me at any time. Find fault with me. After all, I was far from perfect.

Then there were the real and practical considerations. Dylan had said we were a couple. But what did that mean? He spent most of his time away from home—traveling around the country, retrieving stolen art objects and gems. How could a relationship sustain itself when one person was always out of town?

Not wanting to burst my happy bubble of feeling loved and adored, I decided to focus on the murders instead. It was safe to assume the same person had stabbed Benton, Mariel, and Tom Quincy. Had the victims been killed because of the gems? Mariel and Tom Quincy were both found murdered near the Darbys' home. Paul Darby had been seen with the two male victims shortly before their deaths and had found Mariel's body. Paul was involved because his wife had had an affair with Benton Parr.

Was it possible that Jennifer had killed three people?

Most unlikely. Which brought me back to the gems. Was the killer after the gems, and did he or she think that Jennifer had them in her possession?

Then why not break into the Darbys' house and search for them?

By the time I approached the outskirts of Clover Ridge, I was no closer to a theory, much less a preferred suspect. On impulse, I called Dina.

"Oh, it's you. What do you want, Carrie?"

Inwardly I cringed at her hostility, but I forced myself to be pleasant.

"Hi, Dina. I heard about your mother. I'm so very sorry."

"Really? After the way you treated us last night? And now

she's dead." Dina burst into tears. I waited for her sobbing to subside, hoping she wouldn't hang up.

"Do you know what she was doing outside at three in the morning?"

"No!"

The way she shot out her answer made me wonder. "Are you sure? Whatever you know can help the police catch her murderer."

"Right! The way they caught the person who killed my father. For all I know, he'll come after me next."

"I doubt it. The killer must be after the gems."

"Then why did he kill my mother?" Dina asked. "She didn't know where they are."

"Maybe she managed to find them, and the killer took them from her."

Dina sighed. "Those damn gems! All they do is bring bad luck. If they even exist."

"I think they do," I said. "Someone hit me over the head and searched me, thinking I might have found them."

"I wonder why he let you live."

Thanks, I thought but didn't say out loud. But actually, I wondered the same thing.

"No one knows where they are," Dina said. "Not even the stupid murderer."

"Did you know your mother was found near Jennifer and Paul Darby's house?"

"No, Lieutenant Mathers didn't say. But I'm not surprised. Mom suddenly got it into her head that Dad gave the gems to Jennifer for safekeeping. Maybe she was right. Wasn't that where that goon Tom Quincy was murdered?"

"I don't know, Dina. The police searched the Darbys' house after your father was killed and didn't find them."

"I told Mom that. I told her to forget about the gems, but she wouldn't listen." Dina started sobbing again. "She said she needed the gems. She needed the money to lead a decent life. We started arguing. I told her she was selfish and only cared about living well, that she didn't care about me." She sniffed. "She didn't deny it."

I felt a rush of sympathy for her. "My mother never said she cared more about living well than she did about me, but if pressed she'd have to admit it."

"Lucky us, getting stuck with the two most self-centered mothers on the planet."

"I know. Mothers aren't supposed to be that way. If I ever have kids, I swear I'll put them first."

"At least you have a father that adores you," Dina said, the hostility back in her tone.

I laughed. "Right. Cast your vote for Jim Singleton, father of the year. Did you forget he's a thief, and I hardly saw him when I was growing up?"

"Regardless, he loves you, Carrie. My father put on an act that he cared about his family and the welfare of Clover Ridge. He did it all for show, so people would say he was a good and trustworthy person and would want to shop in his store." She made a sound of derision. "The truth is, he was as self-centered as my mother."

"I'm sorry, Dina."

I pulled into a spot in the library parking lot and was about to end our conversation when Dina asked, "Who found the— my mother?"

"Believe it or not, it was Paul Darby."

"Him again? He's always around when there's a murder, but there's never any evidence, so the police can't hold him."

"I don't think he killed your mother," I said. "Why would he?"

"Maybe he's after the gems like everyone else."

"I never thought of that," I said. "He's been out of work for months . . ."

"I hope the police see that as a motive," Dina said.

"Don't you want them to catch the person who's guilty?"

She hesitated, then said, "I might as well tell you, since Richard's a wuss when it comes to coping with stress, and the police will worm it out of him."

A tremor snaked down my back. "Are you saying your brother killed your mother?"

"Of course I'm not saying that," Dina said, sounding annoyed. "But Richard was out most of last night, driving around."

"He told you this?" I asked.

"Yes. He called me this morning after the police informed him that our mother was found stabbed to death sometime between midnight and sunrise. He was upset because he realized afterward that he'd witnessed the murder."

"Really?"

I must have sounded as skeptical as I felt because Dina rushed to her brother's defense. "He and Ginny have serious money problems. Their son, Danny, has medical issues, and they can hardly keep their heads above water. Rich said they had a fight about finances, and then he went out driving. It's what he does when things get to be too much for him. Anyway, he remembered passing two figures standing in an alley or a driveway leading to a detached garage at the back of a house. He couldn't even make out if it was two men or a man and a woman. They appeared to be arguing. Since it was none of his business, he drove past without thinking too much about it. It was only when he got the news that he realized he must have seen the killer and Mom just before she was murdered."

"Maybe he saw something that can help the police identify the killer."

"Maybe the police will think my brother did it. I gotta go, Carrie. Merry Christmas."

Chapter Thirty-Two

I tried to call Dina back, but the phone rang and rang. Clearly, she didn't want to talk to me any longer. I couldn't blame her. Both her parents had been murdered, and once her brother admitted he'd passed the site where Mariel had been murdered, the police would be on him like dogs after a rabbit, at least for a while.

I carried Smoky Joe into the library. It was like entering a sanctuary after spending time in a war zone. All around me were wreaths and menorahs and snowmen in celebration of the season: winter, Chanukah, Christmas, and Kwanza as well as the New Year.

Smoky Joe dashed off to entertain the patrons. I headed to the staff room for a much-needed cup of coffee. I eyed the colorful array of Christmas cookies and gingerbread men and the stack of festive paper plates beside the coffee urn. Heaven! I filled my coffee mug and selected an assortment of cookies and a chocolate gingerbread man, then headed for my office.

I was too agitated to get much work done that day. Another murder had been committed—another member of the Parr family—and I had no idea who had killed Mariel Parr or why. Though I wasn't in the proper frame of mind to make any decisions regarding new projects, I intended to fulfill my responsibilities and see to it that the library's programs and events ran smoothly. And, of course, be available if Sally needed me. That said, three o'clock couldn't come soon enough for me!

I exited the staff room and nearly banged foreheads with Jennifer Darby.

"Oh, you're still here!" I said in surprise.

"Yes. I won't be leaving Clover Ridge until early tomorrow morning." She frowned. "Sally said I'd be docked if I didn't work today."

I lowered my voice. "The police found Mariel Parr's body near your house early this morning."

"So I heard. That's the second murder in the same spot," Jennifer said. "Good thing I wasn't there. I've been staying at my sister's."

"I understand your husband found the body."

"Paul didn't kill Mariel! Why would he?"

I pursed my lips. "I have no idea."

Jennifer's laugh sounded like a cackle. "My poor husband's such a loser. He always manages to be in the wrong place at the wrong time. I can't wait to get away from here and lead a normal life. An exciting life. One with meaning."

"Where are you planning to go?" I asked, curious to hear what place she thought offered a normal life that was exciting and had meaning.

"I'm moving to Manhattan, where else? It's the only place filled with all sorts of possibilities and a new start in life."

"Can you afford it?" I asked.

Jennifer dismissed my concern with a wave of her hand. "I'll stay with my cousin until I find a job. It shouldn't be that hard."

"Really?" I asked. "What can you do?"

Jennifer frowned at my question. "Lots of things. Now I have to open the coffee shop or Sally will have a fit. And Carrie, please see to it that your cat stays away from the shop. He's been disturbing the customers these past few days."

"Really? What has Smoky Joe been doing?"

"Running through the tables and sniffing around the back room. Yesterday I almost tripped over him. It's really annoying having him underfoot."

"I'm sorry, Jennifer, but I think he's after a mouse that gets into the woodwork through the grate at the back of the shop."

"Just keep him away, okay?"

"Sally's hoping he'll catch the mouse. Or mice."

"After today I'm gone; then he can catch all the mice he likes."

I'd taken no more than five steps when I heard a familiar voice: "Our Jennifer's gotten a bit snippy, don't you think?"

I turned to Evelyn, grateful that no one was in hearing distance and would wonder why I was talking to myself. Today she wore a fitted gray jacket over a blue silk dress. Her gray hair looked as if she'd just stepped out of a beauty salon.

"I sure do," I agreed. "Sounds like she can't wait to leave Clover Ridge."

"Do you like my new dress?" Evelyn asked as she unbuttoned the jacket to show me the pleated bodice of her dress.

"I love it. And I see you've had your hair done."

She patted the back of her head. "I thought I'd try a new style for the holidays."

Again, I was about to ask Evelyn where a ghost got new clothes and had her hair done, when she said, "Interesting how Jennifer didn't even blink when you told her Mariel had been murdered near her home."

"I noticed, but it was old news to her."

"Mariel was the wife of her dead lover. Makes you wonder, doesn't it?" Evelyn said cryptically.

"Not really. Jennifer told me she realized that her affair with Benton was nothing more than a fantasy."

"And you believed her?"

"Oh, no!" I stared at Evelyn. "You don't think—I mean, Jennifer couldn't have killed Mariel. She's too—"

"Gentle? Passive? Naïve?"

"No, actually. I might have thought so at one time, but I don't anymore. I wonder how she found out about Mariel."

Evelyn shrugged. "Perhaps she heard the news on the radio."

"I doubt it. They weren't talking about it on our local TV channel when I left the cottage. But maybe Paul called to tell her what happened."

"Do you really think he would?" she asked.

"I know Jennifer left him and they're not on good terms, but there's the possibility that he'd want her to know."

Evelyn disappeared without commenting, and I walked the rest of the way to my office, pondering the possibility that Jennifer had killed Mariel. I'd be sure to tell John how unfeeling she'd been when I mentioned the murder. I was unlocking my office door when Marion Marshall walked over.

"Carrie, stop by the children's room at eleven. We're treating the pre-Ks to a light lunch and a visit from Santa."

I chuckled. "Uncle Bosco had his costume cleaned for the

occasion. Aunt Harriet told me he's gained so much weight, this year he didn't need a pillow to stuff in his suit."

I stepped into my office and hung up my jacket. There were emails waiting for me on my computer—mostly Christmas greetings from presenters and librarians who worked in nearby libraries, whom I'd gotten to know at the few library association meetings I'd attended. They gave me a feeling of belonging and continuity, both of which I'd never felt before, despite the fact that I'd only been living in Clover Ridge since May.

I smiled to think that coming to live here, the hometown of my father's family, had been the wisest decision I'd ever made. Now I had a job that I loved and a boyfriend I cared for. My relationship with my father was improving, and I was learning to accept him for the person he was. I had no idea how long he planned to stay with me at the cottage before taking off to parts unknown. I supposed it would depend on how long he continued to look for the gems that Benton had so successfully hidden.

I was beginning to believe that finding them was a lost cause. So many people were searching for them, including the killer. I wished I knew how to help John discover who it was. Whoever it was had already murdered three people.

My cell phone rang. It was my father, sounding distraught.

"I can't believe Mariel's dead, Caro. We were with her last night."

"I'm sorry, Dad. I know she was a friend of yours."

"This place has turned into a killing zone! That makes three murders since I came to town, not to mention you and me being attacked."

Dylan must have told him about the incident at the cabin. "I'm pretty sure they're all connected to the gems everyone's after."

"As far as I'm concerned, those gems can rot wherever they are. The minute the doctor says I'm okay, I'm off."

"Oh," was all I could manage.

"Sorry, honey. I didn't mean that I want to leave you. It's been wonderful spending time together, but you knew I wasn't planning to stay in Clover Ridge."

"Where will you go?"

"I have no idea now that South America is out of the picture."

When I didn't answer, he said in a false bright tone, "We'll keep in touch. I promise."

"What time did the doctor say you can be released from the hospital?"

"One, one thirty. Dylan knows I'll call him as soon as I get my walking papers."

"Will you be okay on your own till I get home shortly after three?"

"Of course, Caro. Don't you worry about me."

I hung up feeling blue. Of course I knew he'd probably leave after the new year, but hearing it stated so baldly made me sad. I'd gotten used to having my father close by. Once he was gone, traveling God knew where, I'd worry about him and hope he wasn't getting into trouble.

The usual programs were in session that day, needing no assistance from me. The only special event was a group of local carolers who were coming in at two o'clock to sing holiday songs in the main reading room for half an hour.

"Guess what!"

The door to my office flew open. Angela stormed in like a gale of wind. "Mariel Parr was murdered last night!"

"Early this morning," I corrected

"You knew and didn't tell me!" she said.

"Things have been hectic. My father fell after dinner and was taken by ambulance back to the hospital. Then Dylan and I—" My face grew warm as I remembered our night together.

"Go on!" Angela urged. When I didn't say another word, she grinned. "Are you not saying what I think you're not saying? That things between the two of you are finally taking off?"

I nodded. "He told me he loves me."

"That's terrific."

"I'm still getting used to—everything. Then this morning, John called him to say Mariel had been murdered. She and Dina were at the cottage for dinner last night."

Angela reared back, her eyes bugging with amazement. "You have been a busy lady. You must be exhausted. How is your head feeling this morning?"

I touched my scalp. "It doesn't hurt as much, now that you mention it."

"The murderer's been busy too," Angela said, "following you to the cabin, trailing after Mariel in the wee hours of the morning." She paused. "You know, Dina might have murdered her mother."

"Or it could have been her brother or Jennifer or Paul Darby or Chris Crowley."

"Or even his mother," Angela said.

"Why Stella Crowley?" I asked.

"She might not have liked the way the Parrs treated her son. From what you've told me about her, Stella Crowley sounds like a very protective mother."

We made plans to have lunch at noon at the Cozy Corner Café, and Angela departed as quickly as she'd arrived. Sally appeared minutes later with a bowlful of chocolate-covered strawberries.

"Part of a holiday basket from an appreciative patron," she said. "Dig in!"

I took a handful of strawberries and placed them on one of the paper plates I'd learned to keep in the office for just such occasions. We talked about Mariel's murder and how awful it was until Trish arrived and most of our conversation was repeated.

"I see I'm not going to get any work done today," I said.

Sally laughed. "Were you expecting to?"

I shrugged.

"By the way," Trish said, "I just saw Smoky Joe race across the reading room and behind the circulation desk."

"He must be after that mouse," I said.

"I'm afraid the word is 'mice,'" Sally said. "Several more of them. Yesterday I saw two tiny babies dive back into one of the grates as I was entering the storeroom behind the circulation desk."

'Oh, no!" Trish and I shouted at the same time.

"Much as I hate to bring chemicals into the library, it looks like I'll be calling in the exterminator after all."

When Sally left, I looked over my December expenses to make sure I'd recorded every receipt. I'd learned to keep track of every penny I spent so I could fill out those dreadful forms every month. When I looked up, it was five after eleven.

"Trish, Marion invited me to the pre-Ks' party. I'll be there awhile."

"Take your time," Trish said, reaching for a chocolate-covered strawberry from her stash. "I'm enjoying my own little party."

Evelyn reappeared and strode beside me as I walked across the large reading room to the children's room.

"Two visits in one day?" I said. "I'm honored."

"I haven't seen Tacey in a while," she said. "I miss her."

"She is a little cutie," I agreed.

The kiddies' holiday party was in full swing as we entered the room. Alvin and the Chipmunks were singing their well-known Christmas song as Marion and Gayle spooned portions of mac and cheese onto the plates of eleven four-year-olds sitting around two kiddie-sized tables. A few parents stood chatting along the far wall. I waved to Julia, my cousin by marriage, and approached the children.

As soon as she saw me, Tacey jumped out of her chair and ran over to hug me. "Cousin Carrie! You came to our holiday party, and you brought Miss Evelyn with you!"

Oh, no! Now you've done it, Evelyn. I looked around. No one was paying us any attention. No one but Julia.

"Tacey," I said softly. "Miss Evelyn's our secret, remember? No one but you and I can see her."

"I'm so happy to see you, Tacey," Evelyn said. "I wish I could hug you, but I can't."

"I know," Tacey said. "And I won't try to give you any cookies." She took me by the hand and led me back to her table. "Miss Marion said that Santa's coming later, but I know he's only make-believe."

Marion looked frazzled as she walked over to me. "Glad you made it, Carrie. Would you like something to eat or drink?"

"Nothing to eat, thanks, but I'll have some fruit punch."

Marion waved to her assistant, who was pouring drinks for the children. Gayle brought me a cup of punch.

"Thank you," I said.

I stood behind Tacey and sipped my punch. Evelyn knelt on the other side of my little cousin, and the two of them chatted in low tones. I felt a bit guilty, deliberately blocking Julia's view of her daughter, but I'd sensed how much Evelyn wanted to spend time with Tacey. Julia could never understand that her daughter's so-called imaginary friend wasn't imaginary at all.

A roar of excitement arose as the kids noticed Santa Claus had entered the room. "Good afternoon, children!" boomed Uncle Bosco, looking like old St. Nicolas himself in his black boots and belt, his red suit and hat trimmed in white, and a large sack slung over his shoulder. "Were you good children all year?"

"Yes!" they shouted.

"Very good. I have presents for good children."

I noticed Santa's beard was crooked and hurried over to straighten it out.

"These damn toys are heavy, Carrie," he whispered. "Help me set the sack down."

The sack *was* heavy. Uncle Bosco sighed with relief as I slid it down his back to the floor. Marion instructed the children to remain in their seats and promised that everyone would have a chance to talk to Santa and receive a gift.

I joined the parents and watched as Santa spoke to each child and reached into the sack for a present. The little ones ripped open their gifts. They all seemed happy with Santa's choice of presents.

I realized Evelyn had disappeared when Santa joined the party. Something else I'd learned today: that Evelyn cared about Tacey as much as my little cousin cared about her.

Julia leaned over to me and asked, "What did Tacey say when she saw you? I thought it was something about her imaginary friend."

I smiled. "It's just a little game we play."

Julia looked relieved. "That's good to know. She's taken quite a shine to you, Carrie. The two of you seem to share a special bond."

"I'm glad, because I adore your daughter," I said. "Tacey's a special little girl."

Julia beamed. "Well, I think so, but I'm her mother."

I smiled back, wishing she knew just how special her daughter really was.

At that moment Smoky Joe entered the room, causing an uproar as each child called to him, urging him to come closer. Good little cat that he was, he visited each of them in turn, letting them pet him and making him the center of their attention. What a wonderful addition to the library he had turned out to be! I stayed a few more minutes to chat with Santa, then returned to my office.

It was close to noon. I had lunch ahead of me and perhaps a visit from John; the carolers at two; then home at three. By then, Dylan would have brought my father back from the hospital. I looked forward to a quiet evening after a hectic day.

Chapter
Thirty-Three

I found John pacing outside my office when Angela and I returned from lunch.

"Sorry. I should have called to let you know I'd be leaving the building," I said. "Have you been waiting long?"

"I only got here a few minutes ago." He chuckled. "As soon as Sally saw me, she hauled me off to her office and plied me with chocolate-covered strawberries. They look so good, I've saved a few to bring home to Sylvia."

I laughed. "At the rate Sally's doling them out, I'm amazed she has any left."

We entered my office. Trish looked up from what she was doing and grinned. "Uh-oh, the law has arrived."

"Go ahead and treat yourself to a long break while I'm being grilled."

"Yes, boss." Trish stood. "I think I'll check to see if Sally has any chocolate-covered strawberries left."

John sank into the seat she'd vacated and rubbed his eyes. He looked exhausted.

"Can I get you a cup of coffee?" I asked.

"That would be wonderful. Two sugars, a little milk, and any cookies you can scrounge up."

"I'm off to the staff room. Be right back."

Sure enough, there were more platters of cookies and other yummy treats on the table. I made up a paper cup of coffee for John the way he liked it and wrapped a generous assortment of goodies in a napkin. I returned to my office and waited while he downed half his coffee and devoured several cookies.

"Thanks, Carrie. That hit the spot." John patted his stomach and stretched his arms overhead. "Now, would you please run through last evening's events, starting with Dina and Mariel Parr's arrival at your cottage."

"I think I'd better backtrack to Monday evening."

I explained to John why I'd gone to the Crowleys' house and about meeting Dina there. That we had decided to go out for something to eat and ended up making plans to drive up to her father's cabin to look for the gems.

He frowned. "The gems that weren't stolen and no one knows anything about?"

"The very ones. I let Dina think I was her new partner, but if the gems were at the cabin, I intended to hand them over to Dylan."

"To keep your father out of trouble."

I smiled. "There's also a lovely reward for finding the gems."

"Which you would probably hand over to Jim, who stole them in the first place."

I fluttered my eyelashes. "What preposterous ideas you come up with, Lieutenant. Anyway, as I told you yesterday, Dina didn't come with me, after all—supposedly to keep her mother occupied and prevent *her* from going to the cabin."

"Why was Mariel suddenly interested in going there?"

"She wants the gems like everyone else." I was careful not to mention that Jim and Mariel had joined forces. "As you know, I found nothing and got hit over the head for my troubles. Whoever attacked me rummaged through my pocketbook and my pockets. And no, I didn't see him because he—or she—knelt behind me the whole time."

John scowled. "That was a stupid risk you took, going there by yourself."

I patted his arm. "I appreciate your concern, and I'm okay—now. I was seriously annoyed when Dina told me she hadn't spent the day with her mother as planned, because Mariel had to take care of something."

"So either Dina or Mariel could have followed you to the cabin."

"I suppose."

"Did your assailant speak? Wear a fragrance you might recognize again?"

"You asked me that yesterday."

"I did," John said, "but in police work we go over the same ground again and again. It can help jog a witness's memory."

"I heard a few grunts, but I couldn't say if they were made by a man or a woman."

"You must have noticed the color of the assailant's jacket."

I thought a moment. "I did! It was navy. And he wore gloves. They were black leather."

"Why do you say he? What made you think it was a man who struck you?"

"I'm not sure. I just do."

"Was he taller than you?"

"Maybe a few inches." I cocked my head. "Does that help?"

John gave me a half smile. "Every piece of the puzzle makes a difference. We'll check out everyone's alibi for the times of the murders and the time you were attacked, again and again. That's what so much detective work involves, Carrie—painstaking attention to small pieces of information. Often we're like archeologists sifting through sand, discovering shards of pottery that make up a pitcher or a plate."

I nodded, liking his analogy.

"Did you notice the assailant's car when he took off?" John asked.

"No. He left before I got to my feet. I remembered hearing a vehicle passing when I was inside the cabin. I thought it was simply a car driving by."

"Any distinguishing sounds the motor made?"

I shook my head. "I was concentrating on searching every cabinet and drawer. Later in the day, my father called to say he'd be making dinner. I invited Dylan. I discovered my father had invited Dina and Mariel." I stopped, embarrassed.

"Go on," John urged.

"From a previous conversation I'd overheard, I knew that Richard Parr was estranged from both his parents and that he knew about the gems. I tried to provoke Dina and Mariel into admitting they suspected Richard might have killed Benton after he'd refused to lend his son money. All I succeeded in doing was upsetting them both."

"Richard Parr has no solid alibi for yesterday morning when you were attacked at the cabin. He didn't arrive at his job until the early afternoon, claiming he had to babysit their son while his wife kept a doctor's appointment."

"Interesting!" I sat back, digesting this. Maybe I'd been on the right track all along. "I suppose he had a motive of sorts to kill his father, but I'm not sure why he'd want to kill his mother."

"There's a substantial life insurance policy on her life, to be shared by both Dina and Richard upon Mariel's death."

"And he was out driving around early this morning," I mumbled to myself.

"What did you say?"

I bolted upright in my chair. "Dina told me Richard had been driving around at the time of Mariel's murder. According to Dina, when he passed the crime scene, he noticed two people talking in the shadows. At the time, he had no idea who they were."

John nodded as he thought. "I sent Danny to tell Richard Parr that his mother had been murdered. Danny said Parr had a weird reaction to the news. He mumbled, 'I should have known.' Could be he meant that he should have recognized his own mother was one of the people he'd seen arguing. Of course that doesn't mean he's innocent. And he didn't give a satisfactory explanation when Danny asked why he was up and dressed at six in the morning when he usually left for work hours later."

"Dina said he'd gone out driving after arguing with his wife. Do you think Richard Parr killed both his parents and Tom Quincy?" I asked.

"It's too soon to say anything more than that he's a person of interest."

"Jennifer Darby turned out to be a strange bird. She wasn't

at all surprised when I told her that Mariel Parr had been murdered." I repeated our conversation as best I could recall it.

"You've been a busy woman," John said when I finished. He stood. "I'm off to talk to Jennifer. See you tomorrow evening at your aunt and uncle's."

I grinned. "I'm glad you and Sylvia will be there."

He winked. "And say hi to Dylan for me. We had a long chat this morning."

"Did you?" I felt my face grow warm. No doubt our relationship had been a topic of conversation.

I watched John close my office door behind him, musing how our relationship had changed. When I'd first met Lieutenant John Mathers two months ago, he'd been distant and inflexible, unwilling to share any information about the two murders I'd found myself investigating. But that changed after I'd provided the police with a journal written by one of the victims and helped solve both cases. I grinned. And it didn't hurt that John and his wife, Sylvia, were good friends of Aunt Harriet and Uncle Bosco.

The recent unsolved homicides demanded my attention, and I tried to think of them from a different perspective. What did they have in common? The gems. Did the same person kill all three victims, or had Tom Quincy killed Benton?

I wondered if there were two murderers rather than one, each person carrying out his or her part. What if Jennifer and Paul were in on it together, and their estrangement had been staged so everyone would think they were at odds with each other, when, in fact, they were working as a team? They had means, motive, and opportunity. Jennifer had been close to Benton. Paul had been seen arguing with one of the victims and near two of the murder scenes. What if Jennifer had only pretended to care about Benton and plotted with her husband to kill him once she'd learned about the gems?

Then why was she still hanging around Clover Ridge, worried that Sally would dock her if she didn't come to work today? It wasn't what someone would do if she had seven million dollars worth of gems at her disposal. Unless Jennifer knew about the gems, but not where Benton had hidden them, and she was as much in the dark regarding their location as everyone else.

Or she wanted people to *think* she needed to work today so they wouldn't suspect that the gems had been in her possession all along. And once she was in New York or wherever she was really going, Paul would join her.

My cell phone rang, jarring me from my speculations.

"Hey, babe. How are you?"

Hearing Dylan's voice sent a surge of happiness coursing through me. "It's been a strange day. Everything feels surreal— Mariel's murder, us, Christmas almost here."

"I'm on my way to the hospital to pick up your dad. They've given him the okay to go home."

"Thanks, Dylan. Mariel's death has shaken him badly."

"That's not surprising. What time will you be home?"

"Around three twenty."

"I can't wait to see you."

"I miss you too."

I felt the grin spread across my face as I disconnected the call. I'd be seeing Dylan in just a few hours. And tomorrow. And the next day.

And then what? He'd go off to another assignment a plane ride away, and we'd communicate via texts and phone calls. Was it enough? Was that the kind of relationship I wanted?

I shook my head, refusing to follow that train of thought. I had to focus on the positive. Our romance was new and wonderful. The man I loved cared about me, and that was most important right now. Other matters needed attention—like discovering who had murdered three people and was hell-bent on finding the gems my father and Benton had stolen.

Chapter
Thirty-Four

Aunt Harriet called to talk to me about Christmas Eve, which was the following evening. She was delighted when I said Dylan would be joining us and distressed to learn that Jim was about to leave the hospital for a second time.

"He fell trying to straighten out the snowman on top of my Christmas tree," I said, omitting why he'd bothered doing that in the first place.

"Honestly, that man! You'd think he'd learn to act his age and accept his limitations. I won't be able to rest easy until he's gone from Clover Ridge."

"Actually, Dad's been behaving himself pretty well," I said.

"Really?" She sighed. "I don't want him disappointing you the way he always does—running off and leaving his family."

"I don't think he can help it," I said. "He loves me—I know that now—but he can't stay in one place for long."

Aunt Harriet harrumphed. "And we won't get into a discussion of his less than honest ways to make a living. After all his shenanigans, he's lucky he's not in prison."

I laughed. "True. But I must admit I'm glad he's spending Christmas with me."

"Can your little group be here at three tomorrow afternoon? Your uncle and I thought we'd celebrate Christmas Eve early this year. I invited the Claymonts next door to join us. They're elderly, as you know, and prefer to eat early. And John and Sylvia Mathers would like to be home by eight o'clock since they're expecting two carloads of kids and grandkids late tomorrow night."

"It's fine with me, as well as Dad and Dylan. What are you making?"

"The usual—a turkey, a ham. Coquille St. Jacques for appetizers, along with stuffed mushrooms, various veggies. I've made Christmas cookies, but I've yet to bake a few cakes."

"Don't bother, Aunt Harriet. I'll make a batch of my double-chocolate brownies."

"Oh, would you? Your uncle loves your brownies!" She paused, then added, "Thanks so much for taking care of that little matter for me."

I grinned, picturing Aunt Harriet leafing through *Sex for Seniors.* "Don't mention it. Dealt with and forgotten."

"It's so stupid the way I let the overdue fine grow and grow. I didn't want anyone finding the book lying around, so I put it on the top shelf in my clothes closet. Eventually, I forgot I still had it. Then I got that official letter . . . How much was my fine?"

"Nothing. Not a penny."

"Really?"

"Angela said to tell you it's her Christmas present to you."

"What an angel! I'll make up a package of goodies for her, and you can deliver it. Don't let me forget it tomorrow."

We'd no sooner ended our conversation when Smoky Joe

started scratching at my office door. As soon as I let him in, he ran to his dish, expecting me to feed him his afternoon meal. I filled it with kibble and stroked him as he ate.

"And what have you been up to, racing around the library?" I asked.

He turned to stare at me, then resumed eating. He licked the plate clean, then used his litter box. That accomplished, he ran to the door as if he had an important appointment. I, his loyal servant, opened it, and off he went frolicking again. *You have some wonderful life, Smoky Joe.*

I found myself replaying my conversation with John. He was an astute interviewer, I decided, knowing which questions to ask and when to repeat them. This afternoon he'd helped jog my memory regarding the color of my assailant's jacket. I'd caught a flash of his sleeve, remembered it was navy. Dark blue.

I made a mental run-through of the suspects and their clothing. Dina's jacket was navy. So was Chris's. Or was it black? Paul Darby's jacket was dark blue.

And my father's was too.

Besides, people often had more than one winter jacket. I gave a sigh of exasperation. So much for that helpful bit of information.

Trish returned and we chatted a bit. The carolers would soon be arriving to serenade us in the reading room. As their presentation required no preparation, and nothing in my office required my immediate attention, I decided to pay Angela a visit at the circulation desk.

She was busy checking out films for a lineup of patrons. When she noticed me standing to the side of the counter, she nodded in a way that told me she had something to tell me.

As soon as she was free, I asked what had happened.

"I ran into Jennifer in the bathroom. She was in tears."

"That's interesting," I said. "John Mathers came to see me after we had lunch. Jennifer was next on his agenda."

"Whatever they talked about must have upset her," Angela said.

"Maybe we should try to calm her down," I said.

Angela laughed. "So you can find out what he said to her that upset her so much."

"That too. I think she knows more than she's saying."

Just then an elderly couple stopped at the circulation desk with a load of films they wanted to check out.

"Talk to you later," I said and let Angela do her job.

How to pose my questions without upsetting Jennifer again? I pondered the matter as I walked toward the coffee shop. *Did you know about the gems? Did you kill Benton? Are you in cahoots with your husband?*

I stumbled as a flash of gray sped by.

"Smoky Joe!" I called after him. "Where are you off to?"

I stopped to watch him make a mad dash toward the wall under the window of the reading room as a tiny creature disappeared inside the metal grating that was part of the library's heat and air conditioning system.

I'd just seen the mouse! Or one of them.

I walked over to Smoky Joe, who sat sniffing the metal grating, and knelt beside him.

"Sorry, kiddo, he's gone. There's no point in waiting around for him to show up again."

I swear, it was as if he understood exactly what I'd been saying. Smoky Joe looked at me and at the grate, then trotted off in the direction of the coffee shop. Somehow his feline brain had figured out the mice were free to travel inside the library walls and used the grates as doorways to enter and exit the library. He knew that the grate at the rear of the coffee shop was their favorite and that was where he was heading. Exactly what Jennifer didn't want. She'd made it very clear that he'd been a pest recently. Today was her last day working at the coffee shop, and she didn't need him underfoot

He slowed down as he approached the seating area. Three of the five small round tables were occupied. Jennifer stood talking to someone seated at the table in the far corner. Though her back was to me, I knew she was agitated by the way she waved her arms about to get a point across.

Don't turn around! I silently instructed her. *I'll grab Smoky Joe and get him out of your way.*

"Smoky Joe, come here!" I called softly.

The little devil turned his head to look at me. Then, very slowly, he ambled over to the middle-aged couple seated at one of the tables. He lifted a paw to the knee of the gray-haired woman.

"Why, hello, kitty cat," she crooned as she stroked his back. "I was wondering where you've been."

Smoky Joe's purrs were louder than a locomotive. My mouth fell open as the woman broke off a piece of her cake and placed it in her outstretched hand.

"Please don't feed—" I began, but it was too late. Smoky Joe had gobbled it up.

So this was why he loved coming to the coffee shop! He'd learned to beg for food! And the patrons were only too happy to feed him. God only knew what he'd been eating this past month.

The woman caught my expression of outrage. "Oh, sorry," she said, not sounding sorry at all.

"There are signs are all over the library instructing people not to feed the library cat!"

"Well, it *is* the holiday season," she said, as if that excused her behavior.

Her husband sent me an apologetic glance and told his wife it was time they got going. They stood and left.

Smoky Joe padded over to the young bearded man at the next table and put his paw on his leg.

The young man laughed. "I have nothing for you, pal." He stood and tossed his Styrofoam cup in the garbage and left.

That feline had his routine down pat! I heard what sounded like a little squeak. Smoky Joe's ears perked up.

"Oh no, you don't!" Jennifer shrieked.

We both stared at Smoky Joe as he dashed behind the counter.

"Sorry," I said over my shoulder as I ran after him.

"Don't!" Jennifer shouted, chasing after me.

It was tight behind the counter, which, except for the doorway, was actually two sections. The narrower back section was where the shop's supplies were kept on shelves along the wall. Smoky Joe wasn't interested in coffee filters or packages of cookies. The lighting was poor back here, but there was no missing the way he hovered over the grating, staring into its depths.

"Carrie, get out! You're not supposed to go behind the counter!" Jennifer sounded desperate as she tugged on my arm.

"I just want to get him out of your way," I said, yanking my arm free of her frantic grip. I reached down to pick up Smoky Joe, when he nimbly jumped across the grating.

"Come here!" I yelled, stepping on the grating so I could get a firm hold on him. "I'm sorry, Jennifer. I'll have him in a minute, and then . . ."

And then I saw the chamois leather jeweler's bag lying on the shallow floor of the heat register. For a moment, all I could do was gulp down air. I lifted the ornate wrought iron grill and picked up the bag. The gems weighed more than I'd expected.

I leaped to my feet and glared at Jennifer. "You had them all this time!"

"They're mine! Hand them over," she said.

"Are you kidding? Three people have been murdered. These are going straight to the police."

"Benton gave them to me, to start our life together." Jennifer lunged forward and tried to grab the bag of gems. "He's dead and now they're mine, for my new life in Manhattan."

I held the bag high and out of her reach as I staggered back. The wall broke my fall, but I was trapped in the narrow space.

Smoky Joe meowed as he ran out. It was enough to distract Jennifer. I pushed past her toward the opening. As soon as I rounded the counter, I'd be safe! There would be people around, people to stop Jennifer as I called John to come and arrest her.

"I'll take those before you spill them all over the floor."

I halted dead in my tracks as Chris Crowley seized the bag of gems from my nerveless fingers.

Chapter Thirty-Five

"Stop him!" I screamed at the top of my lungs.

Patrons came to see what was the matter, but despite his bulky frame, Chris dodged around them like a star quarterback making a touchdown. Only his goal was the front door.

Sally was the first to reach me. "What's all the fuss about?" she asked.

"Call the police! Chris Crowley just ran off with the missing gems."

We both turned to gape at Jennifer, who had collapsed at one of the tables, her face in her hands as she sobbed.

"I'll make the call," Sally said, reaching into her cardigan pocket for her cell phone.

Angela joined us. "Jennifer had them all this time?"

I nodded. "She'd hidden them in the grate at the back of the coffee shop. I went to get Smoky Joe, who was chasing a mouse, and found them."

Angela gave me a friendly punch on the arm. "I suppose that means you get the reward."

"I don't know about that, since Chris Crowley has run off

with them." I grabbed Angela's arm. "Chris is the murderer! He must have realized Jennifer had the gems and came here demanding that she hand them over. I noticed she was talking to someone, but I couldn't see who it was. She was clearly distressed, probably doing her best to convince Chris that she didn't have them, when I had to announce I'd found the gems and practically handed them to him on a plate."

Tears sprang to my eyes as I thought of how stupid I'd been. Angela sat me down at a table. "Carrie, stop beating yourself up."

I shook my head. "I had no idea who she was talking to. I should have been more careful."

"The police will find him."

"Not if he gets to a fence right away. He probably knows one or two. And he has money now. He can fly off anywhere in the world."

Sally came over to us. "John is on his way. He asked me to keep Jennifer here if I could."

We looked at her hunched in a chair. "I don't think she's going anywhere," I said.

I suddenly had an idea. I jumped to my feet. "Sally, I have to leave."

"Why? Where are you going?"

I ignored her questions and turned to Angela. "Please take Smoky Joe home with you."

"Will do."

"What are you up to, Carrie?" Sally demanded. "You're not chasing after a murderer, are you?"

"Merry Christmas!" I shouted, hugging each of them in turn. "Talk to you both later."

I rushed out to my car and pressed the ignition button. As I exited the parking lot, I called Dylan. "Where are you?" I asked when I heard his voice.

"Almost home. Your father managed to wrangle an escort down to the main lobby. Be there in five minutes. Why?"

"Smoky Joe found the gems! Jennifer had them hidden inside a heat register in the library's coffee shop."

"That's great! Did you call John?"

"He's on his way to the library to question Jennifer."

"I'll come by as soon as I drop off your dad."

"Don't come to the library! Chris Crowley has the gems! I didn't realize he was in the coffee shop when this happened. He grabbed the bag of gems and took off."

"Damn! You're saying Crowley has them? And now he's in the wind?"

"Dylan, I think I know where he went."

"Where?"

I drew in a deep breath, knowing what was coming. "To see Dina Parr. He's crazy about her. I think Chris thinks that if he shows Dina he has the gems, she'll be willing to go all in with him."

"I know where the Parrs live. Soon as I drop off your father, I'll head over there."

I heard Jim saying he was going with him; then both of them were shouting.

"Meet me there now," I said.

"I'm on my way, but promise me you're not planning to go there yourself. If Crowley's the killer, he's already taken down three people for these gems and won't hesitate to kill you too."

I shuddered. "Don't worry. I won't do anything stupid. I'll wait for you outside the house."

Read and Gone

"No, Carrie. Don't—"

I disconnected the call and drove on. *Why am I chasing after Chris Crowley?* I asked myself. I couldn't capture him myself or retrieve the gems. If he caught sight of me, I was in mortal danger. But would he try to kill me in broad daylight? Not in front of witnesses and not in front of Dina, who he loved.

I called John's cell phone. He picked up immediately.

"Can't talk, Carrie. I'm on my way to the library to talk to Jennifer Darby."

"John, Chris Crowley swiped the gems and ran. I think he's on his way to see Dina Parr."

"I'll send Danny Brower to the Parrs' house on the chance that you're right."

"Dylan's on his way there."

"Carrie, you'd better not be thinking of going there too. I don't want you involved in more homicides. You remember what happened last time. Stay put!"

"I'm not in—" I tried to tell him, but he'd already hung up.

I drove on, anticipation becoming excitement. *Dylan and John have no reason to worry about me,* I told myself. I had no intention of doing anything stupid. Right now Chris was as dangerous as a grizzly bear. He'd killed three people and believed the gems were his entrée to a new life—providing the funds to open his own jewelry store and winning Dina back. I'd remain out of sight while John and Danny captured him, but I had to witness the last act of this drama I'd been a part of and helped to screw up.

The Parrs lived a few miles east of Clover Ridge's center village, in a lovely residential area. As I approached the brick-and-stone, colonial-style house, I counted two cars in the driveway and three parked in the street in front of the house. Of course! Close friends and relatives must have stopped by, even though the funeral wasn't for another two days. I parked on the other side of the street, then crossed and followed the cement path to the Parr's front door. I was about to ring the bell, when a guy in his early twenties stepped outside, an unlit cigarette in his hand.

"Are you a friend of Dina's?" he asked. "She's out back talking to this weird dude."

"Thanks," I said.

He lit his cigarette, then reached into his pocket for his cell phone as he continued walking down the path toward one of the cars. I looked up and down the street. No cars were approaching. No big surprise since it would take Dylan and Danny ten or twelve minutes to get here.

I decided to walk around to the back of the house. Tall evergreen bushes hugged the side of the house, giving me good cover. I peered around to the patio where Dina and Chris were having a heated discussion.

"I told you, Chris, I'm not interested. Can I make it any clearer? I have a ton of paperwork to see to now that both my parents are gone. I can't even think of starting a new business."

"But I'll do all the purchasing," Chris wheedled. "You won't have to do anything involving the store until you're ready to start working. I'll set everything up—though I'll run important decisions by you, of course."

"Chris, I've told you before. I don't want to be your partner in any way, shape, or form. I can't believe you're haranguing me about it today. My mother's just been murdered. I have to go back inside and finish making funeral arrangements."

When she stepped toward the door, he tugged on her arm. "I have the gems." His voice was hoarse with emotion.

"What did you say?" Dina turned slowly to gawk at him.

"I have them right here. Want to see them?"

He reached inside his jacket and brought out the chamois bag of gems.

Her eyes never left his face. "How did you find them?"

Chris laughed. "I went to see Jennifer Darby. After checking out every possible place, I figured your father must have given them to her. And I was right! The idiot stashed them in the library until she was ready to leave town. Luckily, I—"

"What do you mean, after checking out every possible place?" Even from where I stood, I saw Dina's eyes register shock and disgust. "Did you follow Carrie to my father's cabin and attack her?"

Chris shrugged. "I had to know what you girls were up to."

"And did you follow my mother last night and stick a knife in her like you did my father?"

"Of course not!" Chris let loose a false laugh. "Are you crazy? Do you think for one minute I'd murder your parents, even though you didn't give a rat's ass about either one of them after the way they treated you?"

Dina backed away from Chris, as if he were radioactive. "Of course it was you. Who else could have done it? You killed my father and took off before Carrie's father came into the store. Then all you had to do was change your clothes and go to work, same as always and pretend you were shocked to see him lying there dead when *you murdered him*!"

Chris put his hand over Dina's mouth. "Stop shouting," he

said, so softly I could barely hear him. "No need to bring any of your relatives out here."

"Why did you have to kill them? *Why?*"

"Because they were both hypocrites, both stupid, selfish people who made our lives miserable."

Dina sniffed. "You didn't have to work for my father. When you found out what he was really like, you should have quit. As for my mother—she was raised to think the right background and appearances were what mattered. She didn't know any other way to think or to live."

"She must have figured out that Jennifer had the gems, same as I did, though I can't imagine how she expected to make Jennifer hand them over."

"You followed her and killed her."

Chris shrugged. "She didn't care about you, what you wanted. She didn't like my background, so she told you not to see me."

Dina stamped her foot. "She was my *mother*, damn you."

Chris made a scoffing sound. "And no longer around to tell you what to do. You should thank me, is what you should be doing."

Dina shook her head and started for the house.

"Where are you going?" Chris demanded.

"Inside."

"Will you tell the police?"

She shot him a look of contempt. "What do you think?"

He sprang on her like a wild animal and wrapped his hands around her neck. "No, you won't."

"Let go of her!" I was amazed at how fierce I sounded, when I was quaking inside.

Chris growled when he saw me. "I should have taken you out when I had the chance."

He ran after me. At first I was too frightened to move, but as he drew nearer, my legs started pumping.

"Help!" Dina shouted. She swung open the back door to her house.

Chris stopped suddenly and let out a string of curses. His eyes darted from Dina to me, momentarily uncertain what to do. He must have decided to deal with me since I was closer, but I raced around the side of the house and made a beeline for the front door. *Be unlocked. Please! Someone come out and stop him!*

I felt his warm breath on my cheek as he closed in on me. A car screeched to a halt in the street. Dylan flew out followed by my father, as Chris gripped my shoulder.

"Let her go!" Dylan shouted.

"Let her go, damn you!" my father yelled, several paces behind.

Chris let loose another string of curses as he released me. His head darted from side to side, searching for an escape route.

"Better give yourself up," I said.

He glared at me, then made a dash for it, past Dylan's reach. I watched him go, surprised at his speed, given his stocky build. But then, he was running for his life.

Of course Chris had no idea that the car speeding toward him was driven by Danny Brower, Clover Ridge Police Department's rookie, who'd broken several Clover Ridge High School track and field records five years earlier. Danny stopped the car. He sprinted after Chris and tackled him. His partner joined them and removed the bag of gems from inside Chris's jacket. Danny handcuffed Chris and led him to their cruiser.

"What are you doing here?" my father demanded of me.

"What were you thinking?" Dylan yelled.

They each tried to hug me, making me feel like the center of a tug of war. I finally broke free. "He was about to hurt Dina. I only wanted to distract him. Thank God you arrived in time."

Another police car pulled up, this one driven by John Mathers. He stopped to talk to Danny. Finally, Danny drove off and John walked over to join us.

"I thought I told you to stay put," he thundered at me.

"I was on my way here when I called you," I pointed out. "You wouldn't have known Chris was coming to see Dina if I hadn't told you."

John shook his head in disgust. "What did you hope to do—convince Crowley to give himself up?"

"Carrie saw Chris was choking me," Dina said. "She was only trying to help."

She'd come outside, as had five or six people whom I assumed were Parr relatives, there to pay their respects because of Mariel's demise.

Richard Parr approached and shook my hand. "I'm Dina's brother, Rich. Thank you for all you've done to ID my parents' killer and for protecting my sister just now."

"You're welcome," I murmured, not sure if that was the correct response.

"What's going on out here?" a red-faced man with jowls demanded of John. "This is a house of mourning."

John raised his voice to address the visitors. "I'm Lieutenant John Mathers of the Clover Ridge Police Department. I'm asking that all of you go back inside the house. As soon as I've had a chat with Miss Parr, I'll explain what just transpired and answer all your questions."

Dina allowed John to lead her up the steps to the front door. Instead of going inside, he spun around and glared at me, "And I'll be talking to you later, Miss Singleton, so don't you disappear on me."

"He's really pissed at you," Dylan observed as the three of us walked toward the parked cars.

"She gave him a fright," my father said. "Caro, dear, you gave us all a fright."

"Me too," I admitted. "I promised myself I wouldn't do anything stupid. I never intended to say a word while Dina and Chris were talking, but I was afraid Chris was going to choke Dina when he realized she intended to give him up to the police."

"I don't think you should drive," Dylan and my father said at the same time when we reached the street.

"I don't think I should, either. Dad, I'll go home with Dylan if you'll drive my car to the cottage."

"Of course. Whatever you say."

Dylan grinned, pleased that I'd chosen him to do the honors. He turned up his palms and said to my father, "Carrie always likes me to drive her home after she's landed a killer."

Chapter
Thirty-Six

Except for the phone call Dylan made—I assumed to his boss saying the gems from the Farthingale heist had been recovered and he'd have more information shortly—we rode to the cottage in silence. As soon as we shed our jackets, Dylan headed for the bar in the living room and poured us each three fingers of scotch.

"Here, Carrie. My father always downed a shot or two of scotch after experiencing a shock to the system. And this one was a doozy."

I sat down on the sofa and sipped. Scotch wasn't my favorite, but I appreciated the feeling of warmth that immediately circulated through my system.

"So that's it," I said. "Jennifer had the gems all this time, and Chris murdered three people to get them."

"Looks that way, though I'm betting his deep resentment toward both Benton and Mariel Parr was a factor." Dylan sat beside me and put his arm around me.

I rested my head against his chest and sighed. "I'm glad everything's resolved, but I feel kind of—left in the air."

Dylan laughed. "That's because the chase is over, the story's ended. It's kind of a letdown, after all the excitement."

"The story's over, but there's no happily ever after."

"That's for sure," Dylan agreed. "Three people are dead because Chris Crowley was determined to get his hands on twenty million dollars' worth of stolen gems that I bet very few fences would venture to touch."

"Twenty million!" I exclaimed. "I thought! I mean, my father said—"

Dylan grinned. "The morning of the heist, Mr. Farthingale placed five very special sapphires in the safe. They were stolen as well. As for the other gems—mostly diamonds and sapphires— the smallest are two carats in weight and go up from there. Some are uncut stones."

"No wonder the bag felt so heavy! I can't wait to get a look at those amazing gems." I turned to Dylan. "I can—can't I—see them before you take them back to their owner?"

"I think that can be arranged. And I won't be bringing them back. There will be a special armored car escorting them back to Illinois."

"Hard to imagine those expensive jewels were sitting in a little space under a heating register in the library."

"And if it weren't for Smoky Joe, we wouldn't have found them until Jennifer tried to fence them. Maybe not even then."

"I wonder what Benton was waiting for. Why he hadn't cashed them in all those months," I mused.

"Could be he didn't know someone he could trust who handled such expensive gems. Or he was on the lookout for an expert diamond cutter who knew how to cut the stones with a minimum of waste."

Dylan glanced at his watch. "I'm going to have to leave you shortly. I need to run down to the police station—talk to John, interview Jennifer, and examine the gems. My boss is expecting a detailed report on them. He shook his head. "I'm afraid I'll be up to my neck in paperwork until we go to Harriet and Bosco's tomorrow. Ordinarily, on a big case such as this, I'd have to fly to the main office in Atlanta, but since it's Christmas, I'm getting a few days' reprieve."

"I understand," I said, biting back my disappointment. *Does that mean he has to fly off on Monday? Is this how our relationship is going to play out?*

A knock on the door stopped my negative train of thought. I hurried to let my father inside. Jim was looking tired and washed out. I felt a pang of guilt. In the excitement of finding the gems and tracking Chris Crowley to Dina's house, I'd neglected to look after him properly. How could I have forgotten that he'd just come from the hospital after falling the night before? Was it only last night that Mariel and Dina were here having dinner with us? After today's events it felt like more than a month had passed.

I took Jim's arm and walked him into the living room. "Come sit down, Dad."

He sank into a chair and closed his eyes. "Caro, dear, I'm beat. Would you mind getting my overnight bag from Dylan's car?"

"I'll get it," Dylan said, rising to his feet, "and then I'd better get going."

"Dad, should you be taking any meds?"

He reached in the pocket of his parka and pulled out a plastic vial of pills. "The doc wants me to take anti-seizure medicine—just in case—and something for the pain. I could use one right now."

I brought him a glass of water, and he swallowed two pills. "I'm wiped out. Think I'll crawl into bed for a nap."

"Need any help?"

"No, thanks. I just want to sleep. Seeing that guy coming after you scared the hell out of me."

"I'm sorry I upset you."

"Don't you ever be sorry, Caro. It's for me to regret missing those years with you and your brother." He turned quickly, but not before I saw the tear trickling down his cheek.

"Here you go," Dylan said. He carried my father's overnight bag into the guest room. " 'Bye, Jim. See you tomorrow."

My father struggled to his feet. I stopped myself from running to help him. "Thanks for picking me up at the hospital," he told Dylan.

"Don't mention it."

He shuffled off to his bedroom. Dylan and I stood in the hallway, holding each other close.

"He's knocked out," Dylan said. "He'll probably sleep most of the afternoon."

"I'm in for a very quiet evening," I said.

"Maybe it's for the best, considering all you've been through." He kissed me. "Talk to you later."

I closed the door behind him, suddenly feeling abandoned. *Silly. Dylan has work to do. He can't stay here and hold your hand.* Still, the silence in the cottage, with my father asleep in the guest room and no Smoky Joe dashing about, added to my sense of isolation.

I turned on the radio to a classical music station and gazed out at the river. I knew I should be feeling a sense of satisfaction for having helped solve the murders and finding the missing gems. Instead, I felt depleted, as though I'd just lost my job. Which was ridiculous because my job was overseeing programs in the library, not chasing murder suspects and thieves. I supposed I was experiencing the letdown that Dylan had described. *It will pass,* I told myself.

I must have dozed off on the sofa, because the sound of the doorbell jolted me awake. I ran to the front door to let in an excited Angela. "It's all on the news! The police have Chris Crowley in custody. He's being arraigned for the three homicides."

Smoky Joe butted his head against my leg to remind me that I hadn't greeted him properly. I bent down to rub the back of his head, which he loved. Then, bushy tail in the air, he led me to the kitchen. As I dished cat food onto his plate, I filled Angela in on what had happened after I'd left the library.

When I finished, she had the same look of horror and dismay on her face as I'd seen on Dylan, my father, and John's. "My God, Carrie! You could have been seriously hurt! Murdered, even."

"Chris had his hands around Dina's neck. I *had* to call out to distract him. I didn't expect him to come after me. Lucky for me, he wasn't carrying a knife."

"Hah! Most likely he didn't want to get caught red-handed with a weapon in broad daylight." Angela shot me a sly look. "You must be especially pleased about finding the gems."

I made a face. "Why? Because Dylan's closed his case? Right now he's making calls and doing paperwork. He'll probably have to fly off after the holiday."

"But think, Carrie, you'll get that hefty reward for finding the gems."

"I'm not so sure about that. I only discovered them because I followed Smoky Joe to the register at the back of the coffee shop."

Angela laughed. "*You* removed the bag of gems from the well beneath the register. Besides, they give out rewards to people, not cats."

"Only to have Chris grab it and take off."

She waved her hand. "A moot point, my dear, since you led Dylan and the police to the Parrs' house, where he'd gone. The gems were recovered. They're going back where they belong. Talk to Dylan. See if he doesn't say I'm right."

My father walked into the kitchen, rubbing his eyes. I introduced them.

"A pleasure to meet you, Jim," Angela said, shaking his hand. "Carrie's been filling me in on her latest murder case."

"Latest?" my father asked.

I shrugged. "I helped catch another murderer."

Too late, Angela realized she'd said the wrong thing. "I'd better get going," she said, reaching for her pocketbook. "I'll call Sally from the car. She'll want to hear every detail of your latest adventure."

"Hungry?" I asked my father, who'd sat down at the table.

"I'd give anything for a batch of softly scrambled eggs and a lightly toasted bagel."

"Coming right up. Coffee or tea?"

"Coffee would be nice."

I retrieved the necessary ingredients from the refrigerator, and what had become my favorite frying pan from the pots and pans drawer, and got to work.

"I'm going to miss all this," Jim said as he gazed around the kitchen.

I stopped beating the eggs to stare at him. "You're leaving?"

"Probably early next week. By then I should be steady on my feet."

"But—what's the rush?"

"Come on, Caro, you knew I'd be moving on, soon as my business here was done. Now that the gems are going back to their previous owner, there's nothing stopping me here from taking off."

Previous owner? Nothing stopping you from taking off? "Well, thank you very much."

"Oh, honey, I didn't mean it like that. You know I love you, but I'm running short of cash. It's time I started earning some money."

"Earning? That's a laugh. I wish you'd find a way to make money some legitimate way."

My father cleared his throat as if he were embarrassed. "Dylan happened to mention that his company might be interested in hiring me as a consultant."

"You? A consultant for an insurance company?" I burst out laughing.

"What's so funny? How many ex-cons work with the police, giving them tips on how houses are burgled, how they choose their marks. And former drug addicts promote anti-drug programs."

"I'd be very happy if you took the job," I said. "That way I'll know you're keeping out of trouble."

"And I wish you'd stop chasing killers. For God's sake, you're a librarian, not an investigator."

Having both said our piece, I poured the egg mixture into the heated frying pan and started stirring.

When I saw my father happily slurping his coffee and biting into his toast, I reheated some of last night's leftovers for my own dinner. John called to say he'd be at the cottage in a few minutes to interview Jim and me.

"Fine," I said and added a generous portion of food to the casserole dish before returning it to the microwave.

John arrived, hungry and exhausted. His eyes took on a glow when I invited him to sit down at the table and have a bite with us. After he'd eaten a good portion of his pasta and meatballs, he brought us up to speed.

"At first Crowley insisted he hadn't murdered anyone. But after I told him what Dina told us, he broke down and admitted he'd killed Benton and Mariel Parr and Tom Quincy. His mother, Stella Crowley, came down to the station and tried to get him to stop talking. She hired a lawyer, who arrived shortly, but we got it down, all legal and proper."

"What about Jennifer?" I asked.

"It depends on the judge. She could end up getting a suspended sentence, or she might spend some time in jail for keeping the gems. She knew they were stolen. The interesting thing is, she asked us to call Paul." John laughed. "He came running down to hold her hand, and they acted like the most in-love couple you'd ever seen. She kept apologizing for her affair with Benton, and Paul kept on forgiving her. Not a word about the way she'd hidden the gems all this time and planned to take off to the Big Apple to start a new life on her own."

After I cleared the dishes, I put on a pot of coffee and sat down to tell John what I'd heard Chris say to Dina.

"He admitted he'd murdered her parents?" John asked when I was finished.

"Yes, as if he'd done Dina and himself both a favor. Dina was horrified."

John shook his head. "That kid's some piece of work." He glared at me, his lips pursed in disapproval. "You knew he was dangerous, yet you had to get involved."

"I was afraid he was going to choke Dina to death."

He let out a deep sigh and turned to my father. "Your daughter's one special woman, Jim Singleton."

"Don't I know it."

To my surprise, John said to me, "Now, if you'll excuse us, your dad and I have some private business to discuss."

Chapter
Thirty-Seven

I never did find out what that conversation was about, but from the contented expression on my father's face, I suspected it had something to do with cancelling a few outstanding warrants against him. It was close to nine o'clock when John bid us good night. I put the dishes in the dishwasher, gave Smoky Joe the few treats he'd been begging for, and had just sat down to watch TV with my father, when Dylan called to tell me how he'd spent the evening. My father disappeared inside his room while we were talking. When Dylan and I finished our conversation, I looked in on him. He was fast asleep.

I watched a bit of TV, then realized I was totally exhausted from the day's activities. I got ready for bed, told myself I'd bake the brownies tomorrow, and quickly fell asleep.

Christmas Eve day I woke up early with a feeling of excitement. Christmas was almost here! My mind filled with childhood memories of TV shows about the holiday spirit of loving one's fellow man, of the one year my father had played Santa and brought us gifts.

Jim was already awake and whistling in the kitchen as he

prepared a cup of coffee for himself in the Keurig. Smoky Joe was chomping away at his breakfast, which was probably why he hadn't bothered to wake me up this morning.

"Morning, Caro. Care for an omelet? I'm in an omelet-making mood."

"Sure."

He opened the refrigerator door and surveyed what I had on hand. "Let's see—I can fill it with cheese, mushrooms, or onions, or all three."

"All three would be nice."

"Rye bread, multigrain, English muffin, or bagel?"

I giggled. "English muffin."

"Sit back and relax."

The doorbell rang. I went to answer it. A young woman with long blond hair that framed her pretty, heart-shaped face smiled down at me from her six-foot frame. Behind her stood a man with a camera, and behind them a white van with big letters on its side occupied my driveway.

"Carrie Singleton?" she asked.

"Ye-es." I said, sounding as leery as I felt. My first impulse was to slam the door in the reporter's face, but I was a public servant of sorts and didn't want to come across as rude or offensive, especially not on local television.

"Good morning. I'm Ginger LeMotto, WTRX news." She stepped to the side of the doorway and turned so the cameraman would get a good shot of both of us. "I understand you played a part in apprehending Christopher Crowley, the man being charged with murdering three people here in Clover Ridge."

"Really?" I plastered a smile on my face. "May I ask who told you that?"

She returned a wider smile. "Ah, that would be telling. Do you think we could come inside for a brief chat?"

She tried to step over the threshold, but I held my ground. "I'm sorry. I'm very busy right now. Christmas preparations, you know."

"I understand." She fluttered her eyelashes. "We promise to take a mere ten minutes of your time. Not a second more."

"Sorry. I wish I could help you, but"—I winked—"that would be telling."

My father clapped as I closed the door firmly behind me. "My daughter has turned into a force to be reckoned with."

I swelled with pride. "Do you really think so?"

"Absolutely. Now back to the kitchen before your omelet gets cold."

Breakfast was usually a rushed event, but that morning I took my time, savoring every bite. Only after Dad had removed my plate and refilled my mug of coffee did I reach for the local newspaper. Sure enough, the lead story told of Chris Crowley's capture and arraignment and filled the first three pages. The two large photos must have been taken when Dylan, Jim, and I were long gone. My name was mentioned in the second paragraph as having been present when the police arrived. Someone must have told the reporter I'd been there and not much else. I imagined Ginger LeMotto was simply fishing for a story. I didn't think she'd be bothering me again.

I'd cleared the kitchen table and was setting out the ingredients for the brownies I'd be baking when Uncle Bosco called, sounding distressed.

"Carrie, dear, what were you doing at the Parr house when the police captured that murderer?"

I didn't want to upset him further, so I downplayed my involvement. "I was there to see Dina," I said, which was truthful in its own right. "How did you know I was there?"

"Your aunt just got off the phone with Grace Brower. Her son Danny seems to think you're some kind of Wonder Woman."

I laughed. "You know I'm not."

"I hope you weren't playing detective again. You know that could put you in serious danger."

"I'm fine, Uncle Bosco. I'd love to talk more, but I'm in the middle of baking a batch of double-chocolate brownies for our dinner."

"In that case I won't keep you another minute," he said quickly.

"See you later." I grinned. Uncle Bosco loved my double-chocolate brownies.

Dylan stopped by while the brownies were baking to give us an update on the investigation. He kissed me briefly, then sniffed the air.

"Hey, does my nose tell me what I think it's telling me?" he asked.

"As we speak, brownies are baking in the oven."

His face took on a wistful expression. "Think I can have one?"

I grinned. "Only if you stick around for the next fifteen minutes."

"That's about all the time I have," he said as we sat down on the living room sofa.

"What's happening with Chris?"

"Stella's hired an expensive lawyer who's doing his best to get

Chris out on bail. He might very well succeed." Dylan grinned. "But not before Christmas has come and gone."

"And the gems?" I asked.

"The latest revised arrangements are that I'll have a special escort when I bring them to Atlanta to be authenticated by our gem expert. After that, if they prove to be exactly what our client says they are, they'll be delivered to his company in Texas."

I swallowed. "Does that mean you'll be going to Texas?"

"Looks like it." He drew a deep breath. "But I told my boss I have to be back here next weekend for a special occasion."

"What special occasion?" I asked.

"Spending New Year's Eve with you."

"And after that?"

"My company's one of the biggest in the country. I'll probably be sent to work another case involving stolen artwork or jewels."

"Oh" was all I could manage.

My father chose that moment to leave his room and join us. From the way he and Dylan greeted one another, it was obvious they liked each other, which made me even sadder.

"Tell me more about the company," my father said, and Dylan was quick to reply.

When the conversation changed to a discussion about the gems, I tuned out. Now would be a good time to ask Dylan when I could catch a glimpse of those fantastic jewels, but suddenly I didn't care if I ever saw them. They'd caused the biggest upheaval in my life. They were the reason why three people had been murdered—and why Dylan would soon be leaving Clover Ridge. I was glad they were safely out of my father's hands and on their way back to their rightful owner. All I could think about was that Dylan would be leaving—again.

The timer pinged. I hurried into the kitchen to test the brownies with a toothpick. Perfect! I let them cool off before cutting them into squares. I placed two in a small Pyrex container and handed it to Dylan, then walked him to the door.

"I'll pick you up at two forty-five," he said, removing the cover and biting into a brownie.

Not even a goodbye kiss.

I returned to the living room, plopped down on the sofa beside my father, and let out a mournful sigh.

"Honey, it's Christmas. I wish you'd cheer up."

"How can I, with Dylan flying off Monday morning? He'll be back next weekend, but then he could be gone for ages."

"You have it that bad, do you?"

I blinked back tears. "Silly, isn't it? We've only been seeing each other since Thanksgiving, and most of that time we've been apart."

"You really love this guy."

"I do, but his job isn't suitable for a long-term relationship."

"Jobs change. People change. Look at me, getting my first honest-to-goodness job in I-don't-know-how-many years." He laughed. "I know my stones pretty well, but I might take a gemologist course so the company has it on record."

I burst out sobbing. "And you're leaving too. Soon as you're feeling all right."

"That's true, but I'm not on the lam. John Mathers managed to vouch for me and see that I got some charges expunged. It turns out some jails are too full, so arrangements have been made to suspend charges against nonaggressive offenders. I'll be traveling for the company, but I'll have time off. I promise to come visit."

"You promise?" I asked. I sounded like a little kid, but I didn't care.

"Caro, honey, I intend to come back here often to spend time with you. I can never make up for the years I wasted being away from you and Jordan, but my absentee father days are over. And that's a promise."

We sat quietly until Smoky Joe leaped into my lap, his way of telling me it was feeding time again.

Suddenly energized, I decided to take extra pains with my appearance for our Christmas Eve outing. I hummed as I buffed and shaped my nails, then applied a vivid fuchsia-colored polish. I put on my new black jeggings, a soft forest green cashmere tunic, and my favorite leather boots. Next, I applied eye shadow, mascara, and blush, which I rarely bothered with, and blow-dried my hair.

"Stun-ning!" my father exclaimed when he saw the results of my efforts.

"Well, thank you, kind sir."

"Really, honey, you look great." He disappeared inside his room and emerged with a small wrapped box.

"Go on, open it."

I ripped through the holiday paper and unlatched the box. "How beautiful!" I exclaimed. The earrings *were* beautiful—a twisted golden hoop with a scattering of diamonds.

"Why don't you put them on?"

"I will," I said as I opened the omega back of one and slipped the post through my earlobe. "They're dressy enough to wear to a party, yet suitable for work."

"Merry Christmas, Caro."

I hugged him, then pulled away. "They're not—stolen, are they?"

He laughed. "Of course not. I bought them in the jewelry store in the shopping center ten miles from here. I wanted to be sure you could exchange them if you didn't like them."

I bit my lip. "And I only have a woolen scarf for you."

"That's all right. Spending the holiday with you is the best gift you could give me."

I burst into tears. "Why couldn't we have had this years ago, when I was growing up and needed you?"

"Because things don't always work out that way," he said softly. "Let's enjoy what we have now for as long as we have the time together."

He left to get the box of tissues from his room. While I was blowing my nose and drying my tears, he switched on the tree lights and put on a CD of English Christmas carols.

I sat quietly in the living room while he showered and dressed, thinking about the many things I didn't know about my father. Where had he been living all those years he was away from us? What were his favorite foods? Where had he gotten the money for my earrings if he was broke?

I finally managed to put an end to my mulling. I'd been doing a good job of making myself sad about what could have been, what should have been. I had my father back, and that was what mattered.

Chapter Thirty-Eight

"Don't you look great!" Dylan said two hours later when he came to pick us up.

I eyed his suede jacket, breathed in his leathery aftershave, and reached up to kiss him. "You look pretty good yourself."

"Great earrings? Are they new?"

"My Christmas gift from Jim," I said, thinking how much Dylan and I still had to learn about each other. All this learning! It would take time.

My father and I put on our jackets and gathered what we were bringing that night: brownies from me, a bottle of Chablis from Jim, my gifts for Aunt Harriet and Uncle Bosco, and two toys I'd bought for Mark and Tacey. As we headed for the front door, Smoky Joe followed us, his bushy tail high in the air.

"Sorry, boy. You're not invited," I said, petting him. I'd left plenty of food and treats for him to enjoy while we were out.

"Brrr, it's cold," my father said as he climbed into the back of Dylan's BMW.

"It's snowing," I said as I slipped into the front passenger seat.

"Just flurries," Dylan said. "Nothing to be concerned about."

"This is a really good Bordeaux," my father said, reading the label on the wine bottle Dylan had placed in a carrier behind the driver's seat.

"It's my favorite," Dylan said, sounding pleased.

Wine. Something they both know about and enjoy. I tucked away the information for future reference.

The snow was falling more densely when we arrived at my aunt and uncle's home. I gazed up at their white house set back on a rise, then across the Green—past the large Christmas tree lit in all its glory—to catch a glimpse of the library that had become such an important part of my life.

"Looks just like a picture postcard," my father commented.

Just as you'd imagine Christmas would be if you were reading a story about a happy family.

Uncle Bosco hugged each of us in turn and helped carry our packages into the house. He placed the gifts I'd brought for him and Aunt Harriet beneath the Christmas tree that sparkled with multicolored lights, then set about serving us drinks.

Wine glass in hand, I wandered into the kitchen, where delicious aromas were vying for prominence. After clasping me tightly and telling me I looked beautiful, Aunt Harriet handed me a platter of piping hot canapés.

"Be an angel and serve these to the Claymonts. They're in the living room. And offer them to your father and boyfriend, of course."

A fire was crackling in the living room fireplace. I found my aunt and uncle's elderly neighbors sitting side by side on the loveseat. They each took a stuffed mushroom, along with a napkin, and nodded their thanks.

"You're welcome. Merry Christmas."

Mrs. Claymont smiled. "And to you, young Carolinda. Lovely earrings you're wearing."

I smoothed back the hair above my right ear. "Thank you, Mrs. Claymont. They're my Christmas gift from my father."

My cousins, Randy and Julia, arrived with their children, Mark and Tacey. We greeted one another with kisses and hugs, except for Mark, who offered me his hand to shake.

"I have presents for the children," I said.

"Thank you," Julia said. "We'll put them under our tree when we go home."

"Mom, it's Christmas Eve already," Mark said. "Can't we open them now?"

"Please!" Tacey pleaded.

Randy shrugged. "Kiddies rule."

I handed them their gifts.

"Thank you," Mark and Tacey said in unison, then proceeded to rip off the wrapping paper in record time.

Mark's eyes popped when he caught sight of the small electronic toy I'd bought him.

"Wow! Just what I wanted, Cousin Carrie." He cannon-balled into me, nearly knocking me off my feet, and hugged me tight.

Tacey was delighted with her Barbie doll. "I love Barbie dolls. I have two at home and a Barbie house. You should come see it, Cousin Carrie."

"I will," I said.

"We'll have Cousin Carrie over very soon." Julia winked. "Along with her boyfriend."

"You have a boyfriend, Cousin Carrie?"

"I sure do. He's in the den with my father, talking to Uncle Bosco."

While the kids played with their toys, Randy and Julia plied me with questions about my part in catching Chris Crowley.

Randy patted me on the back. "Julia, who would have guessed that my shy little cousin here would turn out to be a great detective?"

Years ago his teasing would have upset me, but now I knew it was good-natured. Furthermore, I knew he was proud of me.

Randy joined the men in the den, and Julia went into the kitchen to help Aunt Harriet. I felt a tug on my arm. It was Tacey. I bent down so she could whisper in my ear.

"Do you think Miss Evelyn is celebrating Christmas where she is?"

I stroked her long, silky hair. "I think so. It's a special place, Tacey, so they probably celebrate Christmas in a special way."

"No cookies for Miss Evelyn."

"No cookies," I agreed.

"Next year I want to give her a present," Tacey said. "She gave me one."

"Really?" I asked, surprised. "What was it?"

"I told Miss Evelyn I wanted Mommy to read me a book about an elephant. And you know what? She showed me where one was. Mommy checked it out so we could read it together."

Bless you, Evelyn Havers, I thought. *And Merry Christmas, wherever you are.*

Sylvia and John Mathers joined us a few minutes later. I took a shrimp toast from the tray Julia held before me and glanced around, curious to know what everyone was doing. Uncle Bosco was horsing around with Randy and the children; Sylvia and

Aunt Harriet were in the kitchen catching up on each other's news; and Julia was chatting with the Claymonts. I chuckled to see Dylan, my father, and John huddled in a corner, where they were probably discussing the gems and Chris Crowley. Two lawmen of sorts and a thief. *Retired thief,* I quickly amended and hoped fervently that it was so. My father let out a hoot of joy. *What is that all about?* I wondered.

I was surrounded by people I cared about and who cared about me. Hard to believe I'd only arrived in Clover Ridge in May, feeling beaten and bedraggled. *You've come a long way, Carrie,* I told myself.

Dylan beckoned to me, and I followed him into the small sunroom at the back of the house.

"I want to give you your Christmas present," he said, reaching into his pocket for a narrow, rectangular, gift-wrapped box.

"Oh! I didn't think to—"

"Shh," he said, putting a finger to my lips. "I wanted to give it to you back at the cottage, but things got hectic."

I ripped through the gift paper almost as fast as the kids had, and opened the box.

"Ooh!" was all I could manage. Inside was a tilted open heart of gold, with diamonds along one side, on a slender rope chain.

"Would you like to wear it now?"

I needed no encouragement. I handed the necklace to Dylan and lifted my hair so he could fasten the lobster claw clasp. The heart fell an inch below the hollow in my neck. Perfect! I ran into the bathroom to see myself in the mirror.

"It's lovely," I said to Dylan, who had followed me. "Thank you."

"You're welcome. I'm glad to see it goes well with your new earrings."

I stared at him. "Don't tell me you and my father went Christmas shopping together."

Dylan laughed. I kissed him until I felt giddy with happiness.

"Would everyone please come to the table," Aunt Harriet called, loud enough for all of us to hear.

We approached the beautifully set dining room table.

"You're sitting here, between Dylan and John," Uncle Bosco told me.

Aunt Harriet whisked Julia and me into the kitchen to help bring out the platters of food. When we were all seated, Uncle Bosco said a few words about the meaning of Christmas and how blessed he and Aunt Harriet felt to have family and good friends and neighbors with them on this special day. Aunt Harriet started doling out salad from the large bowl, and conversation resumed.

I turned to John. "I'm glad that yesterday's events didn't keep you from coming today."

He grinned. "Everything's under control. I even got in my five seconds of fame. I'll be on TV"—he checked his watch—"in about an hour."

"I dodged my moment of fame," I told him.

"So Dylan said." John put his hand over his heart. "I swear I didn't send that reporter to your cottage."

"Any new developments on the case?"

"Now Chris Crowley won't shut up, to his lawyer's annoyance. Half of what he's saying are complaints about his father—that he grew up in poverty because his father never could keep a job, and he—Chris—would have been a big success if his father hadn't been such a loser."

"And so he murdered people to get his hands on stolen gems. Did he explain why he killed Tom Quincy?"

John laughed. "It turns out both Chris and Quincy suspected Jennifer Darby had the gems. Each was watching the house, trying to figure out his best approach. Should he risk a break in? Threaten Jennifer? Quincy spotted Chris and went after him. Chris had the knife and used it. He swore it was self-defense."

"Maybe it was."

"Come on, Carrie. A punch in the gut, yeah, but stabbing someone to death? I don't think a jury will buy it, especially since he used the same knife on his other two victims."

"Do you think Jennifer will go to prison?"

"I doubt it. She's agreed to testify that Benton told her that he and an accomplice stole the gems."

My heart raced. "Did she say who the accomplice was?"

"She claims Benton never told her." John's eyes bored into mine. "And even if she did, it would be considered hearsay."

"Oh," I breathed.

John's face took on a bemused expression. "Interesting how things work themselves out. She heard somehow that the gems' owner was offering a finder's award."

I stared at him. "Don't tell me she had the nerve to try to claim it."

"She did."

"But she's not getting it," Dylan said, sliding his arm across the back of my chair.

I turned to him. "Good!"

"You are!"

I felt light-headed. Dizzy. On the verge of fainting. Not sure that I'd heard correctly.

"You'll receive half a million dollars," Dylan went on. "I explained in great detail how the gems were recovered to my boss and to our client. It was agreed—the reward is rightfully yours."

I reached for my wine glass, which Uncle Bosco had refilled, and gulped down the contents—certainly not the way wine was to be savored.

"Please thank them for me," I said. "I don't know that I deserve it. After all, it was Smoky Joe who led me to the heat register."

"But you retrieved the bag of gems," Dylan said, "and later led us to Crowley. No doubt about it, the reward is yours."

When I realized my father was grinning at us from across the table, I gave him a thumbs up. Half of the reward money was his if he promised never to steal again.

"Carrie, you haven't touched your salad," Uncle Bosco called to me.

"I'm eating it right now," I said, putting a forkful of greens into my mouth.

Things were perfect again, or close to it. I smiled, savoring the moment. If I'd learned one thing these past few weeks, it was they wouldn't stay perfect for long.

Acknowledgments

I want to thank everyone at Crooked Lane Books who helped turn my manuscript into a polished and beautiful book. I love working with you! To my wonderful editor, Faith Black Ross, who knows just which issues need attention; to Sarah Poppe for doing such a great job promoting my series and Jenny Chen for overseeing the production end—both so responsive to my questions and concerns. To my copy editor, for her careful attention to detail, and to the fantastic Griesbach/Martucci team of illustrators for my series' outstanding covers. My readers adore them!

A special thanks to my agent, Dawn Dowdle, for being so diligent and helpful. And a very warm and heartfelt expression of gratitude to my many readers who have told me how much they loved reading *Death Overdue* and can hardly wait to read *Read and Gone*.